AMBA TROTT

Nutting ~~But...~~

NONSENSE

IN

NEVIS

HHS

A Hamilton House Studio Publication
Charlestown, Nevis, West Indies

Hamilton House Studio Publications
P.O. Box 547
Charlestown
Nevis, West Indies

Nonsense in Nevis First published by Hamilton House Studio Publications, 2005.

10 9 8 7 6 5 4 3 2 1

Manufactured in CARICOM (Caribbean Community)

ISBN 976-8173-92-0

Cover conceptualised by:	Amba Trott
Cover designed by:	Peter Ngunjiri
Illustrations by:	Jimmy Simmons
Photo acknowledgments:	Mensa Adams (page 112); Lorette Brand (page 165); Samuel Hunkins Family (Page 264); GIS Nevis (page 267); Peter Ngunjiri (pages 203, 215, 250, 271, inside back and back cover); Llewellyn Parris (Page 168); Amba Trott (page 148).
General acknowledgments:	Nevis Historical and Conservation Society; *The St. Kitts-Nevis Observer* and *The Leewards Times*.
Edited, designed and typeset by:	Peter Ngunjiri, Key Stone Complex, Cedar Trees, Charlestown, Nevis, West Indies.
Printed and bound by:	Caribbean Paper & Printed Products (1993) Ltd. 60 A Boundary Road Extension, San Juan, Trinidad, West Indies.

To William and Marion Trott,
Who made me possible in the first place...
To the island and people of Nevis,
Whose existence made this book possible in the second place...
And to Louise vanWijngaarden, Hope Trott and Marc Beaudin,
Who have always encouraged and supported my forays in the arts
and my efforts at writing.

Nuttin But.....

Nonsense in Nevis
Is an opinionated social commentary expressed through the use of
fact, fiction, fable, and verse.

FOREWORD

Several years ago when I was a regular columnist for a local newspaper, an irate reader who frequently disagreed with my point of view,
claimed that my writings were "nuttin but nonsense!" I readily admit to
writing a certain amount of nonsense. I think, though, that to say my
writings are "nuttin but nonsense" is really stretching things quite a bit.
But that is only my own self-serving opinion - others must decide for
themselves. I do firmly believe however, that there is actually much
more 'nonsense in Nevis' to be discovered than what little may be
contained between the covers of this book. For that, my sincere apolo-
gies.

Amba Trott
Nevis
West Indies
May 2005

BOOK I

SMILEY STORIES

Smiley Stories are strictly a work of fiction. The characters, incidents, and dialogues are products of the author's imagination or are used fictitiously and are not to be construed as real. Any resemblance to actual events, or persons, living or dead, is entirely coincidental.

THE BIG DONKEY MOSQUITO AFFAIR IN NEVIS

When he was still in his teens, Smiley Smitten was one of those characters that everybody in Nevis knew, but hardly anybody ever took seriously. One reason for this was that Smiley was born with a facial condition that made him look as if he was always smiling. It caused him plenty of problems at school when he was a kid, and as he grew older, it developed into an incredibly lopsided grin, which he wore even at the gravest moments. Needless to say, he seemed quite out of place at funerals, which he loved to attend for some unknown reasons. But another reason why people rarely took Smiley seriously was that throughout his teens, he was regarded mostly as a buffoon because of the hijinks and pranks he seemed to be constantly involved in.

Some people claimed that Smiley was retarded, but those who knew him really well didn't support that opinion. For instance, by the time he was sixteen, Smiley could do some wonderfully imaginative, creative, and remarkable work with his hands, so some people said he was gifted. They agreed that he might be a little slow mentally, but certainly not retarded. Still, Smiley did some weird things at times that made people wonder. His supporters always defended him though, by claiming that he had an offbeat sense of humour. People often made fun of Smiley, but occasionally he turned the tables by doing something that gave everybody a good laugh – at someone else's expense.

For instance, one Sunday morning a few years ago, Smiley rushed excitedly into the Charlestown Police Station to report that there was a donkey mosquito down at the bogs. It so happened at the time, that the Health Department was conducting a campaign against mosquitoes, because of the danger of contracting the deadly dengue fever. The sergeant, a little annoyed at the interruption while doing his crossword puzzle, looked up. "Smiley, what you comin wid now? I killed tree a dem dinky maskeetoes dis mawnin already, an' look…" he clapped, an inch from Smiley's face. "Dat makes four," he said, brushing the dark specks from his hands.

Smiley persisted, and insisted that what was down at the bogs was no ordinary little mosquito, but a mosquito that was as big as a donkey and that someone should really investigate, especially since the Health Department was issuing warnings about "Donkey Fever," as he called it. The sergeant guffawed so loudly that soon all of the other officers at the station came to see what was going on and join in the fun. The sergeant made Smiley repeat his story, obviously so that everyone in the station could have a rollicking good laugh.

9

No one missed the opportunity, and everybody was trying to get Smiley to elaborate on the details to prolong the mirthmaking scene. It certainly helped to break the monotony of that particular Sunday morning. No drug busts had taken place recently. No rapes, no break-ins, no murders, no assaults, nothing. Things were unusually quiet and dull in Nevis, especially since cricket hadn't started yet. So the personnel at the station didn't have anything of interest to chat about aside from mundane domestic problems, until Smiley dropped in with his lopsided grin and ridiculous story.

The sergeant, who was a bit of a practical joker, couldn't resist the temptation to have a bit of fun. Pulling Smiley to one side, he glanced at his watch importantly. "Smiley," he said, trying to keep a straight face, "I can't spare a soul dis mawnin to go to investigate dis situation. It's ten-terty already and we all as busy as bees around here. However, even one donkey maskeetoe is serious business an' somebody mus' do somet'ing about it. Is a serious tret to public healt'." Smiley nodded furiously in agreement as the sergeant looked around the room.

The sergeant motioned for the corporal to come over. "I going tell de Corporal to take de jeep an' drop you off at Chapel Street right away. When you get dere, run up de street to de Metodiss Church, you hear me?" Smiley nodded eagerly as the sergeant continued. "De pastor should jus be finishin' his sermon. You explain to him as forcefully as you can, what de situation is. I understand he is a resourceful man wid lotsa experience. He might even fine somet'ing in de Bible to deal wid dis ting. Anyway, I'm sure he will know jus' what to do. But mind you, you have to stress de importance of it all!"

The corporal sped off in the jeep with his excited passenger. It wasn't every day that Smiley got a ride in a police vehicle. He enjoyed the feeling of importance as he sat up front with the driver while the jeep rocketed down Main Street. The fellows at the station were killing themselves with laughter. Smiley's grin seemed to be enlarging, if that was possible.

The corporal got Smiley's attention. "Smiley, is only because de sergeant realise how important dis is dat he mek me bring you to Chapel Street. I busy as hell today man. I busy real bad!" Smiley nodded knowingly. At the corner of Main and Chapel Streets the jeep screeched to a stop and as Smiley stumbled out, the corporal issued last minute instructions. "Smiley, hurry man, no time to waste. We all countin' on you bwoy!"

Fortunately, the church service had ended and the congregation was just preparing to leave when Smiley burst in, babbling about a mosquito as big as a donkey that the sergeant wanted the pastor to investigate. In a few moments, church members were spilling outside, holding on to each other with side-splitting laughter. The pastor had only recently come to Nevis from Barbados, and had not encountered Smiley before. Smiley lived in Stoney Grove and often attended other churches, although this was really the church he was brought up in.

All church members knew Smiley and were familiar with some of the remarkable antics he had been involved in from time to time. These incidents occurred not only at the church, but also at various places such as the bakery, the airport, the market, the hospital, and the Four Seasons Resort. Smiley liked to get around. He certainly wasn't shy. But the curious, incredibly lopsided grin he wore, was enough to start people chuckling before he even uttered a word. Even the doctors at the Alexandra Hospital didn't take him seriously when he complained of a bad pain in his side the year before. He was lucky they discovered appendicitis in time, but only because a friend who had gone with him was able to convince the doctors that he was serious.

So Smiley's encounter with the new pastor that Sunday morning, really had the parishioners rolling in the aisles. Like the sergeant had indicated however, the pastor was a resourceful person, and because he was interested in environmental issues and had not visited the bogs before, he thought this would be a splendid opportunity to do so, while at the same time, humouring this "rather curiously unconventional character." So he rounded up his Polaroid camera, and with the sexton who knew the bogs well, sallied forth in his car with Smiley and the incredible grin.

The officers at the police station were still having a great laugh at Smiley's expense. Nearly everyone had a bit of knowledge about some of Smiley's escapades, so they were having fun swapping "Smiley" stories. The laughter would scarcely die down from one story, when someone would remember another even funnier. If whoever was telling the story left something out, others were quick to interrupt, filling in the missing details. The corporal, now giving his version of a Smiley story, was getting plenty of interruptions. This incident apparently happened a few years earlier when Smiley was still in his mid-teens.

According to the corporal, he happened to be at the scene one day when Smiley fell into the water near the end of the Charlestown pier. Smiley couldn't swim and so had to be rescued. The corporal was telling the story in a way that made him appear to be some sort of hero, but the rest of the boys were having none of that. "No man, dat ain't de way I hear it," charged a constable through bursts of laughter. The corporal staunchly defended himself, saying that he was the only officer on the scene when it happened, that he was the one that made the report, and all the details as he had reported were on record.

"No man, nuttin' go so!" It was the voice of the sergeant who had left the room for a few minutes to relieve himself and was now returning. He told the gathering that what was on record was the corporal's version of the event and that he wasn't going to officially disturb that, but he had gotten, unofficially of course, unimpeachable eye-witness accounts which are more reliable and believable.

The sergeant looked around at the raised eyebrows and expectant faces and another version began to emerge. The corporal's version had been funny enough, but the way the sergeant portrayed the scene with the corporal playing a much less heroic role, made it seem even funnier. The laughter was almost constant as the sergeant described the event.

The *MV Caribe Queen* had left on its afternoon run to St. Kitts. As usual, there were several groups of people lolling around the pier. Smiley liked to watch the ferry until it was out of sight, so when a porter who was turning his cart around told him to move out of the way, Smiley, his eyes still on "The Queen," absently moved and fell into the water. Several people rushed over to see Smiley thrashing about in the water with this incredible grin on his face. It soon became apparent that even though he was grinning for all he was worth, Smiley was in great difficulty and the situation was grave.

Noticing the commotion, the corporal who was nearby, walked over to the edge of the pier, asked what had happened, and thinking Smiley was only playing around, ordered him to come out of the water. But Smiley only grinned desperately as he floundered around. Someone in the crowd told the corporal that Smiley was having trouble and urged him to jump in and "haul out de bwoy!" But the corporal had declined saying "Not me – me cyan' swim!"

The officers in the station were doubling over with laughter. Even the corporal was giggling and nodding furiously in agreement with this version of the event. He dug a fellow officer in the ribs with his elbow. "You could swim?" he asked. The fellow officer ignoring the question, implored the sergeant, "Go on wid de story, it getting sweet, man!" The sergeant described how finally, three young boys who had been lolling about casually stripped, dived into the water and got Smiley out, making it seem like it was all a game. But, he said, the fun was just beginning.

When Smiley was brought out of the water, he was acting in a strange manner, making uncoordinated jabbing movements with one hand inside his shirt. When an onlooker who had just come on the scene, asked what was going on, the corporal who was now taking notes and trying to get Smiley to stand still for questioning, told the man to stand back, he was in charge there and would ask all the questions.

He then instructed someone else to call for an ambulance. Next, he ordered the three young rescuers to put their clothes back on or he would arrest them for indecent exposure. He then ordered the large crowd, which had gathered, to disperse or he would arrest them for unlawful assembly. Finally he turned to the porter who had unwittingly started the chain reaction of events, and asked him what happened.

At this point, two buttons on Smiley's shirt popped open and a three-pound flounder squirmed out and fell flopping about on the pier. While Smiley awkwardly tried to retrieve the fish, the crowd laughed, hooted, and shouted out various comments. "Look, Smiley come a fisherman!" "Lawd, what a technique!" "Is dat why de bwoy jump in de water – oh me God-oh!" After Smiley had recovered the fish, someone offered him five dollars for it, waving the money in his face. While trying to grasp the money, Smiley dropped the fish again and before he could reach it, it had flip-flopped off the pier and back into the water. The crowd called out encouragements, "Go after it Smiley bwoy!" "Get one for me too!" "Lawd, what a fisherman, oooweeeh!"

The sergeant was a master story teller who knew how to pause for effect, how to let the fellows catch their breaths before feeding them another little tid-bit deliciously spiced with his special brand of embellishments, guaranteeing gut-wrenching belly laughs from those who still had anything left, while man-sized tears freely rolled down the cheeks of others, whose vocal chords having given out on them, had only this means left for expression.

With the whole station in a rollicking uproar as the sergeant recounted his version of the Smiley Fish Story, it was awhile before anyone took notice of the two wild-eyed men who had entered the station and were trying to get some attention. It was the corporal who first noticed the pastor and the sexton. He gestured to the sergeant who barked a command, which quickly quieted the others down. "Yes?" said the sergeant, addressing the two men. Both men blurted out something, which was completely incoherent. "One at a time please," said the sergeant, "say it again?"

The pastor spoke up rapidly, while the sexton followed his words, nodding nervously with intense agreement. "At de bogs, Mon – a maskeetoe, big, big, big, like so, Mon." The pastor spread his arms wide. "Big as a donkey!" "Me arm!" muttered the corporal, involuntarily. "No Mon, bigger dan dat!" protested the pastor.

One of the constables snickered.

"Shut up," ordered the sergeant, glowering at the man.

"Beejeeze," the pastor continued, "I never see dat befar!" From his accent and unique phraseology you could tell he was a 'Bajan.' A mixture of quaint West Indian expressions from the sergeant's Barnes Ghaut in Nevis and the pastor's Bridgetown in Barbados spiced the air as the sergeant conducted the questioning.

"Start from de beginning," he advised the pastor. "And Corporal, take some notes. I want a clear picture of dis, dis, dis…"

13

"Picture?" blurted the sexton, "I have it, see it here!"

He waved a Polaroid photograph at the sergeant who took it, holding it this way and that, peering at it from different angles.

"You have any udders? Dis one is kinda blurry."

"Lawhawd, Sergeant, is de only one. Me could hardly hole de camera – me fraid for so!"

The sergeant passed the picture for the other officers to look at. "Way you was standin' when you take de picture?"

"I was standin' right dere 'pon de groun' at de bogs."

"I mean how far you was standin' from de ting?"

"Sergeant, we had just pushed true some bushes an' dere we was – right on top of it!"

"On top of it," said the sergeant, "how you mean?"

"Well, maybe ten feet away."

"Twenty," said the pastor. "Well, anyway it was too close. An when de ting start to tun towards us – Lawd, me nearly trip an fall over Smiley in me rush to get outta dere!"

"Smiley was wid you?" queried the sergeant.

"Is he showed us de way," and the two men began to describe how Smiley had burst into the church with his incredible story, and how everybody had laughed, and how insistent and forceful Smiley had been, especially mentioning that the sergeant himself had requested the pastor's assistance in the matter, and how finally, the pastor had decided to go along just to humour him and to take some pictures of the local flora and fauna around the bogs.

"Where Smiley is now?" asked the sergeant.

"Beejeeze…!" the pastor's eyes widened with horror as he looked around questioningly. "Oh me God, he mus' still be dere!" The mounting hub-bub created by the officers who were still examining the picture made it difficult to think.

"Oh me arm!" said the corporal.

"Shut up!" snapped the sergeant who was now clearly disturbed. He had been the one Smiley first told his story to. He had been the one who first thought it was a joke. He had been the one who sent Smiley rushing to the church. And now he was the one who had to deal with this situation, which he obviously didn't relish.

The photograph looked pretty convincing and the sergeant's imagination was working furiously.

The corporal looked at him with apprehension, "What you goin' do Sarge?"

The hub-bub was starting to build again as the sergeant struggled to consider his options. He pulled out a handkerchief and wiped his face. Took off his cap and mopped his brow. Folded his handkerchief with thoughtful deliberation, and carefully tucked it into his pocket. Then with a sudden shock of vitality he was galvanised into a burst of action.

He swung up his arm to look at his watch with great urgency.

"Oh-mi-God-oh! I was supposed to pick up de Madam after her Sunday school class an' completely forget. I late as hell, man! Corporal – take care of tings, I gone!" And he was out the door, into his vehicle and spinning its wheels in a cloud of dust before anybody could say anything.

The corporal was of course, completely nonplussed. The other officers were looking at him expectantly.

"What you going do, Corp?" one of them ventured eventually.

"Quiet." He barked, "I'm tinkin." He knew he had to do something, he didn't know what. But he was in charge now and needed to show some initiative, needed to show that the responsibility was placed in the right hands, needed to show that he was a man of action and resourcefulness. After a few thoughtful seconds, he moved over to the pastor with his pad and pencil, ready to take notes.

"You say you went to de bogs dis morning wid Smiley?"

The pastor nodded his concurrence.

"You say a donkey-mosquito was dere?"

The pastor agreed.

The corporal reached for the photograph. "You say dis is a picture of de said donkey-mosquito?"

The pastor nodded.

"An you run 'way when you see de donkey-mosquito, an' you lef' Smiley behind?" The corporal's manner insinuated that the pastor may have acted negligently. The pastor being greatly embarrassed, tried to explain, but the corporal cut him off. "Just answer de question please Pastor, you lef Smiley behind?"

The pastor's admission drew murmurs from the officers in the station, indicating their disapproval.

Things might have gone on like that for quite awhile had their attention not been distracted by the sounds in the street made by an approaching crowd of people. The gathering drew closer, and the sounds of raucous laughter and revelry became clearer.

As the crowd came into closer proximity to the station, it soon became evident what all the uproar was about. Smiley Smitten was riding down the street on a donkey. But it wasn't just any old donkey.

The animal had been outfitted with materials and paraphernalia that made it resemble a giant mosquito.

The resemblance was truly a remarkable testament of Smiley's extraordinary talents, for at first glance the effect was startlingly realistic.

The officers poured out of the station to witness the spectacle and add to the vocal chorus with their shouts and laughter. The pastor and sexton chortled with relief and admiration and begged Smiley to pose for some pictures. The corporal however, seemed to feel that he needed to exert some authority. Hadn't the sergeant left him in charge of things? He viewed the scene before him with a critical eye.

The sergeant in the meantime was having a bad time of it. When his wife asked what he was doing home so early, he told her that he wasn't feeling well. He said that the mosquitoes at the station had been particularly troublesome that morning and he may have been bitten and infected with the dreaded dengue fever. The way he pronounced dengue it sounded like donkey, so his wife laughingly corrected him and asked what his symptoms were. He was unable to be specific about what ailed him, so she forced him to take a sedative and packed him off to bed, promising that he'd feel much better later.

16

He now mumbled, tossing and turning fitfully, evidence of his encounters in a troubling dream in which Nevis was under attack by a horde of giant mosquitoes as big as donkeys. In his dream, Smiley had burst into the police station babbling about mosquitoes as big as donkeys down at the bogs. The sergeant instantly grasped the enormity of the situation. He remembered that environmentalists had been warning for years that waste oils and other noxious substances could drastically alter and affect the ecology of the bogs. His agile mind was quickly able to realise that the inevitable had finally happened and transmutation on an incredible scale had taken place.

Quick action was needed to avert a disaster of unimaginable proportions, but he knew that going through regular channels would waste too much time. He needed to go directly to the top, but the Premier was in Sri Lanka, the Prime Minister was in Lebanon, and he didn't want to waste any time with lesser authorities. So he placed a direct call to the US President in Washington who promised to send planes as soon as the Kosovo conflict was settled, troops as soon as Congress would permit, and a personal visit as soon as his wife trusted him when he was out of her sight again.

The sergeant was now faced with the fact that the fate of Nevis was squarely in his hands alone. His decisions and actions would determine whether Nevis survived or perished under attack from horrible donkey-mosquitoes. With his mind working feverishly, he ordered every available police officer to proceed to the bogs armed with plenty of weapons and ammunition. The fire truck was to take the lead in order to flush out the mosquitoes. But before the plan could be put into action, the mosquitoes made a pre-emptive strike, spreading panic and disorder as they buzzed into Charlestown.

The sergeant was outdoors when the assault came, and witnessed people scrambling frantically for safety. The only person who wasn't running for cover was Smiley who seemed to be enjoying the hullabaloo around him, as if he were orchestrating it all. But as the sergeant moved towards Smiley to ask him a few questions, a giant donkey-mosquito streaked towards him. He ran back towards the station but couldn't reach in time.

He stumbled and fell before he could reach the door. The giant dipteran insect was upon him in an instant. Its horrible mouthpart moved closer. He gasped, shrieked, and jerked away when his wife reached out and touched him. "Man, wake up," she said. "You mus be havin another one a dem bad dreams!" The sergeant woke up with a start, heart pounding and gasping with fright. It took his wife a few moments to get him to realise he was safe from whatever troubled him in his dream, but he wouldn't talk about it with her. Wouldn't tell her what it was that spooked him so. He didn't want her laughing at him.

Back at the station the corporal had made his decision. He thought the ruckus in the street would get out of control if he didn't do something. He would put an end to this nonsense and restore order to the area. After all, it was Sunday. People shouldn't be doing this stupidness on a Sunday, he thought. He stepped up to the front of the crowd and ordered everyone to disperse or face arrest for unlawful assembly. He demanded to know if Smiley had applied for permission to conduct a parade, and threatened to arrest him for obstructing traffic. Nobody paid him any mind however, and the crowd grew as it wended its way down Main Street. And Smiley – well, he just went on smiling his incredible smile. And best of all, nobody came down with the dreaded dengue fever!

But that is typical of the sort of thing that Smiley used to be noted for. And though over a period of time the nature of his activities changed somewhat, people never tired of talking about his past exploits and wondering what he was going to come up with next.

CONDUCT REFLECTS CHARACTER

ROCK OF AGES

Although Smiley Smitten's grandmother had not said a harsh word to him in ages, he knew when she was upset with him by the abnormal way she would suddenly begin treating him. Normally they got on fine together in the modest home they still shared. She had raised him since infancy after his unwed mother died.

She had fed him, clothed him, taught him right from wrong. And in the early years, she had few qualms about using a switch to straighten him out or "knock some sense" into him when occasion demanded. But that was a long time ago, and not since the time he turned to her calmly and said "you done yet Granny?"

She knew then that he'd grown too big for her to whip anymore, even though he was still in primary school. And besides, that incredible smile he was born with which never left his face, made it hard to tell if she had whipped him enough or if he was laughing at her. So for awhile she resorted to raising her voice a notch or two and flaying him with harsh words of reprimand.

Granny soon tired of that method of correction however. She couldn't always think of the right words, and she didn't want to say things she might later regret. She decided to think of a different tactic to use. It didn't take her long to come up with a new strategy, and it worked so well she wondered why she didn't think of it before.

She actually got the idea after hearing a sermon in the church she attended. It was based on "The Power Of Soft Words And Kind Deeds." So that became her modus operandi. Whenever Smiley did something that displeased her, she would modify her voice to sound as syrupy sweet as possible. She would praise any useful little thing he might have done no matter how trivial. She would remind him what a good fellow he usual is and tell him that his mother would have been as proud of him as she was.

She would also do various things for him. Things that he preferred to do for himself. Hanging up his clothes, putting away his shoes, wasn't so bad. But it made him extremely uncomfortable when she insisted on clipping his toenails, his fingernails, or his hair. Or she might want to squeeze a pimple on his nose, or check his ears for dirt and wax. These were only a few of the things she might do, and all the while she would exaggeratedly be singing his praises or repeating assorted homilies which she remembered from church.

When she first began to use these tactics, Smiley became confused and asked Granny what was going on, why she was behaving so strangely. Then she would relate some transgression she believed he had committed, and told him that the fault must have been hers for not raising him properly. She would apologise for not giving him enough love, kindness and attention in the past and swore that if he just gave her a chance, she would make up for it in the future in hopes he would mend his waywardness.

This was usually enough to give rise to feelings of guilt and remorse in Smiley, who loved his grandmother dearly and intuitively knew that she had already sacrificed so much in her life to give to his. He would promise then to try to be more thoughtful in his actions and behaviour so as not to cause her any more problems or distress. Then things would agreeably get back to normal, until the next time he did something, which upset her.

This particular evening, Granny was exceedingly lavish with soft words and kind deeds. For supper she had heaped Smiley's plate with his favourites, salt-fish and rice, okras and fungi. The ginger-beer she had concocted was the best he ever tasted, and he was actually full by the time she placed her delicious coconut tarts in front of him. Yet he was determined to consume every morsel of the goodies that she had prepared especially for him, lest she feel that he was rejecting her labours and her love.

As he uncomfortably stuffed himself, Smiley's mind groped in search of some method of appeasement, for he knew what had upset Granny even though she had not as yet mentioned it. At least not directly. She had however, solemnly intoned a phrase from one of her church hymns, "Rock Of Ages," as she was putting the food on the table. Smiley knew the hymn well, having learned and sung it many times at the church services he attended with Granny when he was a child.

But Smiley now only went to services at this church sporadically. Unfortunately, that very afternoon he had gotten into a dispute with the local pastor who claimed that those who do not attend church regularly are not good Christians. It was the same pastor who sometime before, had scolded people about what they wore to church saying "You are not welcome in my church in that attire. I will not allow you to turn this place into a circus."

On that occasion Smiley earned the pastor's wrath by stating that he did not know the church belonged to the pastor but thought it was the Lord's House. He also pointed out that he had attended several funerals there where the costumes of policemen, nurses, oddfellows, the Lions Club, Girl Guides, and other orders made it look very much like a circus indeed.

Another time when the pastor had chided someone for wearing sandals to church instead of more formal closed shoes, Smiley pointed to a portrait of

Jesus wearing sandals and asked whether the pastor would complain if Christ wore sandals to church. Though the congregation had a good laugh, the pastor wasn't amused. He told Smiley that the Church was not the place to make jokes, but to worship God and to pray for salvation.

Probably the most serious incident occurred after a sermon in which the pastor exhorted the congregation that "we now know that we should have chosen Barrabas to die instead of Jesus." Smiley questioned the wisdom of suggesting that Christians should choose anyone to die. And he didn't understand why the pastor seemed so upset with him afterward.

Smiley wasn't trying to be difficult or make problems for anybody. He certainly wasn't intending to be disrespectful in church. He was probably more reverent than most of the most pious-looking members of the congregation. And he actually could recite more scriptures and passages from the Bible than most avid Sunday churchgoers. But he had his own way of looking at things. And of course, his custom of saying whatever was on his mind whenever he felt like it, was not always appreciated, and very often misunderstood.

So for awhile, Smiley changed his usual weekly habit of going to this church with his granny, and tried visiting churches of other denominations. He soon encountered difficulties when he questioned the differences in the way things were done, or when he inevitably made comments or observations which seemed to be at odds with the established religious practice or theology. This particular Sunday though, he accompanied Granny to the old church he was brought up in, because he hadn't been there for awhile and he wanted to keep in touch.

But he had been finding it difficult to fit in with any church congregation unless he was willing to keep his mouth shut except when singing hymns or praying. This was simply too difficult for Smiley to do. Especially when he could think of so many questions that needed answering, and so many observations that needed commenting.

This morning's church service was a case in point. The service started off smoothly enough, but the turnout was low and the pastor decided to mention that declining attendance could create problems for the church, threatening its financial viability. When the pastor said that those who do not attend church services regularly were not good Christians, he happened to be looking in Smiley's direction. Smiley felt compelled to explain that he had been attending services regularly, but at different churches.

If he had stopped at that point, things might not have been so bad as everyone was enjoying a little chuckle. But Smiley was only beginning. He looked around with that incredible smile of his and said that a number of people who came to church regularly every Sunday, practiced shady business dealings during the week. He also said that some known wife beaters and child molesters never missed a Sunday in church and wondered if that made them good Christians.

By that time the congregation was in a holy uproar. Granny was of course, mortified to the point of speechlessness and went home as quickly as she could manage. Amazingly, the pastor was able to restore order and finish the service, but he abandoned his main theme about regular church service being central to the development of "Good Christians." Smiley was late getting home because the pastor and other church officials felt it necessary to discuss with him, his future relationship with the church.

When he finally reached home, it was with heavy heart for the discussions after church service had not gone well for him. The pastor was of the view that Smiley's behaviour was too disruptive and that he should not return to church services until he had learned to curb his "outrageous outbursts." The church elders fully supported the pastor and were not at all sympathetic to Smiley's defence, that if other members of the congregation were allowed to shout out "Hallelujah," or "Amen" during a sermon, he surely should be allowed to say something too.

Granny started fussing over him as soon as he came in the door. She made him sit right down in a comfortable chair while she fixed him a glass of ginger beer with plenty of ice. It was a hot day, she told him, and he must be tired after spending so much time at church. She didn't say anything about what had happened in church, nor did she mention her embarrassment or explain why she had rushed home before the service ended. She just bustled about, making him comfortable, asking if he needed anything, praising the way he looked, and setting the table for supper.

As he worked his way through the sumptuous meal, Smiley fretted about what to say to Granny. How could he tell her that he was practically kicked out of the church that she had been going to for ages, the church that she had brought him up in? How could he tell her that he wasn't welcome there anymore? It would break her heart, he was sure.

She asked how he liked the salt fish and the fungi. His guilt mounted as he told her it was fine. And that the peas and rice and okras were fine too. He awkwardly praised the meal that she had prepared for him, while his mind skittered about, remembering. Remembering how when he was a tot, she would take him to Sunday school at that church.

She was not so old then, and would often lift and carry him part of the way. He recalled that she used a lot of talcum powder and it sometimes caused him to sneeze when she held him close. He smiled at the memory and Granny asked why he was smiling, what he was thinking. Over the years Granny had learned to read his face and could tell by the expression in his eyes, when he was happy or when he was sad. She was the only one who could do this.

She laughed when Smiley told her about this particular recollection, and they reminisced through the meal about old times, each recalling the way they remembered things. Gradually they began to recall things of more recent vintage and Smiley's mood became sombre as he remembered the time Granny tripped and fell and bruised herself.

Then in a sudden flash, though he didn't say anything, he recalled that Granny was now having trouble going up and down the church steps, needed more help going to and from the market, and was a lot slower doing things than she used to be. Granny was getting old.

Suddenly Smiley realised he had the solution to his problem and although he was absolutely stuffed to the gills, he finished off his dessert with great gusto. Then he reached across the table and took Granny's hands in his and after thanking her for the scrumptious supper, told her he realised he upset her by his actions in church that day and wanted to apologise.

She started to speak, but he cut her off saying that he didn't mean to embarrass her in church the way he sometimes did, but that he couldn't help it.

Things just came out of him before he could even think sometimes. Then he told her that he thought the best thing for him to do would be to stop going to church services altogether.

Granny started to protest but Smiley cut her off again, telling her that he noticed that she was not as spry as she used to be, and that the walk to church and climbing all those steps was taking a lot out of her. He reminded Granny that the church's outreach programme brings the word of God to the homes of those unable to attend. He said that he thought that programme might be the best solution for the both of them.

He spoke about how they could recite the scriptures, sing the hymns, and witness and pray with the visiting church members. And he pointed out that she wouldn't be taxing herself, walking that distance and climbing the steps, and he would be in no danger of upsetting the whole church congregation with an impulsive outburst.

Granny smiled and rubbed his hands. She wasn't protesting anymore. She was genuinely happy and pleased with her grandson, and herself. She had raised him well. She looked at his face, beyond that incredible grin into his eyes. She saw warmth, tenderness, honesty and love. She drew a deep breath and joyously began to hum that old standby, the hymn she relied on to lift her spirits in good times or bad, "Rock of Ages."

Smiley knew everything was all right again between him and Granny. He could relax now.

CONDUCT REFLECTS CHARACTER

SOUND EFFECTS

Smiley Smitten's grandmother had not had a good night's sleep in more than a week. Though she tried to make up for this lack by taking naps during the daytime, Smiley could see that she just wasn't her usual self and became quite concerned. The trouble was that a neighbour's son had received one of the latest "boom-boxes" for his sixteenth birthday, and played his cassettes on the thing nonstop whenever he was home.

It didn't bother Smiley much at first. He was accustomed to the loud sounds, which had gradually permeated almost every aspect of the community. And he actually enjoyed the tricky rhythms and relentless booming sounds routinely produced by electronic equipment owned by so many young people. But when he realised that the neighbour's loud music was having a negative effect on his dearly beloved grandmother, he decided that something must be done.

At first he approached the boy, asking him to please play the music more softly at night so that his grandmother could sleep undisturbed. But the boy, who had picked up some bad habits somewhere, loudly told Smiley to move somewhere else if the music bothered him. He was annoyed that Smiley had asked him to be quiet, and claimed that would spoil his fun. He fired some bad words at Smiley and turned up the volume a notch or two.

The next day, Smiley tried to reach the boy's mother but had great difficulty because she held two jobs and seldom seemed to be at home. She was furious when he contacted her at her workplace and told him to stop interfering with her and her son. Because there was nobody else in that household that he could talk to, Smiley was unsure about what next he should try to do.

Because the neighbour's son was still attending school, Smiley approached one of his teachers, then the principal, then the Department of Education, but they all spurned Smiley's entreaties saying it was a matter that could only be resolved by the parties concerned. Later Smiley learned confidentially, that the boy was considered an "enfant terrible" at school, the mother had a reputation as a regular battleaxe, and nobody wanted to get involved in any dispute with either of them.

Smiley next tried the pastor, who advised him to learn to be more tolerant of others. Smiley explained that he only wanted the loud music at night to stop so that his grandmother could get some undisturbed rest. The pastor replied that he understood the problem, sympathised wholeheartedly, and would pray for dear old granny. He said he would ask the congregation on Sunday to pray for Granny too.

Smiley tried the Government Ministry of Health and was referred to the Department of Community Affairs, which referred him to the Police Department. Smiley didn't especially want to go the police about this matter. They had never ever taken him seriously about anything. The first thing the police would say if he entered the station was "Smiley boy, what story you comin' wid now?" And they would laugh and joke at him no matter how serious a problem he might try to report.

So after awhile, he stopped taking the police seriously too and would dream up funny, harmless pranks to play on them from time to time. He didn't expect them to take him seriously now and he was right. The minute he complained that his grandmother's sleep was disturbed by loud music from his neighbour, they began making jokes about his granny.

They said things like "Bwoy, when you get to be dat ole, you lucky to hear anyting at all!"

"She shouldn't be so cantankerous and try tap people having fun. Why don't you all move bwoy?"

So Smiley gave up on the police. They had been his last resort but just as he expected, they hadn't been any help at all. Now he was forced to take matters into his own hands. He bent his mind to carefully plotting what he considered would be the most effective strategy. Though he lacked academic qualifications, Smiley's native intelligence could often bring superior results when searching for solutions to problems. A lot depended of course, on what the problems were.

It so happened that Smiley had an old portable radio and cassette player with dual speakers in his possession. He had acquired it for next to nothing at one of those rummage sales the Red Cross is always having. It wasn't in working condition when he got it, but by cleaning the battery terminals and tinkering with the innards, he got it working again probably as well as it ever did.

He didn't use it much except for going to the beach or hikes in the country because the batteries were expensive and he didn't want to run them down unnecessarily. But now he was a man with a mission, so he checked the batteries in preparation and made sure he had a number of spares before putting his plan into action. And that plan was amazingly simple.

He spent a few days surreptitiously making himself familiar with the grounds and surrounding areas of various residences. Among the many homes he scrutinised were those of school teachers, church ministers, the police chief, government officials, and assorted businessmen and women. Then during a three week period he traumatised various neighbourhoods around Nevis with bold tactics, striking first in one area and then another.

His modus operandi was to secrete himself at some vantage point close to the victim's house, preferably near a bedroom, anywhere between the hours of midnight and two or three o'clock in the morning. Then he would turn the cassette player on full blast and wait for a reaction from someone in the house. Although his portable battery powered set did not pack the power of newer, more sophisticated equipment, the volume it could produce on a quiet night was truly amazing.

If someone came to the window and shouted to turn off the music, Smiley just switched from one cassette to another, playing something equally loud and irritating. He would never stick around too long, just long enough to make sure that somebody was roused and angry enough to get out of bed, turn on the lights, shout for the music to stop and threaten to call the police. Three or four minutes was the most he would spend at one place though, then he'd go off to torture someone else.

Smiley would "strike" at several places during the course of an outing, so during the first few nights the police were receiving calls from plenty of irate residents. At first the police didn't pay much attention to these petty complaints, but after the magistrate, the Premier, and the hospital matron all complained on the same night, their priorities began to shift a bit.

The police didn't know how to begin, who to look for or where to look. They hadn't a clue what they were up against. Their training hadn't prepared them for anything like this. Two lawyers, a government minister, a doctor, two nurses and three prominent businessmen complained the next night. The police didn't know what to make of it. They wondered how many people were involved in this kooky clandestine activity. And they wondered what the motive was, what was the purpose.

Smiley showed up at the police station again during all this, to ask the police to please deal with the noisy neighbour so that his granny could get some sleep. The police didn't laugh this time, but they still weren't interested in helping. "Bwoy, we busy bad today. Granny could wait awhile," was the curt response. So Smiley stepped up his activities during his late night forays and the police were kept busier than ever, answering the phones. Three church ministers, two school principals, a librarian, several senior civil servants and a couple of housewives kept them hopping.

After the first week, the media began to pick up on the phenomena, publishing Letters to the Editor and interviews with some of the "victims." By the second week the media were mentioning "Phantom DJs," "Guerilla tactics," and "Midnight Musical Marauders." The radio call-in programmes with their panels of experts allotted extra time to air the questions and comments from citizens who were heavily critical of the police and government handling of the situation.

As the nights and days went by, calls pouring into the police station from upset residents seemed to reach panic proportions. Even owners of guesthouses were angrily complaining about the "Phantom DJs" and demanding that the police do something. Newspaper editorials suggested that the police were not a force to be reckoned with. One columnist even went so far as to say that in the current situation the police actions were less of a force and more of a farce. Needless to say, the police were not amused. The calls to police and government headquarters increased.

During the third week, the Nevis Island Administration announced that it had created a "Task Force" to study the situation and present its findings and recommendations within six months. They also appointed a cadre of "Sound Wardens" to immediately begin functioning in each village. The wardens were armed with portable tape recorders, and were authorised to make recordings of any loud or unnecessary sounds in their areas, and to gather the names and addresses of any perpetrators for the police.

The Police Department created a special "Anti-Sound Squad", which was designed to work under cover for maximum effectiveness and the element of surprise. Not surprisingly, the first few suspects they pulled in had to be released for lack of sufficient evidence. They all produced police permits authorising them to use "noisy instruments" at the prescribed times.

Oddly enough, the Nevis Historical and Conservation Society started a campaign against sound pollution, and were denied permission by the Police Department to use "Noisy instruments" at their first public meeting in the square. A day later, the Health Department made its own appeal against unwanted sound in a public meeting at the same square. They used "noisy instruments" themselves but it was unclear whether they required or received police permission.

The two Nevis newspapers ran similar headlines; "Sound Madness Muddles Nevis!" and "Nevis Assailed by Sound Psychos!" A St. Kitts newspaper whose motto is "Sound speech which cannot be condemned," Published a front-page story titled "Federation's Stability Threatened by Sound Hysteria in Nevis!" The other publication which styled itself as "The Federation's Leading Newspaper," said in its front page story that the Federal Government was sponsoring "agent provocateurs" to create a diversion from its problems in St. Kitts by stirring up trouble in Nevis.

A special session of the Nevis House of Assembly was scheduled to debate newly proposed sound legislation. The Nevis Chamber of Industry and Commerce said they would endorse any local initiative to reduce unnecessary loud sounds, "especially in the Charlestown area." The Christian Council adopted a resolution "supporting measures to restore peace and tranquility to our homes and neighbourhoods."

The Education Department issued a bulletin stating that students raised in quiet environments were more disciplined and performed better academically. The Health Ministry followed closely with a communiqué saying that scientific studies have proven that exposure to loud sounds could lead to serious health problems, citing increased stress levels, ear damage, and possible birth defects. And the Ministry of Tourism sent out a press release urging "a return to the peace and quiet which Nevis is famous for, which visitors find attractive, and which is so essential to the optimum development of our tourism product."

The Evangelical Association announced a series of "Silent Services" based on the idea that "Silence is Golden." The AYPA organised a "Crusade Against Offensive Sound," and thirty of their members marched through Charlestown carrying portable sound equipment playing so softly that you could not hear it if you were more than six feet away.

Other groups and organisations produced displays and presentations too, including the Lions Club with a cleverly designed T-shirt showing a fully-grown lion softly mee-ewing to a tiny kitten. The Nevis Red Cross got into the act by offering rehabilitation workshops in Sensitivity Training for DJs, Truck and Bus drivers, or other persons who commonly commit sound offenses.

VON Radio which normally trumpets itself as "The Powerhouse Of The Eastern Caribbean," powered down a little to provide special programming featuring hours and hours of quiet music. Old time favourites such as "In The Still Of The Night," "Softly, As In A Morning Sunrise," "Tip-toe Through The Tulips," "Whispering Grass," "Sweet And Low," and "Hush-A-Bye, My Baby" were being heard anew by a generation that never heard them before.

A remarkable change quickly took place in Nevis as police began enforcing noise abatement laws, issuing fewer permits for DJs and "Noisy Instruments," especially in residential areas, and paying prompt attention to all complaints about loud or unwanted sounds. The noisy youngster who had caused Granny so many sleepless nights, suddenly became much more amenable and considerate after a sound warden turned incriminating evidence over to the anti-sound police squad, health officials suggested that his loud music could be considered a health hazard, and the Department of Education equated it with his low grades at school.

A few motorists fussed after being cautioned about tooting their horns unnecessarily. Some young bloods actually had to pay fines for driving around neighbourhoods with "boom boxes" blaring. And some eateries and bars that normally played loud music "to attract customers," found that they did just as much business when they played the music softly. In some cases, business actually improved.

The funny thing though is that through all of this hullabaloo, Smiley had faded completely into the background. Although there were a few rumours that he might have been involved, nobody really realised that it was his action that sparked the movement towards a reduction of unwanted sound in the community. Nobody was paying much attention to him except his dear old Granny, who sang his praises every day, and now slept soundly every night.

CONDUCT REFLECTS CHARACTER

SMILEY FALLS IN LOVE

That Smiley Smitten fell in love is really not so surprising as the fact that it took him so long. And maybe even that isn't so surprising when you consider that for most of his young life, none of the girls he knew showed any interest in him. Except on occasions when they would tease and make jokes about his permanent lopsided grin, the girls that he encountered in Nevis took no notice of him at all.

So to avoid being subjected to the inevitable taunting and ridicule, Smiley avoided being around girls as much as possible. The only females in his life that he knew and felt comfortable with, were his grandmother who raised him after his mother died in childbirth, and older women who were members of the church he used to go to but no longer attended because of a dispute with the pastor. But of course that is another issue.

Suffice it to say that girls were not high on Smiley's list of priorities. In fact, Smiley's priorities were not listed at all but just sorted themselves out according to the general laws of serendipity. For instance, one day he accidentally bumped into someone who had just left Evelyn's Travel Agency on Main Street in Charlestown.

The impact jolted travel tickets and other paraphernalia from the person's grasp, causing them to flutter to the ground. Smiley stooped to help retrieve the items and apologised as he handed them back to the owner, a white girl in her twenties, with dark hair and eyes and lightly tanned skin. She might have been a year or two older than Smiley, but then, he always looked a little younger than he really was. She apologised at the same time as Smiley; thinking the accident was her fault. Then, noticing the incredible smile on his face, asked why he was laughing at her.

When Smiley explained that he wasn't laughing but was born with a facial condition, which made it seem that way, she apologised once more, saying that she hadn't intended to be insensitive. Smiley told her that he wasn't offended and could see that she wasn't poking fun at him the way so many others did.

She seemed disturbed that anyone would make fun of him and they stood there for several minutes discussing the issue. When she realised that passersby were staring at them with curiosity, she suggested that if he had the time, they could continue talking over some cool drinks at Unella's Restaurant. And so they spent the better part of the afternoon there chatting about all sorts of things.

He found out that she was spending her last few days in Nevis after a two-week break from her college studies in the US. She was majoring in Theatre Arts and pulled out a book of plays by William Shakespeare, which she would be working on when she went back. He said he had heard of Shakespeare but never read any of the plays. She learned about his family life – what there was of it. That his mother died in childbirth, he had never known his father and he was raised by his grandmother whom he loved dearly.

She found out that even though he had only a primary school education, he had a good inquisitive mind and was an avid reader of all sorts of books and periodicals. So he knew a lot more than most people realised. He also knew a lot of things about the history of Nevis, the places of interest, plants trees, nature trails, old forts, sugar mills, the mountain. She told him that she wanted to do some hiking, horseback riding, climb the mountain and visit some historical ruins before she left Nevis and asked if she could hire him as her guide.

Smiley was happy to agree and for the next few days, the two of them were seen in each other's company all over the island. Local tongues began to wag and one rumour, which spread like wildfire, was that a rich white woman was using Smiley for sexual purposes. It wasn't true of course, but Nevisians love to spread those kinds of rumours.

They had been seen at Pinney's Beach where the girl quite innocently was trying to teach Smiley to swim. Everybody knew that Smiley couldn't swim, but one fellow who saw the girl patiently trying to hold Smiley and instruct him on what to do, joked that it looked like they were having sex in the water.

What started out as a crude joke was soon being bandied about and accepted as an actuality as various versions of the incident spread rapidly through the community. This affected some people in remarkable ways. Local young women, who never took notice except to make fun of Smiley before, suddenly began to fluff themselves up when they saw him, as if they wanted him to notice them now. Older churchwomen criticised him mercilessly behind his back, saying it was shameful that he preferred white women to black. And the young bucks around town wildly speculated about what Smiley had that they didn't.

Smiley had a certain innocence of mind and purity of heart that the visitor he was guiding around the island found charming. He exhibited great patience with her ineptitude at climbing the mountain and hiking the nature trails and he displayed keen knowledge about the areas they visited. He enjoyed telling her the names of various plants and flowers and the medicinal uses of certain kinds of plants. On a trek around Saddle Hill she found a few curious bits of shards and he picked up a gnarled branch that had broken off from an old tree.

With a few deft strokes of his cutlass he severed the gnarled knob from the rest of the broken branch. Holding it in the palm of his hand, he asked her what she thought it resembled. She started to turn it over, but he insisted that she view it only in the way he held it. At first she frowned, but soon a smile spread over her face and she said it looked like a small-scale model of Nevis. He was delighted when she asked if she could keep it.

When they went horse riding she was more expert, so he willingly acceded to her instructions. When they went to the beach she insisted on trying to teach him to swim, and although he was previously terrified of the water he had no trouble entrusting himself to her guidance. And afterwards, they lay on the sand and read passages from her book of Shakespeare's plays to each other. These two young people though hailing from vastly different backgrounds and cultures had rapidly developed trust and confidence in each other.

She was grateful for the ease with which they were able to relate to each other. Her first ten days on Nevis had been a little difficult. Many of the locals she encountered were not as friendly as the travel magazines had led her to expect. Some people mistook her efforts to be sociable, as "forwardness" or worse. Women seemed suspicious or resentful. Men thought she was a woman of easy virtue and made lewd remarks or unwelcome advances. She felt safe in Smiley's company though, even when others were not near.

For Smiley, being near her was the first time as a young man that he was able to be comfortable and happy in the presence of a young woman. She didn't laugh at, taunt, scorn, or belittle him in any way. She didn't pay undue attention to his permanent, lopsided grin. He learned that she was a year or two older than he was, but she showed genuine interest in him, and respect. He loved that. He needed that. He loved telling her about things she didn't know, and showing her ways to do new things. It gave him a new sense about himself that he had never known before.

But their time together was coming to an end. She would soon be going back to her studies in America. She told him she wanted him to keep the book of Shakespeare as a remembrance. For the first time in his life he began to experience some strange and confusing feelings, making him happy and sad at the same time. He needed to express these feelings but didn't know how. He said he would like to give her something for remembrance too but couldn't think of anything. He'd never given anything to a girl before. She insisted that he'd already given her so much of Nevis – she couldn't possibly expect anything more.

On her departure date, he saw her off at the airport and felt perfectly miserable. He didn't want to say goodbye. He didn't want her to leave. He carried her bags to the check-in counter and stood around in misery while the departure arrangements were being made. Then there was a long uncomfortable period waiting for her flight to leave.

They stood awkwardly, trying to make conversation, struggling for words. It was the first time in the four days since they first met that they were at a loss for words. The first time they felt any discomfort. He cleared his throat and tried again but the words wouldn't come. It was just as well, because his mind wasn't clear and the thought that he wanted to express hadn't fully formed yet. He gave up and stood gazing out at the tarmac. The woeful expression in his eyes belied the incredible smile on his face.

She knew she had to say something before she left, but it was difficult. She moved close to his side and brushed at his arm with her warm fingers. His heart thumped wildly at this brief contact and he turned to look at her face. He wondered if she knew what he was feeling and if she had those kinds of feelings too. He noticed a strange expression in her eyes and felt a sudden tingle along his spine.

Her eyes became watery. She squeezed them shut and told him she wished she could stay longer, but her vacation was over and she had to go. She thanked him for the time he spent with her and said that they would always be among her fondest memories. She told him that outside of her family, he was the dearest, kindest person she had ever known, and that it was a great privilege for her to have been in his company. She said that was a gift she would always treasure.

Her flight was suddenly announced. She took his hand and squeezed hard. Then she drew closer and pressed her cheek to his as she said a breathless goodbye. She looked at him expecting a response, but he could say nothing.

He couldn't have seen her as she turned and left to board the aircraft. Hot tears had welled up in his eyes, so he had shut them to stem the flood. When he opened them again, she was gone.

He wiped the tears away and looked out towards the tarmac again, just as her flight was taking off. Finally, he expressed what he couldn't quite understand before – and couldn't find the words for. "I love you," he whispered before he turned and walked away.

CONDUCT REFLECTS CHARACTER

'X' ME OUT

Smiley had been pondering about a mystery for several days and the more he tried to examine the phenomenon from different perspectives the lesser it seemed to make any sense to him. It seemed to him that politicians in power are the only people in Nevis empowered to have big ceremony and celebration every time they do a job that the public pays them to do.

It made Smiley Smitten wonder, but only after he noticed that certain ordinary people seemed to spend a lot of time going to various government functions where special ceremonies were held to open something, to close something, or just to generally celebrate something or other.

Now, some people used to think that Smiley wasn't very bright because he always wore this incredibly lopsided grin on his face, even at the most serious moments. But Smiley couldn't help it. He was born that way. Still, Smiley liked to play some weird pranks at times, so some people were convinced that he was a little light in the head. But don't let anybody fool you.

Smiley may not exactly have been a Rhodes scholar but despite appearances, he had a goodly amount of natural intelligence. Anyway, Smiley was wondering one day, why it was that some people would leave work, leave their home, or leave whatever they were doing – even close up shop to attend some government shindig where the "poo-bahs" would "big-up" their chests and say how much good they were doing for the country.

Sandwiches, cakes, cookies, fruit punch, and all sorts of refreshments were lavished on the people afterwards. At more elaborate affairs, cocktails or rum punch might be served. Of course the press corps with notebooks, pencils, tape recorders and cameras would capture it all for posterity. And if they didn't capture all, at least they would capture some. And if it wasn't exactly for posterity, at least they'd make believe it was.

Smiley couldn't see the point of it all. He'd been to a few of these events, so he knew what went on. He had sometimes helped to set up the seating and hung around to watch all the fol-de-rol. During one period of time, he noticed an increase in that kind of activity and wondered about the reasons for it. He decided to ask one of the politicians in power to explain it to him. So one bright morning he went to the Administration Building and stopped the first government minister to show up.

Smiley is not a person who will ever be known for finesse. He probably doesn't even know the meaning of the word. He just boldly up and asked the minister why the government was wasting so much time and money on all the unnecessary hoopla. The minister, although taken aback at first, was up to the task. He insisted that no money was being wasted, it was simply being invested in "educating" the people of Nevis. He said that the people needed to know what their government was doing. He told Smiley that this was the best way of letting them know. Talk about finesse!

But Smiley wasn't biting. He wasn't having any of that. He told the minister that when people leave their jobs in the middle of the day, stop working, close up shop to attend government receptions and things, they are not producing, serving the public, or helping the economy.

He said that if the baker down the street held a big ceremony every time he baked a few loaves of bread, you'd think he was cuckoo. And if the plumber who fixed your toilet said "let's open a bottle of champagne and celebrate," you'd probably tell him to take a hike.

The minister almost fell over. He didn't realise that Smiley's thought processes were so well developed. Still, it was nothing the minister couldn't handle. He told Smiley that it was basically a matter of boosting public confidence and morale. He said that when people take time out to see and hear their government in action, and to rub shoulders with them and have refreshments and chat with them on those occasions, they become more productive when they go back to work. Their morale is higher, and so on.

Smiley said he couldn't see any evidence of this, and he also wondered aloud why there suddenly were so many of these functions. The minister smiled and told him to go home and listen to the radio and be sure to read the newspaper the next day. When Smiley asked why, the minister said that the date of the election was going to be announced.

Suddenly Smiley understood the reason for all the government frolic and fancy. He understood that the government politicians were trying to make themselves look good so that people would vote for them again and keep them in office. He understood that all the ribbon cutting, fancy speeches and showy presentations were designed to impress ordinary people. And all the awards, ceremonies and free food and drinks were attempts by these politicians to ingratiate themselves with the public in a popular, tangible way. And of course, to influence the votes of the electorate.

Smiley's thoughts, like his vocabulary, were not refined and sophisticated. But at a basic, earthy human level, he could analyse things well enough to understand that certain enticements and inducements were akin to bribery. And in his simple, artless way, he told the government minister so.

The minister wasn't accustomed to dealing with such direct openness and honesty in the circles he travelled. Most people were a little more careful about the way they spoke to a high government official. But he didn't let it ruffle him much. He was clever, cunning, and knew just how to deal with difficult people in his constituency. He turned on his most ingratiating smile, which curiously was almost the mirror image of Smiley's permanent lopsided one. They made an odd, comical looking pair, grinning at each other in front of Administration Building.

The minister leaned closer and in a conspiratorial tone told Smiley that secretly he agreed with him and didn't really like all the fanciness and showiness and free food and drink and the indigestion that followed it all. He said it grieved him sorely to have to do it, but that the public demands it. He said that if the government didn't put on these showy displays, the people would think they weren't doing anything and wouldn't support them at election time. That's the way things were and the way things had always been.

He patted Smiley on the shoulder and told him that he knew Smiley had a good head and could understand. But Smiley wasn't going to be so easily persuaded and told the minister he still didn't like what was going on. The minister sighed and threw up his hands in a gesture of resignation. He told Smiley he appreciated his honesty and that under the circumstances there was only one thing he could suggest.

When Smiley asked what that was, the minister told him to vote against him in the election. Although Smiley was registered, he told the minister that he had never actually voted in an election before. The minister assured him that it was a simple procedure, that all Smiley had to do was to "X" him out on the ballot.

This was a ploy the minister had successfully used before with naïve voters and he had developed this practice to a fine art. He said that Smiley had the God-given right to vote as he pleased and that he, the minister, respected that right. He said that he had nothing but the highest regard for people who voted according to their conscience and if Smiley's conscience didn't like what he was doing, "X me out!" He said that he would still respect Smiley and regard him as a friend.

Smiley nodded appreciatively. Although he never let on, he knew the minister was trying to hoodwink him. He had frequently put up with that sort of thing from people who grossly underestimated his intelligence. It never bothered him very much though, because he had come to realise that it gave him certain advantages. Most people reveal their true selves when interacting with those they consider simple-minded or lacking intelligence. So Smiley was actually able to find out more about others than they would ever realise.

By the time they parted, Smiley was beginning to feel that the minister wasn't such a bad fellow after all. Although he still didn't like what was going on, at least the minister had been honest with him when he said the public demands all the showy displays and free food and drinks. Smiley personally knew a lot of people who went to every government function they could possibly manage. When the free food was served they would take extra plates of it home to their families. That's all that many of them went for. So Smiley began to ponder about these things and wonder if it was such a bad thing for government officials to try to hold onto their jobs by having functions with free food and drink from time to time.

The election campaign swung into full gear with public meetings being held by the contesting politicians all over the place. Smiley attended some of the opposition party's public meetings, but couldn't quite get a handle on what was being expressed. He thought they were saying that the government politicians were nothing but a bunch of crooks. But he wondered why they would be saying that when it was common knowledge that some of their own candidates had themselves been involved in shady dealings. And he wondered why they were saying that the government politicians had done absolutely nothing while in office, when that obviously wasn't true. The government had done a lot of things that the opposition was loudly criticising them for.

So one day he asked the opposition candidate point blank what the point was in calling the government politicians crooks. Wasn't that like the pot calling the kettle black? And then he rattled off a series of changes that had taken place under the latest administration. The candidate, although a little surprised at Smiley's savvy, countered smoothly and suggested that Smiley must have misunderstood what was being said.

He claimed that the message he and the other opposition politicians were trying to get across, was that the government had done absolutely nothing useful about certain things that needed attention. He said that in areas where the government did do something, it was too little, too late, and badly done in the bargain. And he was adamant that none of the opposition candidates had ever been convicted of larceny, and swore that any reports of unscrupulousness on the part of any of his colleagues were merely falsehoods, exaggerations, or ugly rumours spread by unprincipled government functionaries.

Smiley pressed the candidate to outline how his side would perform if elected and could form the new government. The candidate waxed enthusiastically about all the plans they had to improve the economy, upgrade the infrastructure, increase wages, provide better education and health facilities, affordable housing, special provisions for the elderly, the youths, teenage mothers, lower the crime rate and food prices, and raise the standard of living.

Smiley wanted to know what methods the new government would use to acquaint the populace with all of these improvements. The candidate swelled up his chest and explained the use of official ceremonies, receptions and all sorts of celebrations with free food and drink to educate the public about what was going on. Smiley said that the old government did that and he wasn't impressed. The candidate said that the old government didn't know how to do these things. He called them "a bumbling set of amateurs" and said that when his team took over the reins of power, they would do things right.

They would pull out all the stops and leave no stone unturned in putting on a proper spread at official ceremonies. Plus there would be a choice of wines and liquor, not just rum punch or fruit punch. And he promised more ceremonies than ever before; reflecting a "proactive and progressive government" that was going to do a lot more than the "tired old bunch of nonstarters." The candidate, sensing that Smiley was not properly impressed, asked what was wrong. Smiley told him that he thought those plans were too extravagant, although that wasn't the actual expression he used.

A crafty gleam crept into a corner of the candidate's eye. He leaned close to Smiley and with a conspiratorial tone, confessed it was true that all those official ceremonies and free food and drink was extravagant and wasteful. He said that he agreed with Smiley completely. But he said that things had always been done that way and it would be impossible to change now. The people would never stand for it.

He could see that Smiley wasn't buying this pitch so he decided to 'try a

ting.' He told Smiley that his forthrightness and sincerity impressed him and that he had the highest regard for an honest man. He said he could see that Smiley was a man of principle and would vote accordingly. He told Smiley to look for his name on the ballot on voting day and "X me out." He promised to have no hard feelings. They could still be friends. As they parted, Smiley realised he had a tough choice to make on Election Day. Each political party would essentially be doing the same thing as the other if elected to office, but one would be more extravagant than the other.

A heavy sigh rose in his throat as he thought about what he should do. The incumbents had been in office so long that they thought they were invincible. They were unlikely to ever change their way of doing things, regardless of whatever friends or foe might say. But the opposition, although coming from the same mold, might become more malleable and responsible if the voting public more vigorously probed the doings and behaviour of the next government. Suddenly his choice seemed clear. He chuckled as he thought about it. He would "X out" a certain candidate. And he would try to convince a number of his friends that they should do the same for the good of the country.

When the results came in, the defeated former government minister couldn't figure out why he'd lost his seat, which his party had always considered "safe", and why all of his colleagues had suffered the same fate. The margin of defeat wasn't great, but for him it was a bitter pill nonetheless. Smiley Smitten came to offer his condolences. He said he was sorry the minister had lost because he was not as bad as the opposition candidate was. And he explained how he had done his best to help the minister to win by "X"ing out the other candidate and getting all his friends and relatives to do the same.

The former minister could hardly believe what he was hearing. He struggled to find words and gasped as though having a heart attack. Smiley asked if anything was wrong and offered his help. The ex-minister managed to compose himself and with much remorse, told Smiley the truth about the "X me out" scheme. Smiley was moved by the man's contrition and told him that if the new government did not satisfy the expectations of the people of Nevis, perhaps the old one would win again in the next election. Especially if it learned something in the interim and could adopt more sensible approaches. But he said it was clear that the country needed a change and whoever provided the right changes would likely satisfy the people of Nevis for a long time.

The ex-minister tried to speak, but nothing came to his mind so he merely coughed and cleared his throat. Then Smiley revealed that he knew from the start that the minister was trying to bamboozle him with that "X me out" business, and said that he found the opposition just as bad. He wondered if there were any politicians to be found in Nevis who could be trusted. And he pointed out that when there is not much to choose from in these situations, at least a different face might seem more promising.

The ex-minister didn't know what to say. He was stunned by the awareness of a person he'd always assumed was retarded or simple-minded. That incredible lopsided smile was misleading, he now realised. He wondered how many others he may have misjudged. He tried clearing his throat again, but Smiley wasn't finished yet. This was the first time he had voted in an election he said, and he hoped he had voted wisely. He voted according to his conscience, after candidates on both sides of the political fence had tried to deceive him. He said it was a great learning experience for him and that he held no hard feelings towards anyone. Then he turned and quickly walked away. The politician suddenly regained his senses and tried to reach out with a hand of friendship. But it was too late; Smiley was already out of reach. He would always wear his incredible smile of course, but his visage seemed clouded as he walked down the street.

CONDUCT REFLECTS CHARACTER

SMILEY WINS A CROWN

The Cultural Complex in Nevis was in a state of pandemonium. Over two thousand people had turned up for the finals of Culturama's Calypso King Competition. It was almost 1:00 a.m. and the show was over. But even though most of the people had been at the complex since 8 o'clock, five long hours ago, nobody seemed interested in going home. At least not yet.

The 1st, 2nd, and 3rd place winners had been announced almost thirty minutes ago and although the judges' decision was supposed to be final, almost to a man, the two thousand plus crowd of avid calypso fans decided they weren't accepting it. So they rushed the stage, rushed the judges' enclosure, rushed the Culturama Committee members, and held the whole caboodle hostage.

Police, who were on duty at the event, were so surprised by the sudden reaction of the crowd that they didn't know what to do. So they did nothing, which was of course, the wisest course of action for them to take under the circumstances.

A dispassionate onlooker might have been somewhat perplexed at what had taken place, because up until the moment they erupted spontaneously against the judges' decision, the crowd had been very well behaved. Enthusiastic and demonstrative to be sure, but all in the fun-filled spirit of Culturama.

A serious, angry mood however, had suddenly transformed hundreds of smiling faces into a threatening, howling mob. A thousand shouting voices were trying to be heard above the din; "Dem tief im!" "Crooks!" "Bandits!" "Moodoh!" At first only these few short phrases were plainly discernible through the general uproar. Then gradually other remarks sifted through the hullabaloo and a clearer message began to emerge.

"Dey rob Smiley, man!" "Smiley shoulda win, or at least come first or second runner-up!" "I tell you, Smiley better dan all a dem!" Smiley Smitten was well known around Nevis for the permanent lopsided grin he was born with, and his happy-go-lucky disposition. He had never tried to gain permanent employment, preferring the freedom of his own little casual business enterprises, but he sometimes took on odd jobs whenever he felt the need of a little extra money.

It was during one of these periods that Smiley took on a little job cleaning a rehearsal house for one of the local bands that was preparing calypsonians for Culturama, Nevis' annual arts and culture festival. When Smiley learned that every calypsonian would get some money whether they won anything in the

43

competition or not, he decided to enter, just for the easy money because he considered singing calypso play, not work.

Smiley had an active creative mind and had often thought of some trick to play on somebody or some fancy story to tell – so it wasn't much of a switch for him to try his hand at writing calypsos. In next to no time he was back at the band house asking them to try him out with his calypsos.

At first the band tried to dissuade him because they were accustomed to working with real calypsonians like "Dis Ain't Dat" and "Mee-Toe." They didn't consider his tunes or his lyrics up to par. But Smiley was so insistent that the band members agreed among themselves to take Smiley on, just for a lark, for laughs, a joke. They figured he wouldn't get past the preliminaries, but Smiley couldn't have cared less because he'd have earned a few easy dollars.

When Smiley practised with the band they played the music the way he wanted, but they told him he needed to strut and emphasise his movements more. They showed him how to roll his eyes, wave his hands, wag his head and execute a few fancy steps with his feet. And they told him that once the actual performance started, he must continue without stopping until the conclusion, no matter what happened.

Privately they plotted to play the music differently on the night of performance. They conspired to miss a beat at strategic moments, or add a beat. They planned to change tempo every now and then, or to hit a few wrong notes and pretend that he was at fault. They weren't intending to be mean or anything like that. They genuinely liked Smiley. But since he had absolutely no chance of winning anything, they saw no harm in adding a little more fun to the proceedings.

At rehearsals, the band members came to realise that Smiley's performance was going to be a very funny thing indeed, much funnier than they at first had envisioned. They now decided they wanted him to perform in every show including the finals, simply for the hilarity he was sure to provide. But in order for Smiley to advance to the finals, the Culturama Committee and the calypso judges had to be brought in on the action. The band knew this was taking a big risk, but they were betting that these officials would see the entertainment value of what they were about to propose. And they were right.

And so it was agreed that the band would make Smiley's performance seem as waggishly comical as possible. The judges would see to it that Smiley advanced from the preliminaries through to the finals. And the whole scheme would have the blessings of the top Culturama officials. They would milk him for all the laughs they could before elimination.

Things went precisely according to plan. At the prelims, Smiley came on last and glided, strutted, and gesticulated his way through a song that nobody could follow the words to because they were so busy laughing at the antics between Smiley and the band. They seemed bent on avoiding meeting each other on the same beat, the same key, or even the same tune at times. Smiley's performance was so bad it seemed good. People laughed heartily all the way home and vowed to come out to see Smiley's next performance.

Smiley's impact on the crowd at the semi-finals was even greater than his previous performance. He wore a more colourful costume and displayed more confidence and pizzazz than before. His trademark lopsided grin when directed toward the band seemed timed to provoke a sour note, a missed beat, or some other musical anomaly. The crowd went wild with laughter and applause. The band, the Culturama Committee and the judges rejoiced to see their little scheme working so well. And they made sure that their protégé was among the eight calypsonians advanced to the final round.

On the night of the finals, Smiley was pumped up with enthusiasm. He could hardly wait to get on stage and begin his performance. He knew this was the last night of the competition and he wanted to savour every moment of attention and applause that the crowd would lavish on him. And he had prepared a new song to sing which he felt would delight the audience even more.

The band members were all charged up and rarin' to go. This was going to be one of the best calypso finals of their experience. It would be a night to remember, they were sure of that. They would be playing for three of the top calypsonians on the island who would be unveiling their newest songs. "Dis Ain't Dat" would be singing "Something Fishy in de Market," "Flea-Mango" was coming with a cleverly crafted composition "Ah Going Tell Mama on You," suggesting scandal in the family. And "Mee-Toe" had a hard-hitting commentary on the quality of life titled "Hard Times in HardTimes!"

The band was sure that one of these three performers would win the crown and the other two would be the first and second runners-up. The only thing they didn't feel certain of was the order in which they would finish, they expected the competition to be that close. They also felt that the crowd would go along with the judges' decision if these three were the top finishers regardless of the order. They knew the other five finalists had no chance of upsetting the top three because the gap between the standard of performance and quality of words and music was too great.

Smiley's newest song was called "Face de Facts." But despite the catchy title, the words and the tune were not good enough for anything but laughs as far as the band members were concerned. So they planned a barrage of ridiculous antics and gave Smiley instructions for his performance that would make it seem like he didn't know which way to turn in order to "Face de Facts." When added to their routines of hitting wrong notes, missing the beat and changing the tempo, they were sure Smiley's final appearance would be the funniest thing ever seen at Culturama.

The show went off without a hitch and just as the band expected, Smiley's act which was the last on the programme, brought the audience to tears with rib-tickling laughter. People in the audience were only able to catch their breaths and compose themselves when the MC came out to tell a few jokes while waiting for the judges' decision. It wasn't long in coming and went pretty much the way the band members had predicted.

"Dis Ain't Dat" was pronounced second runner-up. There was general applause. "Mee-Toe" was pronounced first runner-up. More general applause, then a hush of anticipation. Flea-Mango was announced the winner and new calypso king. There was more general applause – then a murmur swept through the crowd and a voice suddenly rang out, "What about Smiley?"

Two thousand voices quickly took up the chant and in a flash the audience surged forward surrounding the stage and officials, demanding that Smiley be given a better deal. This swift unexpected crowd reaction had been completely unanticipated. The officials didn't know what to do or what to say and were completely flummoxed by this turn of events.

"Smiley shoulda win," somebody shouted, and the crowd roared its agreement. A couple of sturdy young fellows located Smiley, hoisted him to their shoulders and paraded him around the stage. "Smile-ee, Smile-ee," the crowd chanted in unison.

The Culturama officials and the judges had been herded together and surrounded by a band of people who linked arms together to prevent any escape. The officials wanted a few days to work something out, but the crowd was having none of that. They insisted on an on the spot resolution to the debacle. Too many times in the past when a controversy had arisen, the officials either did nothing until it had all blown over, or they "worked out" something that hardly satisfied anybody. The crowd was determined that it shouldn't happen again. A just solution had to be found now.

The band was trying to play something to calm the temper of the crowd, but the boys couldn't agree on what to play. It was doubtful that music could have pacified the crowd at that point anyway. It was clearly evident that Smiley had won the hearts of the audience. What the band had intended to be a ridiculous joke had boomeranged. Smiley had become the newest entertainment idol on Nevis.

The judges, huddling with the Culturama officials, were angrily pointing fingers and apportioning blame. The Culturama officials were blaming right back with all the authority they could muster, but they realised the situation was serious and something had to be done to give Smiley some kind of official recognition.

They couldn't strip Flea-Mango of the crown he had just won and give it to Smiley. They couldn't pronounce Smiley third runner-up and award him a few prizes, because the remaining four finalists would probably protest strongly and they had more than enough trouble to deal with already. They couldn't afford to make things worse.

The trouble was, that based on the criteria that had been established, Smiley had earned far fewer points than any of the other finalists. The judges thought they had been reasonable and realistic, yet here they were, faced with this enormous problem. It just wasn't fair, they thought. But this was no time for prevaricating. The mood of the crowd was getting ugly. Something had to be done and done fast. They drew the Culturama officials into serious discussion and after a few minutes of heated argument, an agreement seemed to have been hammered out.

The Culturama Chairman implored the crowd to let him make an announcement – a solution had been reached. The crowd parted to let him get to the microphone on stage. The band struck up a brief fanfare as he cleared his throat. Smile-ee, Smile-ee, Smile-ee, the crowd chanted, but the Chairman held up his hands to signal that he was about to speak and the chant diminished to low mutterings.

The Chairman's first words were apologetic, saying that he deeply regretted the confusion and any embarrassment or inconvenience that may have been caused. He magnanimously took full responsibility and tried to absolve any others of blame by saying the fault was solely his. The band members exchanged glances sheepishly. The judges shifted their feet, avoided each other's eyes, and swallowed hard.

The Chairman stated that the judges had strictly followed the rules, awarding points to each contestant according to the criteria. The judges relaxed a little and nodded smilingly towards each other, but the crowd started to grumble. The Chairman went on to say that in the emergency discussions which had just taken place, it was argued that the criteria was not broad enough and should have included a category for entertainment values and audience appeal. In view of this omission, he said, it was decided unanimously to establish that category separately now, with its own separate prizes and award.

The Chairman then announced that the award would be titled "Most Popular Performer," and that the winner was Smiley Smitten. The crowd went wild with enthusiasm and Smiley's lopsided smile stretched like an elastic band. The band struck up the chorus of Smiley's song, "Face de Facts," and everybody was able to eventually go home happy – justice had been done.

On the weekend, one of the leading newspaper headlines proclaimed "SMILEY SMITTEN BECOMES THE CLOWN PRINCE." Other papers had similar headings, and lauded Smiley's success with lots of photos and descriptive stories. Much was said about his sudden rise to prominence and the fact that all the major businesses had hurriedly agreed to contribute to a generous pool of cash and other worthy prizes for him.

Little attention was paid to the real calypso king and the runners-up in this entire hullabaloo, but they didn't mind. After all, they had won their share of accolades and prizes many times before, so they weren't going to begrudge Smiley his moment of glory. And besides, they were already making plans for next year's Culturama. Little did they know, so was Smiley.

CONDUCT REFLECTS CHARACTER

48

THE PLAY'S THE THING!

Smiley really had no intention of being involved in the play that was under rehearsal at the Cultural Centre. He had merely popped in out of curiosity one fine evening, when he noticed lights in the building as he was passing by. It was the first rehearsal of the schedule, but only a few members of the large cast had arrived. The others were more than an hour overdue and the director was leading the actors through one of the scenes of Shakespeare's Romeo and Juliet, while reading the parts of the missing characters at the same time.

So when Smiley showed up, the director was annoyed that he wasn't one of the absent cast members, especially the leading man upon whom so much depended. Smiley was told that rehearsals were not open to the general public and that he would have to leave unless he was ready and willing to play a useful role in some aspect of the overall production. When Smiley said that he had nothing better to do, the director told him that he could be a stage assistant, moving furnishings and settings, as well as doing other chores when required. Smiley agreed and when the rehearsal resumed, he volunteered to also read some parts of the script for any of the missing actors.

The other actors smirked at this, and even the director chuckled, but at least tried to diplomatically dissuade Smiley without hurting his feelings. The fact is though, that nobody thought that he had the slightest ability to do any serious reading. They all knew that he had never completed his primary school education, so nobody expected that he had ever read anything of substance, or could even have the sensitivity to appreciate classic literature and drama. And of course, because of the lopsided grin indelibly engraved on his face, he simply "didn't look the part". But nevertheless, the director told Smiley that he could study the script, get familiar with the action, and perhaps later on in the schedule, might become useful as a prompter, when actors working without scripts forgot their lines.

The first few rehearsals were supposed to be for "blocking"; the actors loosely going through the different scenes with scripts in their hands, with the director pointing out specific areas on stage where certain actions should take place, and plotting what each actor's relative position should be. At each rehearsal, Smiley not only paid diligent attention to everything the director said, but also began to take notes in his own peculiar style. Sometimes he would later ask the director the reason for arranging things in a certain way. The director was at first surprised at the keen interest Smiley showed in all of the

49

proceedings, which certainly was much more than the others did, but took the time to carefully answer all his questions.

The cast members' sporadic attendance and constant tardiness in the early stages, was a chronic problem and caused the director to drastically revise the original six-week rehearsal schedule and extend the opening night performance two weeks beyond the date that had first been set. In this way it was expected that the additional rehearsal time, would surely help to offset the slackness in attendance and punctuality. Unfortunately, these modifications although sorely needed, did not help much. In fact, some of the actors seemed to think that because of the added rehearsal time, there was less urgency, and so acted accordingly.

After the first three weeks of rehearsals, the entire cast had not been assembled even once. Most had committed very few lines to memory and were still heavily reliant on their scripts. The leading actor playing Romeo was the worst offender. He was always late to rehearsals. He would never come on Friday evenings because of his religion. And he seldom appeared to have studied his lines. Most of the others were not any better, and seemed to have been following his lead. But at least a few members of the cast were behaving quite differently now. They were arriving on time to rehearsals, and were making considerable headway in memorising lines and towards character development. They had initially been among the worst offenders, coming late, hungry, tired, or in other ways unprepared to cooperate and put out a decent effort. But inexplicably, their attitude had changed and they were now among the most reliable and diligent members of the group.

The changes had gradually begun to take place during a rehearsal in the third week. The company was working on Act Two, which was the shortest and used the fewest characters in the play. Even so, two actors were absent and so the director resorted to asking Smiley if he would try to read some of the lines until they showed up. This was the first time that Smiley had been given the opportunity to actually read aloud at rehearsal, but it was not to be the last.

The way that Smiley read the lines was such a complete surprise that all of the others, including the director were filled with amazement. He read with more accuracy and fluency than any of the actors. Even some of the strange words and phrases that others awkwardly stumbled over, seemed to cause him no trouble at all. Not only did he read with credible vocal expressiveness, but his involuntary movements and gestures were aptly suited to the character and the scene. The only thing that seemed at all out of place; that jarred a little, was the incredible lopsided grin he always wore. Despite that, some of the actors were so impressed that from then on they unconsciously tried to copy his manner. Smiley had won some respect.

When the rehearsal was over, the director coaxed him into discussing how he had become such a proficient reader. Smiley wondered why anyone would be interested in what he thought was something so ordinary. But he explained how he was raised by his grandmother who used to read fables like Tom Thumb and Anancy Stories to him when he was a tot. After he learned to read himself, they would read to each other from a collection of several old volumes of books she had accumulated, besides the Bible. He said it was a great way to pass the time on rainy days, and that he enjoyed stories like Treasure Island and Robinson Crusoe when he was younger.

Later on, the works of authors like Wordsworth and Tennyson stirred his imagination more and more, even though the only one he shared this enthusiasm with was Granny. And finally, he told about The Works of Shakespeare, which he'd received as a gift from a visitor about a year ago, and which he loved to read over and over. His favourite of all was Romeo and Juliet, because even though they die in the end, their love and commitment to each other is stronger than the forces that keep them apart. By the time they went their separate ways home that night, the director had gained a new perspective of Smiley.

At the next rehearsal, the director again assigned Smiley the task of reading the parts of any absent actors, and also urged other actors to adopt a little of Smiley's style of vocal and physical expression. This did not go down well with one actor who had missed the previous rehearsal and had no idea of how impressive Smiley had been. This was a very handsome and popular fellow who had been cast in the role of Romeo. Physically he was right for the part, but he was quite temperamental and egocentric and felt somewhat insulted to be instructed to use Smiley as a model. Instead of adopting the director's suggestion, he tried to ridicule by imitating Smiley's unalterable grin with mocking cruelty when he spoke his lines.

Some of the cast laughed at this rude imitation, but the director became incensed and immediately warned that that sort of thing was mean-spirited and out of place and was not going to be tolerated. He pointed out that ever since the first rehearsal, Smiley was the only member of the company to consistently show up, and usually even earlier to prepare the stage and set everything up before the others arrived. When he filled in for missing actors, he read with more animation, sensitivity and understanding than those who were assigned the parts.

The director stressed that some of the actors playing major roles were setting the wrong example by habitually coming late or being absent, and that if everyone had been as diligent and attentive as Smiley, there would have been no need to change the date for the opening of the play, or to schedule extra rehearsals.

Things progressed normally for a while when the rehearsal resumed, but the male lead, apparently still smarting from the director's remarks, began to slyly imitate Smiley's grin again whenever he thought the director wasn't watching him. He wasn't quite quick enough one time though, to turn it off when the director suddenly whirled in his direction. Caught in the act, he tried to brazen it off with a shrug, but the director was livid with indignation and told him to leave the hall, he had done enough clowning for the night.

Although there were no further antics of that sort at subsequent rehearsals, the leading actor did not make much progress in memorising his lines and appropriate actions and required a great deal of prompting when trying to work without a script in his hands. Yet whenever the director criticised his lacklustre efforts, he would bluster and claim that he would "have it all together on opening night." But the rest of the company steadily made progress, though not all to the same degree.

By the end of the sixth week rehearsals were often in full costume and with almost all of the props. With only two weeks left before opening night, excitement was running high amongst the cast and even the director was beginning to feel more confident about the possibility of having a pretty good show. The only thing that really bothered him was that 'Romeo' kept fumbling lines and still needed a lot of prompting.

Smiley had turned out to be a real godsend for the production, making himself useful in many different ways. Even if he had done nothing else, he would still have become indispensable as a prompter. For although Smiley followed rehearsals with a script in his hand, he seemed to know every word without looking at it. He kept his eyes focused on what was happening on stage and would effortlessly prompt any actor who suddenly needed it. His dependable example had come to influence most of the others and consequently, it seemed that some of the performances were going to be outstanding by opening night. The director was certain that this cast would never have reached this level without Smiley's contributions.

Opening night found everyone in a predictable state of jitters. Everyone except Smiley, that is. He just went about his duties in the usual way. Helping to set up the chairs in the hall, checking the stage props, making sure the lighting technician and stage assistants were there and ready. Some vendors had already set up for business outside by seven p.m., even though the show was advertised to start at eight and audiences in Nevis customarily arrived later.

At seven-thirty the box office opened and a few early birds got tickets and chose their seats in the hall where they consumed the refreshments they got outside and gossiped while waiting for the show to begin. Around this time the director had become extremely annoyed. The leading man had not yet arrived although the whole company was supposed to be there an hour ago. The other actors started grumbling, voicing their displeasure about his tardiness and lack of consideration on opening night. Some were even getting worried.

Shortly before eight o'clock the delinquent arrived backstage, but the company's relief was short-lived when he stated that the opening would have to be postponed until the following night because he needed one more day to work on memorising his lines. The director with remarkable control, ordered him to put on his make up and costume – there would be no postponement. Smiley would prompt whenever needed, as usual. When the actor refused and said he'd only be ready the next night, the director calmly told him to "leave then, and we'll see what happens tomorrow night."

When the difficult actor left, Smiley was instructed to put on Romeo's costume and take over the role for the night. He was about the same size as the other actor. He knew the lines much better. And the director had complete faith in him. The cast members seemed shocked, especially the girl playing Juliet. As Smiley went off to get ready, she took the director aside and told him she would feel uncomfortable playing Juliet with Smiley as Romeo. When asked why, she replied that Smiley didn't look the part – that people would laugh – that her boyfriend wouldn't like it and was about to specify additional objections when the director cut her off.

He told her he knew exactly how she felt and would not actually force her to do anything that she didn't want to do. He said that he would respect her decision if she really could not agree to do it. But he pointed out to her the way that Smiley had joined the company and willingly done everything that was asked of him. He spoke about the impact he had on most of the cast when he filled in for missing actors at rehearsals. He reminded her that she had rehearsed all of her scenes with Smiley when the original Romeo was absent. She had to agree that she played better with Smiley because he never missed lines and also spoke with more feeling. And everyone seemed to act and react better when Smiley was on stage. She began to see beyond the lopsided grin, and then it didn't take long for her to smilingly make her decision.

*** *** *** ***

At twenty minutes past eight the director steps out onstage to make an announcement. There is a small audience with less than a hundred people sprinkled among the seats. He apologises for the delay, and then announces "due to unforeseen circumstances, the role of Romeo will be played by Smiley Smitten tonight." A ripple of chatter flows through the audience. There are some sounds of disappointment, a couple of loud guffaws and quite a few snickers. The houselights go out, stage lights come on and the play begins.

It is about ten minutes into Act One before Romeo makes his first entrance. By then, the audience has been introduced to about a dozen characters; the Montagues, the Capulets, the Prince of Verona and an interesting assortment of other people. They are all in colourful or elegant costumes of the 1600's. There is some sparkling dialogue, though it sounds a little quaint to modern ears; some fancy swordplay, and all in front of some charming background scenery.

The audience is entranced. They know all of the actors on stage. They've seen them every day but never like this. The language of Shakespeare is rich and poetic. They've never heard people that they know so well, speak like this before. Never knew they could. And then, Smiley Smitten enters as Romeo. He looks magnificent in his costume. He carries himself with so much confidence and grace that it is hard to tell that this is Smiley, except for that lopsided grin – a dead giveaway. But the audience is hushed. Every eye is on him. Every mouth is open in anticipation as he speaks.

His first few speeches are in very short sentences. Extremely short – only a few words at a time. He does them well, but then, anybody could do them. Then suddenly he launches into a much lengthier speech, at least a dozen lines of pure poetry. He does it so well it almost takes one's breath away. The onlookers exchange glances of amazement. This is Smiley…? Most mouths still hang open as he exits at the end of the first scene, for he has delivered four more richly poetic speeches with such sensitivity that the audience is dazzled and filled with admiration at this display.

There are many other actors in the play and all have raised their level of performance to match Smiley's. At the end of the night's performance they are given a well deserved standing ovation, but it is Smiley who clearly gets the most applause.

The next night there is a huge line up at the Cultural Centre before the box office is opened, and the vendors that came early do such a brisk business that they are sold out before the show starts. Many people are talking about how good they hear the show is, but especially about Smiley. Some were there the previous evening, but arrived late and missed the early scenes. So they came to see the whole thing this time, from beginning to end. This sort of enthusiasm has caused the word to spread like wildfire and sparked a sudden surge of interest and ticket sales.

At seven-thirty the original Romeo shows up at the dressing room and tells the director that he has spent the day memorising his lines and is now ready. But he is bluntly told that he is too late and that Smiley is already in costume. He insists that he is early because it is only seven-thirty. The director leads him outside to mingle with the crowds of people who are trying to get seats, or even standing room admission. Everywhere he turns people are commenting about what had transpired the night before.

It doesn't take him long to recognise that those crowds really only want to see Smiley perform. He eases out of the crowd and smiling cheerlessly at the director mutters ironically, "all's well that ends well" as he walks away. He is not really disappointed at all though, for despite his physical suitability for the part of Romeo, he simply couldn't quite get the hang of the language of Shakespeare. It really just wasn't his thing. And he still didn't know the lines very well anyway.

***   ***   ***   ***

The final two shows were sold out, and the seats filled to capacity well before

55

starting time. The performances kept improving and the audiences responded with greater and greater appreciation. The actors of course, were justifiably proud of what they had accomplished. Yet no one could have been more pleased than the director whose critical decisions had paved the way for Smiley to emerge and lead the group to its moment of triumph.

Shakespeare too would surely have been pleased, for the impetus that formed the director's decision echoed part of a well known line from Hamlet, one of his most famous plays. And although it was merely curiosity that caused Smiley to get involved in the first place, '*The play's the thing*' that captured his interest and spurred his motivation. As unlikely as it may seem, Smiley and Shakespeare had a great deal in common.

CONDUCT REFLECTS CHARACTER

THE POWER OF THE PRESS

The "Letter To The Editor" wasn't very long. Short and to the point, it said simply that Nevis people should be sensible enough to clean up their own mess and not have strangers come here to do it for them. It ended by saying that Nevisians should show some pride and self respect in this regard. It was signed by Smiley Smitten, so some locals didn't take it seriously at first.

When it came out, the first person who passed him on the street snapped out rudely, "Humph, yu tink yu could write now Smiley? Bwoy, yu tink yu smart nuh!"

Next, a man with eyes narrowing angrily stopped him and snarled, "You makin too much joke man. Watch you mout!"

True, there weren't very many that actually accosted him that way. But even a half dozen nasties out of the total population can seem like too much, when honourable intentions are misunderstood or unappreciated. So Smiley suffered some discomfort from the first few people he met the day the newspaper with his "Letter To The Editor" came out.

Although people often made fun of him, he had grown accustomed to that and it never bothered him very much. The ignorant often make fun of people who are a little different. But outright malice and animosity was something he didn't often encounter and found hard to endure, because basically he tried to be friendly with everybody.

So after being peppered with an unexpected barrage of unfriendly comments, he wandered along the Charlestown waterfront and sat on the seawall. Staring off into the horizon, he let his mind drift until he started to recall how he had been taking a sea bath at Gallows bay one day, and saw a group of people ambling along the beach in a strange manner. While they were still at a distance, he thought that they were gathering seashells or other curios that had washed ashore, as souvenirs. Most of the people were white, so he assumed that they were tourists. There was just one black person with them whom he recognised when they drew nearer, as a local woman from Church Ground. When they got close enough, he hailed them and asked what they were doing. They replied that they were doing a "beach cleanup." They were part of a committee that was conducting a drive to clear Nevis' beaches of environmentally harmful debris.

Smiley got out of the water and chatted with them for a while. He learned that some of them were indeed tourists who were just in Nevis for a short visit.

And some were expatriates who had homes here. But since none of them were staying anywhere near, he asked why they were cleaning up Gallows Bay. They explained that the committee relies on volunteer efforts to do its work around the island and if no volunteers come from Gallows Bay or surrounding areas, volunteers from elsewhere have to do the job. So he had put on his clothes and joined the group, picking up and bagging junk littering the beach, which was not only unsightly but often hazardous. Sharp edged tin cans, broken bottles, dead batteries and plastic bags, plates, and wrappers, were among the many items they removed.

But he was surprised to learn that there was another group of people who were involved in cleaning up trash from streets in Charlestown and other areas. These were high school kids from the U.S. and Canada who were spending part of their summer holidays doing volunteer work in needy countries. These were not Peace Corps workers who are supported by U.S. government funds, but kids whose parents' hard earned money had to pay for transportation and all other costs for the children's upkeep while they were away on vacation. The idea was to give those kids an on-the-spot learning experience of how people in other places live, and to offer help if needed where they can.

Smiley didn't enjoy the idea that strangers on vacation might come here and gather from first-hand impressions that Nevisians aren't capable of keeping their own place clean and tidy. That is what prompted him to send that letter to the editor, hoping that locals would stop littering and take responsibility for keeping Nevis clean and beautiful seriously. He thought that foreign volunteers should not feel there was a need for them to come here and do it for them. He felt that they should have more self-respect than that.

His mind lurched back to the present and he turned as someone's hand rested on his shoulder. He saw the magistrate smiling broadly at him.

"Smiley" he said pleasantly, "you surprised me with that little piece in the newspaper today. I didn't know you were such a thinker, and a writer too. You put it very well indeed. Very commendable, and I hope that others noticed and will face up to their civic duty. Keep it up!"

He patted Smiley's shoulder and was gone before Smiley could think of anything to say.

He sat there stunned for a few moments. The magistrate had never said anything much to him before. Certainly never any words of praise. In fact, once when Smiley was a witness being questioned in a court case, he drew the magistrate's ire by refusing to answer yes or no to one of the questions. He was trying to offer an account which he insisted was "the whole truth and nothing but the truth," but was told he was supposed to answer only "yes" or "no" to the question, and nothing more. His attempts to get his point across "in the interests of justice," met with a stern rebuke from the magistrate and soon had the courthouse in an uproar. The question was eventually withdrawn, and Smiley was dismissed as a witness and expelled from the courtroom.

So the magistrate's sudden display of approval was totally unexpected. And coming on the heels as it were, of negative and malicious comments about his letter to the editor, it made him a little confused and suspicious. He wondered whether the magistrate's comments were really sincere praise or clever sarcasm. For after all, the magistrate's use of the words "thinking" and "writer" were close to the words used by the first person who had accosted him that morning. And since the magistrate really had no reason to be warmly disposed towards him, he was unsure about the real intention. What should he make of it all?

While he wrestled with these thoughts, someone else approached and quickly got his attention. It was the local woman from Church Ground who was involved in the Gallows Bay clean up day. She was an effervescent type and immediately showered him with sparkling comments. "Oh Smiley, I'm so glad to see you. I adored your letter in the newspaper. It was just great – simply great! How did you think of it? It is just what is needed. It strikes just the right chord. Everybody's talking about it. It's just wonderful, wonderful. You're a real genius!"

Her enthusiasm was almost overwhelming. Still, Smiley managed to tell her about the hostile encounters he had endured that morning, and his inability to fathom just where the magistrate stood. She nodded with understanding and then explained that most people, who read newspaper commentaries, filter the ideas expressed through their own preferences and biases and ability to understand things. Because of this, no matter how reasonably a matter is presented, some people are going to find fault and disagree, or be offended and become negative or even abusive.

But the great thing, is that often large numbers of people can be aroused and stimulated into positive action by the right approach. Smiley's letter took the right approach about a festering problem in Nevis, and if enough people read it and are moved to do something personally and collectively, the problem could soon be resolved. She said that the magistrate's words clearly showed that he was on Smiley's side in this case, and had nothing to do with how he dealt with matters in a court of law. There was no question about yes or no to be answered in Smiley's letter, he was telling what he knew to be the truth, to the court of public opinion. And she said that it was "testimony that simply could not be ignored!"

The truth of this was borne out almost immediately as other people who were passing began to converge on Smiley as soon as they saw him. Almost all directed laudatory comments expressing approval of his letter in no uncertain terms. As the days went by, more and more people sought him out to express agreement with his letter. When the newspaper came out again on the weekend, several other letters appeared supporting what he had written, and a well-known columnist devoted a full page of commentary to the subject matter and stated that more locals must become aware and get involved like Smiley.

Smiley was of course, tickled pink with all the attention, especially after he learned that his letter had been used by some teachers at the secondary schools as a stimulus in certain classes. But what really put the icing on the cake is when the Nevis Historical and Conservation Society invited him to become a member and serve on their Environmental Committee. He thought it would be a great honour and was really looking forward to that. But what he was also looking forward to with even more eagerness was next weekend's newspaper. He had written a brand new Letter To The Editor, with a brand new topic concerning some nasty open drains in Charlestown, and unpleasant public toilet facilities at the waterfront. He hoped a lot of people would be reading the paper. He could hardly wait for it to come out.

CONDUCT REFLECTS CHARACTER

STYLE

There used to be a lot of young fellows in Nevis with seemingly nothing to do. There may be fewer now than there used to be, but at one time you could have seen them hanging about at all hours of the day or night, especially around Charlestown which seemed to hold some special attraction for them. They could certainly have done nothing just as well somewhere else on the island, where they'd have been less of an eyesore and public impediment. But for some strange reason, they preferred to do their thing around the overburdened areas in the heart of Charlestown. Perhaps because that was where they got the most exposure to flaunt the vacuous lifestyle they had chosen.

They'd line the street as thick as flies in some places, and often were an annoyance for shoppers, visitors, business folks, or just ordinary people who were subjected to their loud aggressive music, foul language, and sometimes downright scary attitude. Smiley Smitten tried hanging out too for a while after he had quit school a few years ago, but soon gave it up. It just wasn't his style. He didn't wear ragged, baggy pants with his hands jabbed in the pockets like some of the others. He didn't shout, and use coarse language. And he didn't swagger around looking mean and rough and ready to rumble. With his ever-present lopsided grin though, that would have been pretty tough for him to do. He just really didn't fit in with that crowd at all, where he more than ever, stuck out like a sore thumb.

Smiley's granny of course, probably had something to do with it too, because she became very unhappy when she discovered how Smiley was beginning to spend his time in those days. And of course Smiley's conscience would not long allow him to do things that displeased Granny. She had done so much for him that he knew he could never ever repay her even though he must try. And besides, he realised he wasn't getting anything out of hanging out with a bunch of lay-a-bouts all the time. He had only begun to do it because at that time in his life he was groping for something, some kind of connection possibly, that he missed and never had.

He had never known a father. The man had simply disappeared, sometime before he was born actually. After his mother died when he was just a tot, there was only his grandmother who raised and nurtured him through all of his developing years. He acquired few close friends even at school, because others would make fun of him and treat him as though he were an imbecile. Even the teachers thought his constant lopsided grin surely indicated a high degree of low intelligence. So they didn't waste their time giving him any serious attention. His resulting poor grades were therefore not an accurate measurement of his capabilities, but rather a sad reflection of inadequacies within the education system. Accordingly, he failed miserably in his schoolwork, even flunking and repeating several grades, before finally quitting the sixth grade and leaving in frustration without any kind of school certificate.

Yet Smiley was no dummy, no matter what other people thought. He had a keen, inquiring mind, became an avid reader and developed an extraordinary facility for doing things in a creative way. But this cultivation didn't begin to flower until after he was freed from the rigid constraints of a school system that had neither the facilities nor sufficiently trained personnel to provide adequately for all of the many different types of schoolchildren. Consequently, Smiley became just one more of those unlucky students that "fell through the cracks in the system". And, as an underachieving school dropout at sixteen, no one could say that "the future looked bright" for him in those days.

Smiley's period of hanging around didn't last very long though, just a few weeks. But he had seen and learned enough about the characters of the other hang-a-bouts to know that this was not a worthwhile route to follow. He knew that some fellows his age had already been in secondary school for a couple of years, and one was even in the fourth form. And several of his former classmates had graduated from primary school and found regular employment. But too many others were doing nothing but hanging about aimlessly. Sometimes he heard them complain about "Dumb-in-knee-cans" or "Guy-an-ease" or "Far-inners comin here an tek all de jobs, dem!"

Some of them used to drink beers and smoke marijuana cigarettes right in front of everybody on Main Street. He would wonder where their money came from, since they never seemed to be making any serious effort to find employment. Smiley on the other hand, at least had some ambition. True, he had not devised a well-formulated plan, nor could he even coherently describe an ultimate objective – a goal he wanted to attain. But deep down he believed in himself and had faith that he was capable of bettering his condition. That he could somehow make a respected place for himself in this world.

So when Smiley heard the grumblers complaining about "outsiders takin all de wuk", he had turned things over in his mind and recognised that these fellows had no serious aspirations. He knew that even outsiders could not find work or keep a job if they only sat around doing nothing most of the time. And he had seen himself as an 'outsider' too because of the way others had treated him most of his life, even though he was born here. That lopsided grin on his face made him different, and those who were different were not treated the same as everybody else in Nevis.

But Smiley understood that being "different" could also be an asset. He knew that most outsiders were willing to do jobs that most locals were reluctant to take. He knew too, that outsiders were often more dependable and productive, and realised that those kinds of differences could work to the advantage of anyone who seriously wanted to get ahead in Nevis. And although it was not widely known, he had already established a modest reputation for being a dependable and productive worker.

Smiley had been accustomed to doing odd jobs for people in his neighbourhood since he was about fourteen years old. He had long practised tinkering around with things in Granny's house even before they needed repair, and developed a remarkable degree of dexterity and skill in repairing mechanical and electrical devices, as well as having a natural affinity for carpentry. Once, Granny had boasted to her church group about how Smiley could fix anything that needed repairs in her house, and soon he began earning some money doing little repair jobs in the neighbourhood.

At first people thought that they could just get him to repair things for free. But he quickly let it be known that he expected payment if he did a good job. If he couldn't fix something, or did the job poorly, that was an entirely different matter. He might also choose to do something free, for an elderly person who had no income. Other than that though, the only free labour he was prepared to do was for Granny or volunteer community services.

Scoffing at this, some people ignored Smiley, preferring to have their things repaired at well-established places that charged as much as ten times the amount that he would have. But others who tried Smiley's services were quite pleased with his workmanship which was speedy, well done, and economical. By the time he quit school, this casual, part-time activity was providing a reasonable, though somewhat irregular income. And that income had become the mainstay of the household for him and Granny. But it was not an income that could lead to the fulfilment of his dreams, vague though they were.

He knew that many people were living in better homes than they were a few years ago. There were more cars on the island, better roads, bigger shops with more items to sell. More people seemed to be going places, even if they never left the island. There was an air of well being and prosperity in Nevis. And because or along with all of that, more people than ever before had achieved a certain amount of respect. When Smiley closed his eyes and visualised himself in the future, he pictured a man who had earned respect and all the accoutrements that seemed to go along with it.

He smiled inwardly as the image formed in his mind. He knew it couldn't happen overnight. But he was willing to apply himself and work at it. And he knew he would surely fail unless he did more of the kind of things that could be acknowledged by others as useful, beneficial, desirable and respectable. He remembered the days when he used to do a lot of goofy things and played a lot of outlandish pranks. He knew he was more widely regarded as a joker than anything else. He knew that if he truly expected to become successful and earn respect, he would have to adopt a different way of doing things. He would definitely have to change his style.

Gradually a new persona began to emerge – as creative as ever, but more astute and considerate. Less prankish, and more proper and prudent. More class and less clown. As the new persona gradually grew, so did Smiley's influence. Just as people were once attracted by Smiley's clownishness, they became enticed by his benign sensibilities. When Smiley first deserted the crowd of lay-a-bouts blemishing the charm of Charlestown, a few others also quit, saying that if he could find better things to do, so could they. And when word began circulating about some of the positive new things he did from time to time, a few more young fellows thought it would make sense for them to also find better things to do.

Quite a few ribald jokes though, made the rounds one time when Smiley was seen all about the place in the company of a beautiful white girl who was visiting the island. But at the same time people were becoming more and more aware that Smiley was a decent and responsible fellow. And before that episode, rumour had it that Smiley had a hand in the affair that resulted in the anti-noise campaign and subsequent legislation against unwanted sound. But since there was no actual proof, it remained a well-founded rumour.

It was known for a fact however, that Smiley's talks with his neighbours had a deciding effect on the outcome of the local election the following year. Or at least, that's what certain people who are in the know, say. It is incontestable however, that what happened at Culturama soon after that, elevated Smiley's status in the community and gained him wider acclaim. Next came an even more unexpected and astonishing success from Smiley's performance in Romeo and Juliet, the Shakespearian play. But when he began to write Letters To The Editor, his popularity soared beyond anything he could ever have dreamed of. People didn't laugh, but smiled their approval and urged him to write more and more letters. He was finally being taken seriously and earning much deserved respect.

When other young fellows he formerly hung about with saw what was happening with Smiley, even more of them began to change their ways. Maybe that's why there seems to be fewer of them hanging about and Charlestown seems much more charming than alarming these days. It certainly couldn't have hurt any of those young fellows to follow Smiley's lead and change their habits. And perhaps they really began to admire and emulate his style.

CONDUCT REFLECTS CHARACTER

BOOK II

TROTT TALK

Articles in the following pages first appeared in *The St. Kitts-Nevis Observer* and *The Leewards Times* newspapers and Hamilton House Studio Publications.

TROTT TALK

STATE OF THE ARTS IN NEVIS

I have been involved in drama and allied arts for nearly fifty years, and I'm disturbed by the rapid disappearance of most of the old traditional cultural activities and art forms that once existed in Nevis. In almost a single generation we have lost much of a rich cultural heritage that has not been replaced by anything of value. Adding to my distress are those apathetic attitudes so endemic in our community, which militate against efforts to salvage what we can of our cultural past and develop those art forms which best reflect our experience as a people.

Few individuals or organisations have made any serious or noteworthy attempts to minister to our weakened cultural condition, in fact, most people seem blissfully unaware of the state of affairs in this respect. Culturama, our biggest cultural event, takes place at the time of the year when there are few visitors. And the manner of organising and presenting what was once our proudest annual event has been in serious decline in the past few years. We owe a debt of gratitude to those few who have managed to persist in practicing, performing and displaying such elements of our culture.

Ironically, most Nevisians seem eager to talk about development in our country. They expound proudly and knowingly about infrastructure, education, agriculture, tourism, land and housing. Many Nevisians have money to spend on new cars, televisions and expensive consumer goods. They talk about buying, leasing, loaning, selling, expanding old businesses, creating new businesses and jobs – all in the name of development. But very few people are saying anything or doing much about our culture.

A healthy, vibrant cultural situation is critical to the proper development of our country. It is the artists who define a country's culture and character. A country's poets, singers, dancers, sculptors, playwrights, painters, musicians and actors tell its stories, sing its songs and write its histories, folklores and fables. They give colour, shape, form and meaning to a national identity.

But this is not solely the responsibility of the artists. They are the way in which a culture is expressed. Without the approval, encouragement and emotional and financial support of the whole community, cultural activity will lose its vitality, purpose and character. I believe this is what has happened here in the last few years. I believe this is the major reason for the attrition of our cultural traditions.

If the people of Nevis are serious about the proper development of our tiny island, then we'd better pay more attention to the encouragement, development and welfare of our artists. There are a number of things that can be done to improve the situation.

I believe the government should be more sensitive to our island's history and cultural development. It should understand why our traditional art forms are rapidly disappearing and try to help find ways to salvage some of them. Government should try to use the expertise of residents who are specialists in the arts in this endeavour. It should not interfere or impose its authority on existing cultural entities, but should be willing to help when asked to do so.

More energy should be put into areas where our cultural development and the arts have an important role to play, such as:

(1) **Education**. A more significant part of the curriculum could be devoted to our cultural heritage and development.

(2) **Tourism**. In most countries where tourism plays an important role, the arts and cultural activities are assisted to ensure visitors are exposed to the richness and depth of the national character. And, of course, to extract more tourist dollars before the visitor departs.

Literature, visual and performing arts are often subsidised to ensure quantity, quality and variety during the tourist season. But in Nevis, tourists can't pay top dollar to see quality shows, dance recitals and concerts because there aren't any.

It is unfortunate that an organisation like the Nevis Dramatic and Cultural Society (NEDACS) was allowed to become dormant. It played a pivotal role in the cultural life of the community for years. If the organisation was functional now, it could help boost our social educational and economic development.

For instance, if NEDACS was able to promote a first-rate annual drama festival during the tourist season, it could offer seasonal employment for some of those involved in the arts and become a tourist attraction.

The whole community could benefit from an active, vibrant cultural entity. The Department of Tourism and the hotels should consider the financial impact the growth of the arts could have on the island.

The general public must play its part by encouraging people with talent to participate and support the industry by working behind the scenes as volunteers or offering financial support.

Government and business sectors could commission artists to produce art, drama and literature. This might help struggling artists to survive and would be an incentive for those who take their craft seriously.

More awareness of the arts, a shifting of priorities, discipline, commitment, and funding are needed to improve the cultural situation in Nevis. If those criteria are met, I believe we can experience a renaissance in Nevis in a remarkably short period of time.

All sectors have to work together to create the climate, offer inducements, make investments and provide incentives, which make it possible to improve the quality, quantity, variety and the state of the arts in Nevis.

St. Kitts-Nevis Observer, October 7, 1994

RUNNING ON EMPTY - GOD SAVE THE QUEEN

Every now and then I become so disgruntled with the way things are going, that I consider running for public office. Alas, I'll never know how much support I might receive. I must resist entering the fray because I realise that if I should win a seat by some slim chance, I could not take the oath of office.

The problem is, I could not in good conscience swear allegiance to the Queen and her heirs. I view the monarchy as outmoded, an anachronistic institution at best. Oh, I wouldn't say "Down with the Queen," or anything like that. Heavens, no!

I like seeing the Queen every now and then, with her crown, gown, and snazzy Prince Phillip at her side. I like watching her ride in the magnificent horse-drawn carriage, waving at crowds lining the streets. As a dramatist, I appreciate the theatrics of it all: Buckingham Palace, the Coldstream Guards. I'd like all that to continue and believe it should be supported.

Museums should be publicly supported because they provide a valuable link with the past. I believe that's what the monarchy is, and that's why it should be kept going. A living museum is a unique thing, and as such, I consider it one of Great Britain's national treasures.

But I feel if I swear allegiance to anything for my oath of office, it should be to abide by ideas and principles I believe in and subscribe to. I would want to swear to uphold certain values beneficial to all.

Queen Elizabeth, in my estimation, is all right as far as queens go. The manner in which she has conducted her affairs in life is, generally speaking, worthy of praise. Her heirs, on the other hand, are all jolly good fellows as far as I can tell and they should certainly be free to live their lives as they see fit. But to swear allegiance to a bunch of jetsetters, who haven't the wit to keep their dalliances under cover, is not something that I would want to do.

I would take the oath of office seriously. And I would want what I'm swearing to, to have more meaning and dignity than that. So, I guess all those politicians who might be worrying about my political ambitions should breathe a little easier. I won't be running for public office anytime soon.

St. Kitts-Nevis Observer, October 28, 1994

TROTT TALK

PERFORMANCE

I recently attended a concert here in Nevis. The admission fee was quite low and, with few exceptions, so was the general quality of the performance. Nobody seemed to mind, as far as I could tell. The audience applauded item after item with great enthusiasm, especially after being urged to do so by the emcee. I applauded too, although with more politeness than enthusiasm. I normally try to find a reason to applaud even performances I may not find satisfactory. So frequently, I applaud the effort a performer makes, despite any flaws of performance. When I am impressed by sheer artistry however, my applause is less restrained and more enthusiastic.

I go to fewer concerts and shows these days than I used to. One reason is economics. Things now cost so much more, that I have less to spend on diversions. Another reason is that generally speaking, I am often unimpressed by what is being offered in Nevis. Instead of improving over the last few years, the quality actually seems to be declining. Quite often, things are too loud, and disorganised for my taste. And I dread going to concerts or indeed, any event which is advertised to start at a specific time, but which really doesn't start until much, much later.

So it's also this lack of seriousness and professionalism that keeps me away. If a show is going to be advertised as good, the artists involved and the promoters have a responsibility to deliver the goods – otherwise, money is taken under false pretences. And if a show is slated to start at a certain time, that's the time it should begin. Let's be honest with each other. Audiences and performers should strive to respect the conditions and conventions inherent in coming together to experience a performance.

If a performance were scheduled to take place at the Anglican Church at 7p.m., it would make no sense for the audience to turn up at the Methodist Church. Any one can see how illogical that is. Is it any less illogical to turn up at the right place, but the wrong time? Yet, that seems to be the habit in Nevis. Certainly, that sort of performance by the audience should not be applauded.

What has frustrated me most in recent weeks, is the fact that performers with high standards have been appearing in St. Kitts, but Nevisians have not had access to them. Internationally renowned organist Dr. Willoughby gave a series of organ recitals and workshops, but none took place in Nevis. The U.S. Information Agency sponsored a Caribbean tour of two accomplished American musicians, Karen Kamensek, pianist, and Heather Gray, vocalist. They appeared

73

in concert in St. Kitts and also ran a workshop for conductors and singers. Again, none took place in Nevis.

A highly acclaimed Jamaican youth group was scheduled for five separate performances around St. Kitts. According to their publicity, this group, through song, dance and drama, teaches lessons of love, self-respect and responsibility. They show positive ways in which young people can deal with peer-pressure and explicitly examine issues such as AIDS. Are we to believe that Nevisians would not find these types of performances interesting, or could not appreciate or benefit in some way from such exposure?

I find it terribly disturbing that highly acclaimed and accomplished artists come to our Federation to perform for the general public, conduct specialised workshops and even sessions for schoolchildren, without Nevis being brought into the picture. If the standards for concerts and drama are expected to improve, Nevisians should certainly be allowed the opportunity and encouraged to experience what skilled professionals have to offer.

In this respect, I have to regard the lack in Nevis of what is made available in St. Kitts as astounding. I am certainly not favourably impressed with this state of affairs. I don't know where the responsibility lies for this situation, but I feel as a citizen of this state, watching the unfolding scenario of our development, that at this stage, this is not the kind of performance I can applaud.

St. Kitts-Nevis Observer, **November 4, 1994**

TROTT TALK

STANDARD PROCEDURE

On the site where Alexander Hamilton was born and where the Hamilton Museum and the Nevis House of Assembly are located, stands a row of three prominent flagpoles. I estimate their height to be about 30 feet and I believe there are few places in Nevis where our country's flag can be more proudly displayed or viewed by a greater number of visitors.

But the flying of flags at this site seems to have become a rather haphazard affair. There is no regularity or protocol that is followed as far as I can see. Currently, the cords on two of the flagpoles are down, and I have not seen any flag flying for quite a few days now.

Earlier in the year, I noticed a period when the American flag alone was flying, for about two weeks or more, day and night. A visitor actually asked if the American Embassy was there. But I believe even at embassies, the flags are lowered at dusk. It seems the cord was jammed and it was a long time before workers were sent to free it.

I think this laissez –faire approach gives our visitors a poor impression. The flag should be a symbol of our pride in our country. And those given the privilege to display it, should do so with love, care and dignity.

I can remember years ago before Independence, before the museum was built on the site, a policeman would smartly march down the street in the early morning, with the flag tucked under his arm. He would unlock the gate, march up to the post, attach and raise the flag, give a snappy salute and march down the street to the station again. There seemed to be some special meaning and purpose to his action, and anyone who witnessed it couldn't help but be favourably impressed.

Of course times have changed and with Independence, so has our flag. But should we treat our own flag – our own symbol of pride in our country – with less respect now than we did then? I think we ought to do better than that.

I think the apparatus for flying the flag should be properly maintained and promptly corrected when there is a snag. I think the task of raising and lowering the flag is an important symbolic gesture and should be the privilege of persons who can appreciate and understand its importance.

I suggest that some outstanding cadet, Girl Guide, or police officer be given the honour to do this duty, and trained to do it with the respect, reverence, discipline and diligence as was so evident in the past. I have no doubt that this would impress our visitors, give locals something to look up to, and help improve the raising of standards in Nevis.

St. Kitts-Nevis Observer, November 18, 1994

TROTT TALK

A MANNER OF SPEAKING

Although I was born and raised by a Nevisian woman, I sometimes have great difficulty comprehending what other Nevisians are saying to me. It wasn't always this way. Part of the difficulty is that I wasn't born and raised here in Nevis. My mother migrated to Canada in the early 1920's, met and married my father and bore all of her children there. We lived in a tightly knit West-Indian community in Montreal. So as a child, I was accustomed to hearing English spoken with accents and lingoes peculiar to people of the Caribbean.

But at that time in Montreal, there were only 5,000 blacks in a metropolis of more than one million people. As I grew and matured and struggled to make my way in the world, I subsequently spent less and less time with contacts in the West-Indian community. In most of the schools I attended, there were very few blacks and often I was the only one in my classroom. Gradually, I lost whatever little West-Indian flavour I might have had and my speech habits became identical with the Standard English, which was more common in the wider community.

By the time I reached my teens, West-Indian dialects seemed as foreign and quaint to me as French or Germans trying to speak English. In fact, at that time, my peers and I would sometimes have great fun "putting on" an accent. We would mimic some of the older members of our community who had a "really bad" accent. Sometimes we would do a "take-off" on a recent arrival whose accent was so broad you could tell "he just came off de boat."

Although I always thought that I strongly identified with the West-Indian community, it came as a surprise to me one day to realise that basically, we didn't speak the same language. It came about this way: In Montreal, I shared a cab with some West-Indian students after a party at McGill University. Three fellows from Trinidad were in the back seat, while I sat up front with the taxi-driver, a French-Canadian. The chaps in the back had had a few drinks and were in a rollicking good mood, chatting loudly and laughing merrily all the way. Since I wasn't involved in the conversation, the cab driver leaned towards me in a friendly way and said in a heavy French accent, "Pardon me, M'sieu, could you tell me where your friends come from?"

"Oh," I said, "they are from Trinidad in the West Indies."

"Aha," says the cabbie, "but what language har zey speaking?"

"Oh, they're speaking English," I replied with a chuckle.

"Non-no," said the cabbie, "hi honderstan Hanglish vary well. Zat his not Hanglish."

I insisted it was English, whereupon the cabbie asked me if I wouldn't mind telling him what they were saying. I was completely stumped. Try as I might, I could not understand what the chaps were talking about, but I couldn't tell the cab driver that.

"I'm sorry," I said, "but it's a private conversation."

Years later I find myself living in Nevis, the place I've always called home. I'm aware that I've lived most of my life abroad and to Nevisian ears, I'm the one with a strange accent. At first I tried to "put on" an accent so I could sound like a local, but quickly realised that I wasn't fooling anybody. I sounded ridiculous, so I quit. There is no way I can convincingly sound like I was born here.

Someone stopped me on Main Street one day with a message: "Missa Trott, Missa Herbert say a tell yu he got one a dem Chicanos hot fe you."

"I beg your pardon?" I said. The message was repeated but made no sense to me. Then I repeated the message to make sure I heard it correctly: "Are you telling me that Mr. Herbert said to tell me he has one of those Chicanos hot for me?"

The answer was affirmative.

I was perplexed. The only Mr. Herbert I knew at the time, was a pastor, and it seemed unthinkable he would send that kind of message to me or anyone else. In North America "Chicano" is a term for Mexican-American, so the picture conjured up by the message, although interesting, was obviously incorrect.

I quickly did some mental callisthenics and after a few moments came up with the answer. I replaced the name Herbert with Hubbard and the rest of the puzzle suddenly fell into place. Vincent Hubbard was the president of the Nevis Historical and Conservation Society. He had gone to the U.S. on a business trip and I had asked him to please bring back a three-cornered hat to replace the one I had donated for an historical display at the Nelson Museum. So the message was, that Mr. Hubbard had one of those three-cornered hats for me.

Sometimes when I'm speaking to locals, I realise they are looking at me with a blank stare. Then I begin to worry whether they understand what I am saying. Can they understand my funny Canadian accent, or are they confused with my manner of speaking. I wonder… seriously.

St. Kitts-Nevis Observer, **December 2, 1994**

TROTT TALK

SETTING STANDARDS

Predictably, this column has been drawing mixed responses ever since its inception in this newspaper. My intention has been to speak my mind and let the chips fall where they may. I have always tried to use a reasonable approach in presenting my opinions, and avoid being accused of haranguing or sensationalism.

I am a little disappointed that no one has taken the time to write a letter to the editor to support or disagree with my comments. A number of people however, have said they enjoy and look forward to reading my column in each issue. Some have been less flattering, saying that seeing my name in print has given me a big head. I find all such comments interesting and try to receive them with grace and tact.

I have more difficulty though, with those people who tell me to take it easy on locals. To not be so critical about things, people, or the way things are done in Nevis. I've been hearing this ever since I came here to live permanently nine years ago. Often when I point out flaws or suggest a better way of doing things, I've been rebuffed with defensive statements, "Don't forget dis is Nevis – we mus' do we own ting!"

I cannot in good conscience accept the idea that because this is Nevis, I should lower my standards and refrain from pointing out flaws or suggesting better ways of doing things.

Some time ago I was directing a play and became exasperated with actors who repeatedly came late to rehearsals and were often inattentive. I proceeded to let the actors know that I found this unacceptable and expected better from them in order to present a first-class production. Someone who had been watching the rehearsal told me that I was being too harsh and demanded too much from the locals. I was told to remember that I was in Nevis now, not Canada or the U.S. where there are different standards.

I was shocked. This person held a responsible position and was a role model for many others in the community. I said that regardless of what others might feel, I would not lower my standards to accommodate laxity. When I am asked to write or direct a play, I always strive to give my best effort. I think that is what should be expected of me, and it certainly is what I want to achieve. And when I am involved in play production, I expect the best efforts of those around me. I would not approach the responsibilities of writing or producing a play with the idea that because this is Nevis, I can be slipshod or lackadaisical. I

79

hope no doctor, lawyer, banker, builder, teacher, plumber, or proud citizen of Nevis, consciously thinks that way either.

This beautiful island is rapidly undergoing changes that will affect the country and the people for many years. Each one of us should be aware that we have an important part to play in our country's development. If we all insist on doing "we own ting" in a slipshod and lackadaisical manner, the country will develop accordingly.

I want better for this island and its people. So I will continue to make my observations with a critical eye, hoping to persuade others to strive to maintain the highest standards. Surely then as our tiny country develops, we can hold up our heads and say with true pride – "This is Nevis!"

St. Kitts-Nevis Observer, **January 20, 1995**

Oops - There I Go Again!

It seems my life is full of ups and downs. I've been told that this isn't so unusual. Everybody has good days and bad. Happy moments and sad ones. Successes and disasters. But often I feel I've had more than my fair share of disasters and wonder why fate is picking on me.

I'm not so much concerned with things like tripping on a stone and fracturing a bone. "That's life," you say. After all, a doctor, a plaster cast and a few weeks with a crutch will get things back to normal and that incident will soon be forgotten. Crashing the front end of a new car can also be pretty upsetting when it happens, but a good mechanic and the insurance coverage will smooth things over until that episode too fades from memory. But I've had moments so excruciatingly embarrassing that it seems time will never erase them from my memory.

I remember as an adolescent in Montreal, going to a banquet honouring the famous baseball player Jackie Robinson, who was soon to leave the Montreal farm club to join the Brooklyn Dodgers. Admission to the banquet must have cost me about a week's salary, which I could ill afford. But I also emptied my savings account to purchase a very stylish sports shirt, which I wore to the banquet. The invitation said "Dress: Optional", which I interpreted to mean something only unsophisticated juveniles would understand. I didn't even wear a jacket, only a topcoat which I had to remove and check before entering the banquet hall.

Scads of people were already there. The fans, the Mayor, baseball officials, the guest of honour, and reporters for newspaper and radio. But it seemed all eyes turned to stare at me as I entered haltingly and looked for a place to hide. To my great horror, utter consternation and complete anguish, I realised that almost everyone was attired in formal dress, long gowns and tuxedos. Corsages and bow ties. I would sooner have jumped into the icy waters of the St. Lawrence River during spring thaw. The shock could not have been worse. It did not even help ease my discomfort when a few minutes later, to my utter amazement, another hapless youth walked in wearing a New York Yankees Baseball outfit, including a fielder's glove! We were both completely out of place, but I think I felt worse.

A few years later, fate found me seeking fame and fortune in New York City. Fame and fortune were not interested in me, but disasters bedevilled me at every turn. Once I wandered into a club where a small band was playing romantic music. I stepped in tentatively and looked over a crowded room. I perhaps stood at the entrance too long, as heads soon turned to stare enquiringly at me. I could have taken a vacant seat near the door, but for some strange reason my legs of their own accord, carried me to a small table near the bandstand where a gorgeous woman sat alone. Instead of sitting and trying to start a conversation, I cleared my throat and invited her to dance. She looked at me with a curious smile, perhaps a sneer, I'm not sure now, but she didn't reply. I don't know why not – I wasn't wearing that ridiculous sport shirt.

Because I am a soft-spoken person, I thought she might not have heard me, so I asked again in a louder voice. Suddenly I realised that except for the music, all other sounds in the room had ceased and all eyes were on me. I realised too late, that no one else was dancing. Perhaps dancing wasn't allowed in this club. Perhaps you were only supposed to listen to the music. How could I have been so stupid! The woman gestured to the saxophone player who suddenly blew a raspy, discordant musical phrase in my direction. It sounded like "Shoo fly, don't bother me!" Forty-odd years later, I still remember the humiliation of the laughs and giggles that accompanied my awkward exit.

Over the years though, I've managed to survive the pain and discomfort of many gaffes. I've come to realise that I seem to have a special knack for them. In fact since coming to Nevis, the quality of my blunders has evolved into what could be considered an art form. For instance, just the other day, in broad daylight on Main Street, I… But no – no, I can't tell you about that one. Maybe after more time has passed and soothed the painful memory. But it is just too soon to talk about that one right now. Sorry…

St. Kitts-Nevis Observer, **March 3, 1995**

The Sound Of Music

There has always been music in my life for as far back as I can remember. And for most of my life, I have welcomed, relished and loved the sound of music. Lately though, because of the volume and times at which it is being played by others, much of it has become intrusive and outrageous and when this occurs, I do not enjoy it at all. But I will come back to that later.

One of the earliest pieces of music I can remember is a song my mother often sang. I believe it to be a local folk song she learned as a young girl growing up in Nevis. But I remember her singing it to me as a sort of lullaby when I was a toddler growing up in Montreal. The melody was simple, but pleasant and easy to remember and the words were well suited to the music with its distinct West-Indian rhythm. I remember she would clap her hands and tap her feet as she sang, and at times she would add a little dramatic movement to her performance:

"Willie, Willie, my sweet Willie
Black up me eye, but stay wid me
Willie, Willie, my sweet Willie
Oh, Willie, don't g'way from me!"

That is the only verse I can clearly remember, but I cherish that song as one of the earliest and strongest influences to my understanding and appreciation of music. The manner in which the music was communicated in that instance, was simple, charming, and clearly enchanted and entertained me.

Another early influence was the Salvation Army band that frequented the area where we lived in the early 1930's. The way they played "Onward Christian Soldiers" always excited me, and though I wasn't allowed out on the streets to follow them, at least I enjoyed standing at the window and marching in time as they passed by. As I recall, while they were marching through the streets, the music seemed loud enough with horns blaring, cymbals crashing and drums booming. And they didn't even have high-powered electric amplifiers back then. When they drew a sufficient crowd of followers they would stop, preach the Gospel and sing and play a few hymns. The music at these times was much quieter than when they were marching. And the low, quiet tones and rich harmonies of such pieces as "Abide With Me" are still embedded in my memory.

Sometime in the late 1930's our family acquired a radio and a gramophone, and both served us well for many years. This greatly expanded my exposure to a wonderful world of music of all sorts, and by the early 1940's I was able to purchase and listen to recordings of my own choice. During those years, the range of music heard in our home was enormous: religious, classical, folk music, opera, Negro spirituals, symphonies, string quartets, piano concertos... And yes, steel-pan and string band and calypso from the West Indies, and a variety of vocal and instrumental music from countries in Africa.

I had three sisters of varying ages and along with our parents, we each had different musical preferences. Harmony was kept in the house mostly by respecting each other's preferences, by sharing and using the equipment at appropriate times, and by keeping the volume at a level, which did not disturb the others.

Because I learned to listen and to love music, my life has been immeasurably enriched. I can recall many favourite melodies in the privacy of my mind. Or I can create new tunes and songs to express various thoughts and feelings musically. I try to do so in a manner that disturbs no one, for I believe that music should be created and played for people to enjoy, not to be bombarded with. But far too often lately, my sleep is being shattered by incredibly loud music being played nearby. It is difficult to enjoy things that are forced on you.

Music has been my closest companion, through the good times and the bad. It has consoled me in my darkest moments and helped sweeten the sunny days of my life. And so I have come to treasure music as one of my deepest spiritual resources. But too much music is being played through high-powered speakers these days, without regard to the fact that it may intrude on someone's need for peace and quiet. At that point as far as I'm concerned, it ceases its function as music and degenerates into something called NOISE! It does not seem sound to me, to allow that to happen to music. I have no choice but to end on this sombre note. I hope someone is listening.

St. Kitts-Nevis Observer, **March 19, 1995**

For Politicians Only

In November of last year, leaders and representatives of political parties met with each other and the Christian Council, the Chamber of Industry and Commerce and the St. Kitts/Nevis Bar Association and negotiated something at a highly touted FORUM FOR NATIONAL UNITY, which was held at the Four Seasons Resort here. I don't remember all of the details, indeed I wasn't privy to them, but I do recall most of the principals being quoted as saying what a fine thing it was that such a meeting was held. And that there now was some sort of a moral commitment from all parties to work together for the purpose of national unity and the benefit of the people of this country.

BUNK! Working together – where, when? The meeting was hardly over before some participants were jockeying for positions to be seen in the best possible light. In doing so they characteristically chose to denigrate others, spreading rumour and scandal, expecting to look good in comparison to a negative picture instead of on their own merits. This is the habitual conduct of too many people in our society, especially politicians and is a sorry example for our youth. In no time at all, the mudslinging and backbiting returned in full force and has remained that way ever since. Day after day, week after week there is no let up in the viciousness of the attacks. This is certainly not the way to national unity! I certainly see no evidence of "moral commitment to work together" in such an atmosphere. Who is kidding who?

The antics of all the political parties in the Federation leave much to be desired. In my opinion, all of the political parties have failed all of the people in the Federation, because none of the parties have focused on the endemic problems of St. Kitts/Nevis with any serious intention of doing anything. The Constitution was riddled with serious flaws from its inception and while it legally joins St. Kitts and Nevis, it is an extremely divisive instrument. Of course many problems existed before independence but the framing of our Constitution instead of eradicating difficulties, perpetuates and exacerbates some of the bitterest problems. While all of the parties have known this, none have made a determined effort to do anything. As we approach the 21st century, we need to change and amend the flaws in our Constitution like other modern countries. Our country needs leaders who understand this and will do something about it.

We need leaders who have confidence and pride in their own performance. We don't need you to come to us at election time and lambaste somebody else's shortcomings. We don't need you to tell us what somebody else didn't do and how poorly they did whatever they did. We're not stupid. We know that already. We've had enough scandal, gossip and muckraking to last a lifetime – in fact, a few lifetimes. Enough is enough!

We are the human resources so sorely needed to develop this country's potential. The young and strong. The skilled and experienced. The teachers and the students, the artists and the labourers, the bankers, the builders, the plumbers, the policemen, the managers and the workforce with which to build a nation. Don't misuse us and abuse us with false promises and pretentious but empty platitudes. Restore our hope and faith and trust by means of competence, compassion and co-operation. Those who are managing the country's affairs should be magnanimous, imaginative, scrupulous and fair. Those who are waiting in the wings, should show by reasonable deeds and attitudes that they would be worthy successors.

Come to us with something new and sensible. Treat us like intelligent, responsible citizens who want to help shape our country's future. Take us into your confidence and tell us your understanding of the problems that beset us and your plans for dealing with them. Start with the Constitution and go on down the line. If you are earnest and convincing, I'm sure you'll get the votes.

St. Kitts-Nevis Observer, **March 26, 1995**

Yer Darned Tootin!

In my column of October 14th last year, I raised some problems of behaviour, which I consider to be antisocial and spoiling the character of Nevis. Included among things I mentioned were "aggressive drivers speeding through town, blasting away with ear-splitting horns." In the May 1993 issue of the now defunct NEVIS INSIGHT newsletter, I raised the same issue. I pointed out that speeding in town is illegal and violators should be dealt with through proper enforcement.

I reminisced about earlier days when there were fewer cars and the "beep-beep" heard occasionally, was then used more as a friendly greeting. But vehicles now are bigger, flashier, more powerful, and certainly because their horns are now so loud, more intimidating. In the two years since I first broached the subject, things have rapidly become worse – much worse.

More people now have more money and are buying cars at an alarming rate! Please consider that in about ten years or so, more and more space in Nevis will become occupied by the rusting hulks of many of these vehicles, which through the process of age and damage, will be discarded as new ones are purchased to replace them. And it seems to me that if many people have personalities to match their driving habits (inconsiderate, brazen, erratic), Nevis is in for a rough time!

Because cars have now become so numerous on this island, it should be evident that more control, direction, or regulation is needed to protect both motorist and non-motorist, our environment, and the character and charm of Nevis. Aside from the obvious dangers and problems associated with speeding, noxious fumes and disposal of discarded vehicles, there has been an incredible increase in the pollution of the environment with excessive and unnecessary sound.

When I say excessive, I am speaking about volume. When I say unnecessary, I am referring to things like drivers stopping in front of someone's house and tooting the horn till the occupant comes out. Or speeders, blasting away on their horns instead of driving within the prescribed speed limits, which would usually require no more than normal awareness and vigilance on the part of both motorist and pedestrian.

If the rules of the road, a little courtesy, common sense and consideration for others were practised by everybody, the sounds of Charlestown would be less frenetic and more idyllic. But at times the sounds in Charlestown are remarkably like Harlem in New York, with tyres screeching, boom-boxes blasting, and car horns blaring away!

All these exert a hidden toll on our society by creating stress and other health-related problems for many individuals who may even be unaware of their sensitivity to sound pollution, but who suffer from it nevertheless. Of course there are many other forms of sound pollution. Motorists aren't the only guilty ones. But in this issue I just wanted to toot my horn at some thoughtless drivers in Nevis who obviously don't give a hoot!

St. Kitts-Nevis Observer, April 2, 1995

PLEASE DON'T MISUNDERSTAND!

As I came out of the post office the other day, a fellow stopped me. "Trott," he says, "what are you going to write about in de *Observer* nex' time?" I wasn't certain of his mood. Was he offended by something I had written last week? Did I have reason to be worried? He expected an answer and asked me again. "Sects," I said. A big smile appeared on his face. "I like dat. Man, I can hardly wait to get de nex' issue!"

As he left, it occurred to me that he might have gotten the wrong impression, he might have thought he heard me say something entirely different from what I actually said. And he just might go around town telling his friends what Trott said he was going to write about in the next issue. But by the time I realised I should try to clarify things, he had disappeared down the street.

So all week I've been worried about it. You see, if that fellow goes around telling people what he thinks I'm going to write about, a lot of people may be disappointed when they read the column and don't find what they expected. I don't want to disappoint those readers, but I don't know what else to do. I can't write about what he thinks I'm going to write about because to tell the truth, I don't know enough about it. I would need to do a lot of extensive research and frankly, at my age, I don't think I'm up to it.

On the other hand – something else just occurred to me. Suppose he didn't misunderstand me after all? Suppose he heard and understood perfectly what I said and was enthusiastic because he had a sincere interest. That's not an impossibility, is it? After all people all over the world these days are exploring alternate religious or philosophical groups. So maybe he's into sects in a serious way. But then, that creates another problem for me. To write and do justice about sects for enthusiastic readers, would require me to do more research than I am willing to do. So it really doesn't matter what that fellow heard me say, I have to disappoint him this time. And of course, if he told you and you had certain expectations, then you will be disappointed too.

The lesson to be gleaned from this of course is; don't ask what I will write about in the next issue. Then there will be no misunderstanding and (hopefully), no disappointments.

St. Kitts-Nevis Observer, April 23, 1995

SOUND POSITION

On April 21st the Methodist Youth Choir performed the gospel musical "Alone On The Altar", at the Methodist Church in Charlestown. This group sang their hearts out in rendition after rendition to an audience that was, if not totally awed, at least thoroughly moved and impressed. But what they were moved and impressed with most, was the quality of the sounds they were hearing: the pleasing melodies, rich harmonies, earnestness of the vocalists and the overall manner of presentation with the inclusion of the Hummingbird String Band performing in crowd scenes, veteran actors Franklin Brand as Jesus, and Frankie Claxton as John the Baptist in non-singing roles, colourful costumes, sensitive lighting and a narrative unifying the whole production under the skilful direction of Victor Martin.

In the printed programme, Easter greetings from the group's Musical Director Lorette Brand, were preceded by a familiar quote from the Bible, "Make a joyful noise unto the Lord… Come before His presence singing." I'm sure that quite a lot of people will be upset to know that I find fault with anything about the Bible, but I have to admit there are a few things that give me pause. One of those things is the use of the word "noise" in the above passage. I prefer the word "sound." The reason is that I believe that noise is loud, unpleasant, disagreeable, or painful. Noise annoys! At least, that's the case these days.

In the *Observer* of March 19th, I complained that a lot of music being played through high powered speakers these days degrades into noise, as it intrudes on some persons' right to peace and quiet. In fact some religious people who are early risers habitually play loud gospel music at ungodly hours, seemingly unconcerned that their "joyful noise unto the Lord" may be playing havoc with a neighbour badly in need of sleep, peace or quiet. I find it hard to believe that this is what the Bible intended. Of course when the Bible was written, there were no high powered speakers. People intent on making joyful sounds could probably not be heard at any great distance and so disturbed no one. When it was necessary for a large number of people to make or hear joyful sounds, they gathered at a special place for that purpose. Nobody had to miss their sleep if they weren't interested.

I am truly sorry however, that more people didn't gather at the special place to experience the joyful sounds of the Youth Choir on April 21st. Yes, they used a modern sound system with a tape deck and hi-fi speakers. But that was just to provide the recorded orchestral background for the singers, not to blast somebody out of bed a block away. The taped instrumental music blended beautifully, supporting the soloists through lyrical passages and providing bouncy, throbbing, rhythmic currents and lush harmonies to underscore the choral efforts.

I cannot say that this is the best choir I have heard in Nevis. But I certainly feel that they are unmatched for enthusiasm. Their performance was the most satisfying I have experienced in a long time. I was pleasantly surprised at the strength of the basses, not the numbers, but the tone and confidence on every note. But every section performed well. The overall impact was very impressive, overriding the few weak spots and giving assurance that there is an abundance of talent in Nevis.

It is a pity that more Nevisians, especially younger ones, aren't involved in more of this type of constructive, creative expression. When something like this is done so well, a tremendous amount of enjoyment and satisfaction is derived for participants and spectators. This production deserved more than one performance. Every schoolchild in Nevis should have been exposed to it. We need more of this type of offering to counter the effects of pernicious material so readily available via TV, radio, and other outlets. This thoroughly entertaining, wholesome type of experience should be more readily available to all. Every adult Nevisian should be urged to attend these performances. And we should not be shy about letting every visitor to this island know when first-class concerts like these are happening. I'm sure they would be even more impressed with our island and its people.

Lorette Brand is doing a superb job as their Musical Director and the entire group should be highly commended for their efforts. If their last appearance was really noise, I can't imagine what they'll be like when they start to make music. But to make sure I find out, I intend to be first in line for tickets to their next concert. Don't bother to make a lot of noise about it – I'm not giving up my position!

St. Kitts-Nevis Observer, April 7, 1995

Say 'No' To Crime!
Stand With Jackie Cramer

Scanning through old newspapers before I threw them away, I came across the column by Gary Steckles in *Caribbean Week*'s March 4-17 issue. He wrote about his experience of Jamaica, a place he has visited many times. He says that even though Jamaica is plagued with an international reputation that isn't exactly savoury, he has been lucky enough to have never had more than the most minor of problems during his visits to that remarkable country.

He explains that just a tiny minority of violent Jamaicans manage to commit enough mayhem at home and abroad to taint not only the name of their island, but an entire race. But what really made me sit up and take notice is where he suggests that even though Jamaica is not the safest place in the Caribbean, "…it might be before too long…" the way some of the other islands are going.

The rapid escalation of crime throughout the Caribbean is shocking and frightening enough. But the situation in St. Kitts and Nevis during the past few years should have set alarm bells ringing long ago. The incidents that led St. Kitts being referred to as "Devil's Island" in the foreign press, did not just suddenly happen overnight with no warning. Unsavoury things, criminal things have been happening with increasing frequency and brazenness for several years. But political posturing and partisanship clouded every issue and instead of developing a united, alert citizenry, capable of co-operating and supporting a competent police force and administration, we seem to have developed factions capable only of supporting selfish interests or engineering the downfall of others.

Such a climate nurtures devious minds, unhealthy attitudes, and encourages the growth of criminal activity. We are now reaping what has been sown and unless we are willing to do some serious weeding, trimming, ploughing, and planting new seed, we'll be overgrown with the problems of crime and corruption. We need to develop attitudes that encourage the growth and influence of benevolent forces in our midst. We need to display the kinds of behaviour that if others emulate, will truly turn our community into a paradise instead of "Devil's Island!" Political posturing, backbiting and pointing the finger of blame simply won't do.

Nevis and St. Kitts are fairly small communities where most people know each other. People always look into my yard to see what I am doing. I seldom go to Gingerland or Barnes Ghaut, without half the place knowing my business. It only follows that criminals and their activities should not be going unnoticed here. Somebody should know that guy who's stealing – that guy who's dealing drugs – that guy who's messing around with guns. But why is nobody exposing them? Are we all "on the take" or all "on the make"?

Every citizen has a moral duty to do what he can to protect his country, from the enemy without or the enemy within. As stalwarts, we must stand against those who do harm. Those who know, but do or say nothing are compounding the problem. Because when criminals know we won't say anything, they become bolder, and their activities increase. Obviously, the more criminal activity that occurs here, the less attractive this place will be as a tourist destination. Then, as Gary Steckles suggests, Jamaica might seem a safer place to be. Let's not kid ourselves, the sickening scourge of criminality will not go away by itself. Determined effort must be made to pry it loose and stop its growth. The police and the administration cannot do it alone. Alert and courageous citizens must do their duty and play their part. It won't be easy, but think of the alternative.

In St. Kitts, TDC Chairman Jackie Cramer led a demonstration March Against Crime on March 21st. He is quoted as saying, "All leaders must live by example…" He was not posturing as a political partisan, he was acting as a responsible citizen. His example says to the rest of us, that crime is unacceptable and he will do whatever he can to eradicate it in our community. If the other residents and citizens of St. Kitts/Nevis really "…love this place", then it is incumbent upon us to follow his lead and do whatever we can to eradicate the blight of crime from these fair islands.

St. Kitts-Nevis Observer, **May 14, 1995**

Contact Points

My daily routine finds me walking along the streets in Charlestown most mornings or afternoons. On these excursions, it is my habit to glance at faces of passers-by. When someone meets my eyes I usually smile and extend a greeting, a simple "good morning" or "good afternoon" in passing, or sometimes a more elaborate "Hi there. How are you doing?" if it is someone I know and would like to stay and chat awhile.

Occasionally I run into a little problem. Sometimes a person is wearing coated sunglasses making eye contact impossible. Extending a greeting then becomes a hit or miss operation, because you can't tell if they're looking at you since there's no eye contact. It's a bit unnerving to smile and greet a stranger who wasn't looking at you after all. Their reaction might make me feel guilty of intrusion. But generally, I like greeting people on the streets. I think important psychological benefits are derived from this activity. And certainly the rewards to be gained are astronomical in proportion to the amount of energy expended.

I don't always verbalise my greeting though. Sometimes I just smile and nod in a friendly manner, and more often than not, my greetings are returned. These greetings are important to me because I have to cope with a lot of stress, difficulties and disappointments. Storing up these positive responses help me to better face the problems of the day. They sort of help to recharge my emotional and psychic batteries. Help me to feel good about myself. Of course I don't greet everyone I see. I've learned through trial and error that some people don't want to be greeted, don't wish to be friendly, don't want to be bothered. So if I suspect a person is avoiding my eyes, looking past or through me, I don't force the issue. I might flash a tentative smile just in case they change their minds at the last second, but I try not to beg for recognition. But my method is not foolproof and has its hazards.

Coming out of Evelyn's Drug Store on Main Street one day, I made way for a woman who was about to enter. As our eyes met, I offered a friendly smile and uttered my usual "Good morning." Her response was a frosty glare, which was most incongruous with the warmth of my greeting and the heat of the day. It was a momentary setback so early in the day, and I wondered briefly if there was something in my manner that might have offended her. But perhaps she wasn't feeling well. A headache perhaps? I couldn't think of anything else that might have caused her negative reaction, but I had other business in town and soon forgot about her.

On my way back home later, I spotted her in the distance coming towards me. As it was obvious that we would pass each other, I almost panicked wondering if I should avoid her eyes, look past her, through her, around her? We drew closer. Although I hadn't yet tried to make eye contact, I could tell she was looking at me. At the critical moment, our eyes met and locked on each other. I couldn't help it – my face relaxed into a smile and my breath formed the friendliest "Hello" I had managed in a long time. Her cold, deepfreeze glare, iced through me. It wasn't a pleasant feeling, even on a hot day. I was chilled to the bone, psychologically speaking. Thank goodness though, I had already collected enough warm, positive responses to effect a quick thaw countering that chill.

I still think about that experience and wonder how to act should we ever meet again. I hope she reads this column because I would like if possible, to dispel any misapprehensions she might have about me. I'm basically a harmless fellow – genuinely friendly. And while it's true I like women, I know how to behave myself. Exchanging "Good mornings" on the street does not commit anybody to anything. Besides, most people who know me would tell you that I'm a perfect gentleman. So you can relax lady, I may smile, but I ain't going bite you!

St. Kitts-Nevis Observer, **May 21, 1995**

Help!

One often feels helpless in the face of confusion. And in the rapid changes and mounting pressures of these times, the amount of confusion often seems overwhelming. I tend to be a meliorist, in that I believe that things can be made better through human effort. I sometimes find it difficult though, to not become pessimistic given the mass of apparently uncontrollable events that are so difficult to understand or give order to. But if I shrink from the task of doing whatever I can towards the improvement of our society, then I fail myself as a man and diminish my capacity as an intellectual and spiritual human being.

There is so much to be done that demands our full intellectual and spiritual involvement. Consider if you will, the impacts of development on our small, unsophisticated communities. Consider the rapid economic, social and cultural changes that are occurring. Consider the growing threat to our security through the escalation of all sorts of crimes that we are not equipped to deal with. And consider that if the law does not protect you, it will not in the end protect me either.

So I struggle on to make whatever contribution I can in the most appropriate ways. Because I am a free thinker and a writer, this column is an appropriate way for me to contribute part of my effort to enhance human development in this community. I believe that a lot of the things I write about will strike sympathetic chords in most readers, helping to better understand, appreciate, focus on and perhaps deal with some of the perplexing problems that beset us all.

For too long the existing print media of St. Kitts/Nevis failed to provide adequate coverage of anything without political content. The two newspapers published in St. Kitts have had the field to themselves for decades. They have been so heavily biased politically, mean in spirit, crude in content and presentation, that I have often shuddered to think that these were the only newspapers available to our young people that are expected to learn from their elders. The general population too, including businessmen, labourers and public servants, should have been better informed about the goings on in their country. And visitors from abroad experience our islands not only through hotels, beaches, and the few locals they meet, but also through whatever print media is available.

I have often been embarrassed to hear the negative comments that some visitors have made about our local press. The main complaints were the lack of objectivity, extreme bias, viciousness and poor taste. These are serious faults, and insofar as these papers have been publishing for quite some time, should have been eradicated long ago. One of the papers uses as its motto, a quote from the Bible, "SOUND SPEECH THAT CANNOT BE CONDEMNED..." How ironic, since almost everything they print is condemned in the other paper which tells us it is "THE FEDERATION'S LEADING NEWSPAPER." But the "Leading Newspaper" is often attacked in the pages of "Sound Speech", as publishing information which is "misleading", and they toss brickbats back and forth week after week with monotonous regularity.

In fact, it appears to me that the main reason for their continued operations is to get back at the other party with as much scandal and ill will as their imaginations and energies can muster. Any other function as newspapers appear to be secondary and sometimes even nonexistent. All this adds needlessly to the mountain of confusion and helplessness I spoke about earlier. Because of this, I have rarely contributed to those papers and in the last few years, not at all, since many local people assume that contributors support the political stance of the papers that publish their pieces. Although there were many things I would have liked to write about, I couldn't find the proper forum, and I believe there were probably others like me, who avoided being associated with partisan political journalism.

In October last year, the *Observer* began publishing in Nevis and I've been able to contribute a regular weekly column about my personal experiences, observations, or opinions. Other personnel gather and write news stories, editorials, contribute other columns or articles, man the presses, and put the paper together. I don't know or care about the political biases of any of the others. I think each of us is just trying to do our best to provide the community with a newspaper that is worthy of the name, and to aim for journalistic standards that are honoured and respected globally. We may be a long way from those objectives, but at least we're trying. Despite the many problems encountered in starting this paper and keeping it afloat, the publisher has persevered and in eight short months, I believe this paper is doing a better job and providing a more valuable service to the community than any other.

Although this paper is in its infancy, and struggling to find its legs, people are saying they find it a refreshing alternative. I am fortunate that this outlet is now available, for I felt frustrated previously. And the positive feedback has been most rewarding, thanks to readers who say that they enjoy the column, and find something of value; a little coherence, a little humour, or a fresh perspective on some of the confusion around us. That encourages me to feel, well – not quite so helpless.

St. Kitts-Nevis Observer, **May 28, 1995**

97

MANGO MANIA

It's amazing, but true; mangoes have the power to bring out the best in some people – or the worst! Although it's a fact that I love mangoes (they're my favourite fruit), I experience mixed feelings whenever mango season arrives. Our family has two properties, each with a large mango tree. The property on Main Street has a grafted tree which gives some of the best flavoured and smoothly textured mangoes I have ever experienced. Our Craddock Road property has a tree, which although not grafted, bears a very succulent and delicious fruit despite the thick skin and stringy pulp. So we obviously have plenty of mangoes when they are in season.

My mother, who passed away recently, loved mangoes with a passion and could eat them all day long if we let her. She would make quick work of the grafted mangoes because of the smooth, fibre-less texture. The stringy mangoes would take her much longer to deal with, but she had patience and relished them as much as the others I believe, and always said "Thank you darling," when I brought them for her. She didn't have much to do in her declining days, so these mangoes when they were available, provided not only nourishment and sustenance for her, but exercise and activity too, as she would work a mango over until the seed was smooth and bare.

But there is one thing I dread about mango season, and that is the craze that seems to descend on the populace as people young and old, go on a mango binge of pandemic proportions. I only eat mangoes at home where there is easy access to a sink, a towel, and a trash bin. But I often see others eating mangoes in public and flinging the skins and the seeds into the streets, oblivious to the unsightly mess and health hazards they create.

That sort of thing is bad enough, but I have been extremely upset on a couple of occasions when our grafted mango tree was completely stripped by unknown persons, before I was able to pick more than just a few for my mother. Another time, when I came home, I found a bunch of young fellows in our tree, picking the mangoes and tossing them to their buddies waiting below. When I ordered them out of the tree and off the property, they abused me verbally with outrageous invective. I wasn't exactly pleased.

Our family has always willingly shared with friends, relatives and neighbours. Sharing a few mangoes is never a problem because when the trees are bearing, we have more than enough for ourselves. We can't hoard them. We don't sell them. We're actually glad to share them with others. But those fellows had climbed over the five-foot high block wall and trampled my mother's precious plants and flowers to get at the mangoes! My mother had spent a lot of time and care, in nurturing that garden. If they had come to the front gate and asked, we surely would have allowed them in to take some of the mangoes. But as things were, I told them they weren't welcome as trespassers and they didn't like that. They simply showed no respect for us or our right to protect our property.

Well, it's mango time again and once more, skins and seeds are flying about. People seem to forget about the anti-litter laws and the Keep Nevis Clean Campaign. Our tree on Craddock Road bore quite a good crop and passers-by and neighbours have been taking a share. Most don't bother to ask, but a few have and we've always allowed them access. One of the few who've asked is a woman who can't speak but makes vocal sounds and hand and facial signals. She came knocking at my window, held up a bag and pointed to the mango tree. I understood her meaning, smiled and nodded "yes" and went on with what I was doing.

A few minutes later she knocked at the window again. She had quickly collected her mangoes and came to thank me and offer me a couple of the nicest ones she had found. I smiled and indicated that she should keep them all, I had plenty in the house. But I wished I knew how to indicate to her how very much I appreciated her thoughtful gesture. Though she couldn't speak a word, she displayed more common sense, courtesy, and class, than many others who have no disabilities.

I had often seen her on Craddock Road or Main Street before, and usually we smiled and waved greetings to each other. But I had never thought about what kind of person she was socially, intellectually, spiritually – until now. I imagine I will never really know. But at least I have a new awareness and appreciation of her personality, a new understanding of her spirit, a fresh insight to her character. By her simple action, she has shown me something few others have and I now see her from a new perspective, and with the utmost respect. In a world of chaos and confusion, she was able to provide a moment of grace. Amazing, isn't it, what mangoes can do!

St. Kitts-Nevis Observer, May 4, 1995

EXCUSE ME!

My formative years in Montreal were spent growing up on the wrong side of the tracks. Literally. Though we actually lived in Westmount, which was one of the ritziest districts of Montreal, we were at the borderline on St. Antoine Street. If you crossed the street you'd be in St. Henri, one of the poorest districts. Westmount was thought to be so ritzy and exclusive that if you committed a crime on the St. Henri side of St. Antoine, then crossed the street into Westmount, the Montreal police couldn't touch you. It probably wasn't true of course, but I was just a young impressionable kid then who'd believe almost anything.

Our side of St. Antoine Street was indistinguishable from the other side with its rows of tenement housing. You had to go up the hill at Green Avenue, and past the railroad tracks towards Dorchester Street, before you could really appreciate the difference. Even the air smelled fresher there. I technically lived in Westmount and went to school there. But my social contacts – the kids I played and fought with, went to church with, hung out and grew up with, came from the poorer parts of Montreal.

I was always a quiet, introverted type, but I wanted to have friends and be popular like everybody else. My mother did not approve of most of my friends during my childhood. If they were not well dressed and groomed, she considered them to be ragamuffins and did not want them in her house. If their speech was a little coarse and uncultured, she considered them ruffians and wanted me to have nothing to do with them. But since we did not have easy access to the ritzy residents in Westmount, I naturally made friends with children from some of the rougher areas nearby.

I had pals from the famous Lacasse Street Gang. From Chatham Street, Notre Dame Street, and Verdun. I never belonged to any gangs myself. My mother would not have allowed that. But I got to know the guys and sometimes played or hung around with them a little. After all, you never know when you're going to need a friend. I was always an oddity in these groups though, and never quite fit in. Never made it to the inner circles. I would join these friends mostly to participate in sports and games in the parks and fields. Baseball, soccer, boxing, wrestling. The play was always hard and rough. Cuts and bruises were a normal part of the proceedings, and several times I had the stuffing knocked completely out of me and thought I was going to die.

TROTT TALK

In most respects when we were together, I was pretty much like the other fellows except for one thing: I didn't cuss or use vulgar language. At least, not very much. My use of profanity was mostly limited to "dammit!" The other fellows couldn't understand it and I never bothered to try to explain it. I realised though, that in the heat of competition when excitement and emotions were at a peak, ordinary language may not suit the moment. But as we grew older I became aware that many of those friends were addicted to using coarse, vulgar profanities to punctuate ordinary conversation. I sensed that they somehow felt that this was a manifestation of their growing manliness. I didn't say so, but I was beginning to feel uncomfortable in their company.

By age 15, I had quit school, had a full time job and wider social contacts. I got together with my old friends less frequently. During one of the last times we were together, an incident occurred in which it seemed to me my manliness was being challenged because I didn't curse. I can't remember the actual spoken words, but the drift is that I was considered a sissy because I wouldn't curse like the others. Hurt and angry, I blurted out that I could out-cuss the best of them if I wanted to, but that I wouldn't because of my upbringing. They laughed and scoffed and called me a mama's boy. That did it! I started cursing. Slow and haltingly at first, as though testing the waters.

After the first few seconds or so, I established a rhythm and when they realised I was just warming up, they could not suppress their astonishment and admiration. I rambled on using all the foul terms I knew they were familiar with and when I had exhausted those, I used my inventiveness and imagination to create new ones. I was on a roll and there was no room for interruption as I incorporated every sickeningly vile and vulgar term I could think of and mixed them with the sacred and profane in ways that left them all in open-mouthed shock.

When I left my friends I think we were all ashamed. I remember sitting alone on a park bench for a while, looking up at the sky and asking for God's forgiveness. I seldom saw those friends after that as my growing interests in art, drama, and literature, occupied more of my time and brought me greater pleasure. Besides, my newer contacts did not require cursing to prove my manliness. Occasionally I now inadvertently utter a curse word or two when something upsets me. Often nobody is there to hear it but me, and sometimes it isn't even uttered aloud, but in my mind. But still I invariably get a feeling of remorse and am prompted to say "excuse me" or, "forgive me."

Nowadays I am appalled at the amount of coarse, vulgar, crude and profane language that can be heard all hours of the day or night around Charlestown. It spoils our environment. Not only men are responsible, but women and children too. This is not a positive reflection of their upbringing, and certainly sets a bad example. I wonder if they can understand how needlessly offensive they are. Or if they ever feel ashamed and ask for forgiveness. I wonder what they are trying to prove with that kind of conduct. Certainly not manliness!

It really doesn't matter where you were born, or what the circumstances of your life were – if you were blessed with intelligence and the power to speak, you have a responsibility to speak intelligently. The constant use of vulgar expletives is an abuse of your God-given powers. Those of you who do it, should think about it. Maybe feel a little shamed about it. Certainly you should try to stop it. And it won't hurt to ask for forgiveness.

St. Kitts-Nevis Observer, **June 11, 1995**

COUNTRY ABOVE SELF - FACT OR FICTION?

Many people have asked me to comment on the local political situation. Too many to be ignored. I don't really relish the idea, because as I have stated in an earlier issue, I am not a political pundit – far from it. So these opinions are offered from my peculiar perspective without any pretensions.

It has occurred to me many times, that our country's motto has not been honoured to any great extent, by either the conduct of our national leaders, or the populace as a whole. Stop me if I'm wrong, but it seems to me that the words "COUNTRY ABOVE SELF," imply a willingness or intention to hold that the interests and welfare of our nation are more important than our individual personal desires. And that if a situation should arise requiring a choice between personal aggrandisement or national interests, we would sacrifice our personal desires and tend to national interests first. I believe this motto is supposed to be expressive of the goals and ideals of our nation and is something we should collectively and individually strive towards. It is also perfectly clear that those who come before us seeking public office have an obligation, a responsibility, a duty to set the proper example and lead us in the right direction.

Quite frankly, I am insulted by the manner in which some people present themselves for public office. Instead of being the ideal we are striving for, "COUNTRY ABOVE SELF" is more like a mirage, a false perception, a lie, in the face of reality – a farcical, cruel hoax foisted on this country and its people. A meaningless platitude employed for convenience and opportunism. In no way has the sentiment it expresses been adhered to as a principle of behaviour by this nation's leaders and politicians. Nor is there any evidence that the behaviour of the majority of our citizens is influenced in the slightest degree by this maxim or rule of conduct. In fact, I believe the exact opposite to be true.

It seems to me that the expression "SELF BEFORE COUNTRY" is a much more accurate description and reflection of the attitudes and conduct of the overwhelming majority of our people. And I believe that some of the reasons for this are the flagrant examples some of our leaders are setting. Our society has become so grasping and avaricious, that those who don't follow the trend are looked upon with suspicion or disdain. This saddening loss of virtue is hardly noticed, as in the stampede to reap the benefits of independence, progress, and development – moral, spiritual and ethical considerations are trampled into oblivion.

These so-called leaders are leading some of us into temptation, chaos and confusion, with agendas rewarding mainly politically astute and dextrous individuals. If all of the leaders of this country had truly adopted and followed the principles implied in the motto "COUNTRY ABOVE SELF", the debacle of the last election which so traumatised our country, could have been avoided. Yet in reviewing the situation a year and a half later, it seems to me that the leaders are preparing to lead us down that same path again.

Selfish interests and partisan politics seem to be determining factors for attitudes and decisions of too many of our leaders. Some methods must be devised to alleviate this tendency in our country. A strict code of ethics and conduct, financial disclosure, practical processes for accountability and recall or removal from office need to be instituted, so that a successful candidate's responsibility is firmly underscored, and the availability of recourse by the electorate, clearly understood by all. Implementation may be quite onerous, but at least some measure of restraint might influence those who might otherwise throw moral cautions to the winds. I also believe that term limits would be beneficial in this regard.

But it is clear to me that the general public has a responsibility too. We must not simply follow our leaders blindly. We must stay alert so that if they start to wander in the wrong direction, we can get their attention before things go too far. We must not remain quiet and wait to see what happens. We must let our leaders know what we want, tell them what we think about their leadership, and encourage others to speak up too. We must dialogue with our leaders, in the best traditions of democracy with its premise of government of the people, for the people, and by the people.

Not every one of us is able to do this of course. Not everyone is able to analyse a situation, organise thoughts, select and present ideas in a clear, coherent manner. But those of us who have the ability, also have the responsibility to do so. Otherwise, what is the purpose of having the ability if you don't use it? You use that ability every day as a matter of course, in business and social contacts. You use that ability for self-interests, to get ahead in life. How about putting "COUNTRY ABOVE SELF" for awhile?

This country is in crisis. It needs fresh ideas and new voices. It needs an enlightened citizenry with the guts and determination to make themselves heard. The leaders are squabbling among themselves. Some seem to have forgotten their purpose, lost their senses, and their sense of direction. Some seem to be actually trying to make us believe in nonsense. Those of us in the general population who have the ability, should speak up now in the interim before elections.

Certainly it would seem safer to remain quiet, wait to see what happens.

Take no risks. Hope for the best. That might be the safest course under a totalitarian regime. But this is supposed to be a democratic state. I believe one of the best safeguards of democracy is participation. It may seem a little difficult at times to make your feelings and opinions known publicly. But when you calculate the risks in terms of how many customers you may lose, or how many friends will turn against you, you are putting "SELF ABOVE COUNTRY" and following the lead of too many others who bury their heads in the sand.

If you have some worthwhile ideas, it is time to let the rest of us hear them. It is time to voice your own opinions. It is time to stand up and be counted, add some weight to the voices of reason. Sure, you may get a little heat. Your spouse may even threaten to leave you. But it's time to call on those inner resources, and find the strength to help make "COUNTRY ABOVE SELF" become a fact of life and a true reflection of our behaviour, instead of this present sorry, pathetic fiction!

St. Kitts-Nevis Observer, **June 18, 1995**

RESPECTFULLY YOURS

Reading and writing have been two of the most important things in my life. Though I lack academic qualifications, these skills have brought me the advantages of better-educated persons. Though I never had the opportunity to travel extensively, through the print medium I've learned as much about different regions as some more well travelled persons. And although I've been exposed to radio in my home since the 1930's and television since the 1950's, I have always preferred by far, the printed word for information and intellectual stimulation.

The different cities in which I have lived in North America all boasted top quality newspapers with first-class editors, reporters and columnists. All of these papers had a page or two where readers with opinions could express themselves through Letters to the Editor. And I of course, would use this forum frequently. Most letter writers would sign their correct names as I did, and occasionally, a reader with a dissenting view would quote something I had written. These exchanges were not only interesting and entertaining, they were also very valuable ways for me to improve my reading and writing skills. I continually attempted to bring my writing up to the level of the professional staff writers at these newspapers.

It has been almost ten years since I came to live permanently in Nevis. I was appalled then and am appalled now, at what has been offered to the public here as newspapers in the form of the *Democrat* and *The Labour Spokesman*. These are not publications that can be relied upon for accurate information or intellectual stimulation. These are not publications I would urge young people to study to improve their reading and writing skills. For while I believe there may be qualified, competent writers on their staffs, these are not publications designed to do anything but further narrow partisan political objectives. The manner in which they have done so has been immature, selfish, vindictive offensive, and as a consequence short-changes the general public.

It is time to call a halt to past practices and turn a new leaf. I urge the leaders of both parties to demand better from the editors and staffs of these publications. I urge the leaders to demand professional quality of whatever is printed in these papers so that students who read them will have something worthwhile to emulate and the general public will be properly informed.

I urge the leaders to demand that the gossip and scandal columns that usually appear as "TALK A DE TUNG" in the *Spokesman* and "WHAT!" and

"QUESTIONS" in the *Democrat*, be eradicated entirely. Furthermore, eliminate such derogatory terms such as "Rubbernose", "Papa Doc", "Sam Dopey", and "The Gremlin". It is time to learn to treat each other with respect, in or out of the political arena.

If the *Democrat* really is "THE LEADING NEWSPAPER", then take the lead in developing responsible journalism in the Federation. Stop spreading unnecessary gossip, scandal and alarm week after week. And if the *Spokesman* really wants us to believe it prints "SOUND SPEECH THAT CANNOT BE CONDEMNED", then it should start printing things that are commendable rather than condemnable. After all, the Labour Party said it intends to "put an end to political tribalism". The tenor of what is printed in the *Spokesman*'s pages will go a long way towards either proving or disproving that statement.

Finally, I believe both papers should stop the practice of publishing letters from people who don't want their names printed. Anyone can write a nasty letter and hide behind anonymity. Frankly, some people suspect that those letters are staff written and not from the general public at all. That certainly isn't a good impression. I'd like to encourage anybody who has an intelligent comment to make, to do so in a statement that is forthright, honest, reasonable, and sign your name to it. I may not agree with you, but at least you will have my attention and respect.

St. Kitts-Nevis Observer, **July 23, 1995**

ANTHING GOES?

In the 1930's the American composer, Cole Porter, wrote a popular song titled "Anything Goes." I remember clearly some of the lyrics which were cleverly critical of the decline in social standards and public morality:

"Good authors too
Who once knew better words
Now only use four-letter words
Writing prose
Anything Goes."

That sentiment is perhaps more appropriate today than it was sixty years ago, as more and more people who should know better words, routinely use foul language in ordinary conversation and everyday situations. In my opinion, the practice has reached epidemic proportions here. Since I have commented on foul language as recently as last month, some readers may not be interested in anything more I have to say on the subject. But I feel almost forced to bring it up again because the practice is so prevalent that unless some of us complain and try to do something, the common use of foul language may become the accepted standard for communication in our community. I find such a development totally unacceptable and ask our readers to do whatever they can to help keep such a scenario from happening.

Consider if you will, that from the dawn of human history, mankind has struggled to improve his condition on this earth. He has struggled to find reliable ways to secure food, water and shelter for his survival. He has struggled to develop skills, which enabled him to compete successfully against other dangerous species on the planet. He has struggled to learn from his experiences and develop the means of transferring his knowledge to others of his species and to subsequent generations.

He has developed various means of communication. Man's early grunts, growls, screams and other vocal sounds, evolved eventually into speech and various forms of language. His marks on the sand, or on tree trunks, or cave walls, evolved into writing. Whistles, drums and smoke signals, were among other interesting methods man used in developing his ability to communicate with others. But it was his unique language skills which set man well apart from other animals, and which enabled him to develop a society, an industry, a science, a future. At present, we are at the threshold of that future. Man needs all of the skills he has acquired up to now, to negotiate a safe passage into that future. For the dangers that confront him now, come not from the other species he has successfully subdued. Not from frightening monsters from outer space. Not from some unknown quantity, some incomprehensible force – but from the well-known, much studied, but little understood, Man himself!

Although mankind is said to have made amazing strides over the millennia, he is still amazingly primitive in certain respects. Consider the situation today in Bosnia, Israel, Nigeria. Or the bombing in Oklahoma, chemical terrorism in Japan, French nuclear testing, or the political problems so recently experienced here in St. Kitts/Nevis. Bombing, maiming, gassing and killing each other does nothing positive for the development of mankind. If we are going to survive as a species in the future, we have to upgrade and improve our communication skills so that we can better understand and appreciate each other. It is a criminal thing to degrade mankind's efforts through thousands of years to develop speech and communication skills, with stupid, thoughtless foul language. Cursing and swearing at each other or about others, does nothing to uplift the spirit, stimulate the intellect, improve one's physical wellbeing, financial situation, or good looks. Cursing and swearing only increases the amount of harmful negativity in the world.

Mankind is still undergoing a process of physical, intellectual and spiritual development. We have not yet reached the end product. If we are ever going to, we had better find more reasonable ways to resolve divisive issues and learn to live with each other. All of us living here in this relatively peaceful, but small developing country, have an opportunity to make a contribution towards the advancement of mankind. That contribution is not in dollars and cents, or goods and services. But in a mental and spiritual approach to things, to situations, and to each other, which recognises, advocates and embraces, coexistence, common sense, and a commitment to work with others to improve the condition of man. That contribution will bring a reduction of negativity in this world, and any reduction of negativity is bound to somehow have a positive effect on something, or someone, somewhere.

Let us begin by eliminating foul language from our vocabulary and using positive, loving, caring words to replace them. Instead of resorting to that overused "f" word when somebody displeases you, try looking at him as if he had just sneezed and calmly say "Bless you." And if you are involved in a conversation with others who start using foul language, explain to them that you are trying something new, which involves eliminating foul language from the atmosphere. If they persist, just excuse yourself saying you are sorry but the atmosphere isn't right for you. And, of course, you can say, "Bless you all," as you leave. Bars and restaurants should be more insistent that foul language is not permitted on their premises. Perhaps signs such as "KEEP NEVIS' LANGUAGE CLEAN" could be devised for them.

But it is mostly the responsibility of parents and adults to set the proper example for children by refraining themselves, and letting children know that foul language is not acceptable and will not be tolerated. As the local representatives of mankind, we should strive to improve ourselves in every way including the way we think, the way we speak, and the way we act. The concept of "Anything Goes" must be exposed for what it is; a warped, selfish ideal seemingly benefiting the individual, but insidiously infecting the whole community. It is the creed of the rapist, the robber, the killer, the drug lord, the liar, the fool and the insensitive, and should have no place in our society.

St. Kitts-Nevis Observer, **July 30, 1995**

In Praise Of...

Most of my offerings in this column have been highly critical about one thing or another. That is not exactly unintentional. My observations about the community around me inform and infuse my opinions and influence the direction of my thoughts. Some people have wondered how I find so many different things to write about. That should never be a problem. There are so many different things to write about that it is often difficult to make a choice. My choice this week is to write about someone commendable.

Keithley Woolward is a young 6th form student at Charlestown Secondary School. He has always done well academically, and hopes to be accepted by one of the five colleges to which he has sent applications in the United States and Canada. In the meantime, he has been holding a summer job as chef's apprentice at Sandpipers. What prompts me to write about him, is that he is one of the people I most respect and admire in Nevis. Though I am some fifty years older than he is, I relate to him more easily than most people in my age group. Keithley is young, energetic, inquisitive and open-minded. He is also ambitious, confident, flexible and very talented.

I first met Keithley in 1991 when I was lucky enough to see him acting in a play at his high school. His was easily the best performance, but I was even more impressed by his composure and graciousness when I went backstage later to say a few words. Two years passed before we had any real contact again, but in the interim he was distinguishing himself with school and other activities.

He has been with the Literary and Debating Society since third form and this year when Nevis won the competition between St. Kitts, Nevis, Anguilla, Montserrat and Antigua, he won two awards including "Overall Best Speaker in Competition." In 1993 he won the National Essay Writing Competition. Was a member of the Nevis Environmental Committee sent to Guyana as participants in the exchange Commonwealth Youth Programme in 1994. Has been elected to the boards of the Nevis Historical and Conservation Society and Nevis Environmental and Education Committee. During Youth Month he was a panellist offering perspectives on youth and crime. He is the narrator for NHCS' recent video "Water, The Liquid Of Life", which is an educational tool for schools and has been shown on TV as well. He was nominated to represent Nevis at the Global Youth Forum in San Francisco Aug. 9-13.

Obviously there's an awful lot going on in this young person's life that is positive uplifting and commendable. Because there are only so many hours in a day, he has to be a very focused and well disciplined person to manage all of these so successfully. I have not spent a great deal of time with Keithley, but time is of the essence, so the time I have spent with him has been 'quality time', as they say.

I began to know and appreciate more of Keithley's qualities in 1993 when he participated in a drama workshop I conducted for a couple of months. The twice-weekly sessions were held after school at Hamilton House Arts Centre and were of one and a half hours duration. Eighteen students had enrolled, but not all attended regularly and I soon had the impression that most of those who attended merely found it a convenient place to 'hang out'. On the few occasions when Keithley couldn't attend, he would call to let me know. He was one of only a few who put enough effort and interest into the sessions to derive anything of value from them.

I often tell students that I can't teach them anything, but if they pay attention, they might learn something from me. Keithley came to learn and was one of the people who made my efforts seem worthwhile. I could see him absorbing what I had to offer and growing in skill and confidence. Health problems forced me to discontinue the workshops and it was not until the summer holidays of 1994 that I was able to try something with Keithley again. I had written a musical comedy and Keithley had agreed to be in it and was doing a marvellous job in rehearsals. But financial and other production related problems were causing me so much stress, that I abruptly cancelled performance plans. I wouldn't have blamed Keithley if he gave up on me. Twice he'd invested his time and energy in projects that I cancelled. But in January this year our paths crossed again.

The Arts Centre had been rehearsing the play *"Cap'n Book And The Bookaneers"* since early December. The cast of four had been undergoing rigorous, specialised training in sword fighting, under direction of J.R. Beardsley from San Francisco. But one of the members had to leave the cast and we were stuck unless I could find a suitable replacement in a hurry. I had not tried to get Keithley earlier, because he had previously told me of his plans and I was sure he would be too busy. However, I was now in a jam and the least I could do was try.

Keithley came through for us in remarkable fashion and helped turn a potential disaster into a moment of triumph for all of us. His rugged determination and dedication to our cause enabled him to rapidly learn the moves, the skills and techniques, making it possible for us to open the show on schedule to an enthusiastic crowd at the opening of NHCS's ART NEVIS '95 week at the end of February.

I expect Keithley to continue to do well. He has the intelligence, determination and sensitivity. He also has my best wishes and of course, my admiration.

St. Kitts-Nevis Observer, August 20, 1995

PLUPERFECT

Someone once accused me of being a perfectionist. At the time, I promptly and staunchly denied it. Not that I felt there was anything intrinsically wrong with striving for perfection. I didn't feel so then, and I don't feel so now. But perfectionism is not a doctrine I have ever believed in or consciously pursued. Besides, I recognise the futility of it all. So it bothers me a little whenever somebody says that I am too much of a perfectionist.

Frankly, I don't think they know exactly what they are saying. According to the dictionary, a perfectionist is (1) A person who believes in or professes any theory of perfection, or (2) One who will not accept or be content with anything short of perfection. Neither of these definitions accurately characterise my attitudes or beliefs.

In the first place, I long ago discovered that many others believed that I possessed too many imperfections. At various times I was told that I was too short, too thin, too slow, undernourished, underachieving, un-ambitious, impatient, impractical, impetuous, incompetent, insipid, insane…

The list of my many supposed imperfections is far too long to catalogue here. Suffice it to say however, that such was my concern that I undertook to devise ways to make most of my imperfections less remarkable or outstanding. Thus when people complained that I was too quiet, I tried to become a chatterbox. When they said that I was dull, I learned to liven things up with a few ribald jokes. Upon being called a wimp, I began elbowing my way through crowds. And I frequently watched X-rated movies after being told I was too prudish.

Alas, my sincere early efforts did not produce the kind of results I expected. One cannot imagine how upset I became at being called a *perfect* bore. How it wounded me to be told I was a *perfect* nuisance, or how it crushed me to learn that some people considered me to be a *perfect* idiot! The one thing that consoled me through those difficult times, was that at least there weren't fifty million Frenchmen telling me those things, because it was a well known fact that fifty million Frenchmen couldn't be wrong. At least not in those days.

I didn't mind in the least however, whenever someone said that I was *perfectly* right about something or other. And I accepted with consummate grace, anyone calling me a *perfect* gentleman. I can very readily accept things, which I find to be *perfectly* true. So I weathered the storm as best I could, knowing full well that it was not my intention, aspiration, or ambition to become perfect in any respect. I'm not that much of a dreamer. In fact, if someone were to call me a realist, I'd be *perfectly* content.

I understand *perfectly* well that this is not a *perfect* world we live in. Therefore, *perfection* cannot be considered a condition or state of normalcy. So, not wishing to become abnormal, or supernormal, I merely set my sights on improving or bettering myself in many of the areas in which I had been made to feel deficient. To do this, I set some personal goals and standards, which I'm sure any reasonable person would recognise, are far from *perfection*. These goals and standards are also not so far beyond reach as to be unattainable. Through reasonable effort I've managed to reach and maintain some of the goals and standards I've aimed for. I'm still working on many others.

But living in Nevis often severely thwarts my attempts to become more patient, tolerant, understanding and forgiving. Many Nevisians exhibit an attitude, which visitors often describe as "laissez-faire", "lackadaisical", or, "laid-back". Locals proudly assert that this is "Nevis Style" or, "We own ting". Call it what you will, it seems to thoroughly permeate the atmosphere here. It affects not only the pace, but also the manner in which things get done, or just as often, not done. It infects all classes and all sectors of the local community, but seems to be a particular affectation in certain areas of the civil service and the business community.

This "laid-back" "Nevis style" attitude may actually seem appealing to many tourists who are only here for a week or so, and whose contact and dealings with locals revolve mainly around the hotels, the beaches, or the local bars and restaurants. They can consider whatever they experience to be part of the culture and colour of this *"perfectly charming"* little island. But to someone who comes to live here, or is trying to contribute ideas and skills that will benefit the community, the lackadaisical manner can be a *perfectly* frustrating and demeaning experience as queries go unanswered, appointments go un-kept, erroneous information is given, deadlines are missed, opportunities are lost, costs spiral uncontrollably, finances shrink ominously, sanity teeters perilously, and health deteriorates rapidly.

In my opinion, "Doing we own ting – Nevis style" is at present, not a cost effective way of doing things here, or of realistically dealing with the rest of the modern world. It has been wasteful of the time, talent and resources of too many who have been actively trying to participate in the development of this country. It discourages the involvement of others who have something of value to offer, but choose to avoid the aggravation and heartache. It ignores and defeats the rich potential in front of our eyes and at our very doorstep. I'm not asking for *perfection*. I simply believe we should do better - a whole lot better.

I expect that saying these things so bluntly will displease a great many people and I may be targeted for some sort of retaliation. But my intention is not to be combative and provoke hostility. I merely wish that more people in Nevis would strive for perfection and of course, failing to reach that impossible goal, at least settle for something closer to excellence rather than simply being satisfied with something closer to mediocrity. I would dearly love to see the day when "NEVIS STYLE" and "WE OWN TING" actually become slogans or trademarks for top quality, rather than excuses as justification for slackness.

I know that to some people, it might seem *perfectly* ridiculous for me to expound on such things in this manner. Of course they have a *perfect* right to their own opinions, which I wish they had the guts to publish in the newspaper. I have only one more thing to say and that is, I hope I've made myself *perfectly* clear.

St. Kitts-Nevis Observer, **September 3, 1995**

TROTT TALK

A Word To The Wise

I used to think that wisdom came with age. Not any more. I mean like, how old do you have to be, for heaven's sake! I'm sixty-eight and going downhill rapidly and yet, I'm sure I'm no wiser now than I was at forty-eight, or twenty eight, or eighteen for that matter. In fact, if I remember correctly, the last time I felt as though I might have possessed any kernel of wisdom at all, was when I was sixteen or maybe seventeen years old.

I was a shy and awkward kid back then. Very unsure of myself – quiet and withdrawn. I had not done well in school and had not in any way distinguished myself elsewhere. My presence in any group was usually so innocuous that others could not notice me, or else forgot that I was there. I seldom contributed anything to discussions for fear of being thought a fool. Mostly I just hung around people I liked, hoping to learn how to be more like them. Hoping some of that confidence, charm and popularity would rub off on me.

I was interested in girls then, you see. But being the hopeless introvert I was, I knew I didn't stand a chance unless I learned to come out of my shell, and overcome my shyness. Not only did I not know how to talk to girls; I didn't know how to talk to anybody. I was never good at making conversations. I could never think of a thing to say. And of course I'd usually panic if anyone else started a conversation with me. My mind would go blank after the first few exchanges. Later though, when I was back home alone in my room, I'd often think of dozens of things I could have said, and I'd torture myself with thoughts of how stupid I must have seemed to others. I'd vow sometimes, that next time I'd do better, but when the next time presented itself, I'd invariably go through the same agonies all over again.

Then one fateful day, something happened. Something, which in a way I suppose was wonderful, because it helped turn things around for me. Well, not completely around, but enough to make a noticeable difference. I was hanging around a group of acquaintances that were having a discussion. It had probably started off as chitchat, but somewhere along the line, serious ideas were being aired. I really wasn't paying much attention, and to tell the truth, I think most of it was over my head. I was just hanging around there in the background, surreptitiously watching the way one of the girls moved, or marvelling over the curves and contours of another. My mind was definitely not on the conversation, when a sticky point arose which the others couldn't seem to resolve.

Curiously, somebody chose that point to recognise the fact that I was there. I hadn't uttered a word all night. Suddenly my opinion was being sought. "What do you think?" I was asked. I wanted to die! I hadn't been thinking. Just eyeing the girls, and … wishing. What a spot I was in. I didn't want anyone to know how foolish I felt, but what could I do? All eyes were upon me, waiting expectantly. I don't know how I managed to maintain my composure. But I had promised myself to do better next time, and next time was here again. I struggled manfully to open my mouth. Speaking slowly, I said something in a few short phrases, which impressed the others, bringing murmurs of agreement and respect. "Amba's quiet", someone said, "but he's deep."

Deep is right. I was in deep trouble from then on. Overnight I had acquired a reputation I didn't really deserve. I was quiet all right, but really not very deep at all. Yet some people had begun to ascribe certain qualities to me, as if I possessed great intellectual powers and wisdom beyond my years. I enjoyed being thought of this way. It boosted my ego and self-esteem. But I also dreaded the moments when people would try to draw me into conversations or serious discussions, which I knew I couldn't handle. I couldn't live up to my billing! And it scared me to death when people wanted my advice on personal or business matters.

I knew I wasn't well enough informed to be offering serious opinions. So most of the time I would fake it, or weasel my way out by saying, "I really need to give more thought to this" or, "John's idea is pretty good, I think he's on the right track, but Susie has some really good points too." It was a pretty precarious business trying to keep a reputation going that way. So over the years I've been trying to do better, by becoming better informed. I read all types of literature and try to keep up to date on current affairs locally and globally. I try to enter into discussions with all kinds of people, to keep an open mind, to observe and analyse situations, and to think of approaches and solutions to various problems.

I don't need to fake things anymore. There really are a lot of things I've observed and experienced and given a lot of thought to. So I really do have opinions now, which I've arrived at on my own. Sometimes others support my opinions, which I appreciate. But it really doesn't bother me if they hold a different view, as long as they are civil about it. What does bother me, is that some people still approach me as though I possess the wisdom of the ages. Alas, although I have attained the age, the wisdom of my youth has not kept pace with me. Nor, as far as I can see, has new wisdom come to take its place.

While this is not exactly devastating, it is somewhat disappointing, and causes me to cast serious doubt on what I was led to believe in my youth – that wisdom comes with age. Here I've been waiting patiently all these years and…

well, it hasn't happened to me yet. Or did it sneak up on me when I wasn't looking and just kept going. Do you think it has come and gone? Perhaps it's just a fleeting thing and I didn't recognise it when I had it. No, that couldn't be right. After all I've been through – that would be too unfair! Probably I'm not old enough yet. After all, they say you're as young as you feel. That must be it.

Say, there's a conversation going on over there. Couple of interesting looking ladies too. I wonder if they'd be interested in my, ahem… opinions. I'll let you know - later.

St. Kitts-Nevis Observer, **October 1, 1995**

Hairs To You

I haven't been to a barber in many years. I began thinking about this the other day, after admiring the tonsorial artistry exhibited by a couple of local lads on Main Street. I'm assuming they'd been to a barber or hairstylist or whatever those practitioners are called these days. The styles they were sporting seemed too elaborate in design and technique to have been created and executed by anyone without credentials from l'Academie de Beaux-Arts in Paris and the London Institute of Advanced Surgery. The local art galleries should really try to find out where this work is being produced and arrange special shows for such outstanding talent. This type of art is really heady stuff.

The height of my attention used to go to those Rasta men and women sporting magnificent knots, ringlets, and braids, which simply could not go unnoticed. But they have become so commonplace now, as to seem "Old Hat." Speaking of "Old Hat", it seems to me that that is exactly what too many Rastas nowadays are resorting to. Lots of them bundle their crowning glory under some oversized head covering which completely diminishes the value of having dreads, in my opinion. Of course some Rastas really don't have a good looking set of dreads and may be better off covering up. So I can exclude those, but I mean, if you've got it, why not flaunt it!

Of course some people like to keep things under wraps, to be unveiled on special occasions. In my case, although I've got nothing to hide, I usually wear a head covering as protection from the sun on hot days, and to keep from getting a chill on cool days. But Rastas with a good head of hair shouldn't have to worry about such things. They are well insulated either way.

Years ago, I didn't have to worry about such things either. I'm talking about many years ago, now. Teenage years ago. I used to have a healthy head of hair then, which nobody seemed to appreciate but me. My folks were always trying to get me to go to the barber, and even my friends used to tell me which barber gave the best haircuts. I seldom listened to any of them. I liked my hair the way it was. Natural. And I didn't like anybody messing around with it. The result was that it grew long, extra long and bushy. Some people didn't like it, but I didn't care. I didn't know it at the time, but I was a pacesetter. The "Afro" didn't come into vogue until the Sixties, but there I was, sporting one in the 'forties. Going against the grain, as it were.

Being ahead of the times (note: ahead is one word), even I didn't understand the trend I was setting in motion. By the time the rest of the world caught on, my

120

style had changed and started a new trend which Yul Brynner, Isaac Hayes and others, quickly followed.

But I'm getting ahead of my story: Let's go back to the 'forties and this huge head of hair that I was sporting, or supporting, depending on how you looked at it. Even though others were not very considerate of me at the time, I at least, tried to be considerate of others. For instance, I usually sat in the back row in church, or at the theatre, so that others wouldn't have to change their seats or crane their necks to see around me.

As fate would have it, I went to the theatre once to see a play called "Dark of the Moon." The story is about a "Witch Boy" who falls in love with a human girl named Barbara Allen, and I think it might be based on the American folk song "The Ballad Of Barbara Allen." The production was haunting and sad and beautiful, and I fell head-over-heels in love with Barbara Allen. Fancying myself as the witch boy whom she would humanise with her love, my diary was filled with secret thoughts about my feelings towards her.

Coming home one day, I was shocked, baffled, confused, when my cousin greeted me teasingly; "Amba, Barbara Allen is looking for you. Barbara Allen wants to see you, Amba!" I couldn't believe it. He had invaded my privacy, found my diary, and exposed my secret to the world. Then my sister chimed in, "Barbara Allen's been waiting for you, Amba. You're long overdue!" Being teased by my sister was always more aggravating, but this was humiliating beyond belief. It was too much too bear. How many others knew my secret, I wondered, as I stood there dumbfounded, pained, squirming with embarrassment. And then, quite suddenly I was blessed with sweet relief as she blurted out, "When are you going to get your darned hair cut. It's growing into your eyes!"

I realised then that my secret was still safe. My privacy had not been invaded. They had not been talking about my secret sweetheart Barbara Allen, but about a local barber whose last name was Allen. After that, I visited barber Allen on a number of occasions. But no love affair ever developed between us. He could never quite trim my hair the way I wanted it, although he tried his best. And I'm sure I made him work a lot harder for his money than anybody else. "A little more off the top", I'd tell him. He'd invariably take too much off the top, then the sides seemed lopsided.

Our relationship did not bloom, so I tried other barbers over a period of time. I don't know what they taught fellows in Barber College in those days, but if I were the one handing out certificates, they wouldn't have been able to get jobs mowing grass. Anyway, the only thing left for me to do was to get my own home-barbering set with clippers, scissors, comb, brush, mirror and powder for $29.95 at Sears.

By this time, I was living alone and didn't have anyone to help or hinder me. Holding a hand mirror in one hand, scissors in the other, and trying to see what you're doing to yourself in the wall mirror, is a tricky business. Luckily I still have both ears. But pretty soon, the inevitable happened: I bobbled the clippers and gouged out a big clump of hair right down to the scalp. Needless to say, I had to even things up – all over. It was a lot easier than I thought and surprisingly, it looked good too. At least, I thought so, although some friends disagreed with me. I was vindicated though, when "The King and I" opened on Broadway sometime later with Yul Brynner. Then Isaac Hayes cut off all his hair and began making hit records. Telly Savalas picked up on the trend, and it hasn't done his career any harm either.

I sometimes wonder what did it for them. Was there a Barbara, or a barber Allen in their background that started things off. Or were they just copying me, following my lead? Coming back to the locals with the heady art, and those Rastas too: I'm sure these styles weren't influenced by me. Much as I'd like to, I can't take credit for everything. Some things just happen by chance. And some barbers really know what they're doing these days. They've got it down to a Fine Art!

St. Kitts-Nevis Observer, **October 15, 1995**

Don't Get Me Wrong

I've made a lot of errors in my time. Mistakes, miscues, goofs, gaffes, boners, blunders, whatever you choose to call them, errors are errors – there's no getting away from that. Wrong is wrong and two wrongs don't make a right, everybody knows that. So what else is new?

Each of us came into this world helpless and dependent on mature others for survival. If those mature others had made too many errors handling us in our early stages, our chances for survival would have been pretty slim. But those who were taking care of us wanted us to survive and grow healthy and strong to adulthood, and we have the obligation to do the same for the younger generations. But their survival is at risk if we make too many mistakes.

We should remember how carefully we were nurtured and raised until we were able to fend for ourselves. Human development is a long, slow process and the primary method of learning for each of us was through trial and error. Gradually we learned after repeated tries and repeated errors, the correct way to do things. To walk, talk, hold objects, move things and a lot more.

One of the most important things we learned early in life was to correct our errors so that we could feed ourselves, climb the stairs safely, use the toilet properly, as well as thousands of other things. Just imagine the mess we'd be in if we never learned to correct our mistakes!

Can there be any doubt that without the ability to recognise and willingly correct errors, mankind would probably not even have made it to the stone-age? After all, the act that results in procreation, for most of us I believe, is learned through a process of trial and error. And if most of us hadn't learned to get things right, there'd be a lot fewer of us around. Of course a scenario like that might help to solve the global problems of overpopulation, but life would probably not be worth living under those conditions anyway.

So mankind learned to correct errors and survived the stone-age and a few other ages like the bronze-age, the iron-age and the machine-age. Now we're in the electronic-age or the computer-age, I'm not sure exactly which, but we're there anyway. And mankind has developed a stunning array of ingenious devices to help ease his workload, to entertain and amuse him, to solve many difficult problems and to help eliminate certain factors commonly known as "human error."

Unfortunately, the influence of these devices has had a deleterious effect on certain categories of the population. Bureaucrats and public officials are most susceptible and in Nevis, have been the hardest hit. But it has been noticed that others are not immune to the strange malady, which renders those affected, unable to admit, recognise or correct errors. Experts believe the condition is not terminal, although it can be very disruptive, frustrating and embarrassing for others. They also predict that locals' confidence will plummet as Nevis becomes the butt of jokes abroad and an air of anger and depression settles over the land.

When asked to assess or quantify the damage in human terms, the experts refused stating that they had a strong suspicion that the results of the last census were seriously flawed, and it would be almost impossible to arrive at a consensus. They said that some people had been counted more than once, some not at all, and some, maybe.

The ones who were not counted at all said they did not want to be victimised, so they refused to stand up and be counted. The ones who were counted more than once, thought they were going to be paid for their efforts. The maybes were trying to see which way the wind was blowing. And some of the enumerators had destroyed their forms, saying that if the data were released, the public would kill them! The experts said that under those circumstances, the plus-minus factor couldn't be calculated, the margin for error being too great.

I've heard it said that Nevis has a lot going for it. The trouble is, where is it all going? I've got a sneaking suspicion that some of our officials are headed in the wrong direction. We don't want to go back to the stone-age, do we? We can't afford those kinds of mistakes. I'd like to see them correct their errors if at all possible. If not, make no mistake about it, I'd rather not see them at all!

St. Kitts-Nevis Observer, December 2, 1995

TROTT TALK

INSPIRED BY EXCELLENCE

Around four o'clock on Monday, I was helping Grace Corpus and Marilyn Curtis with preparations for the Stoney Grove Adult Education group's "Light A Tree" project in Walwyn Plaza. I had promised to set up a P.A. system and stage lights for the event, which was scheduled to start at 6 p.m. There was ample time for me to set up the amplifier, speakers microphones, scoop-lights and still be able to help out doing other chores if necessary, before leaving to keep another appointment at six o'clock, so I was not feeling at all pressed for time.

Pretty soon a familiar red vehicle approached and stopped by the plaza. Recognising Lorette Brand's smiling face, I hustled over to assure her that I would be finished in plenty of time to get over to the Methodist Church for the six o'clock rehearsal. Lorette, as everybody should know by now, is the director of the Charlestown Methodist Youth Choir. Their production of the gospel musical "King Of Kings", was to have its second performance on Tuesday. I was responsible for lighting the show and Monday's rehearsal would be the first with the lights in over two weeks. "I'll be there on time", I told Lorette. She told me not to rush myself if I needed a little more time. "Amba, you know none of my people are going to be there at six, so you shouldn't have to come and wait for everybody else. You come at six-thirty and that'll be fine."

As fate would have it, several unforeseen problems arose and at six-thirty I was still at the plaza. I made a mad dash for the church, arriving at six-thirty-five. The choir was already assembled and in their places in the dark. And just as I was switching on the power supply for my lighting, the music for the overture began. Up to now, I don't know if Lorette realised that I wasn't in the building at the appointed time. I assume she was counting on me to be there as I usually am. Anyway, we ran through the show once with very sloppy lighting. The equipment I have is rather antiquated and the setup for this show is best handled by two people, but I was alone that day. I was not happy with the result, but Lorette didn't complain, at least, not about my work.

After a brief rest, it was time to go through it again. Lorette told me I could go now if I needed to, but the only thing I felt I needed to do was improve the quality of the lighting, so I stayed. Steve Huggins who helps me with lighting showed up, and I immediately felt more confident with two of us to handle things. The choir assembled in their places again, but before we dimmed the lights, I could see some of them were tired and lackadaisical. The music started, and then the voices blended in, "ALL HAIL KING JE-E-SUS, ALL HAIL E-MAN-U-EL!" It's a riveting opening with rich harmonies right from the start. It sets the tone for everything that follows and is the signature moment of this production. It has to be done right. "KING OF KINGS, LORD OF LORDS…" chanted the choir. "Stop, stop, stop." ordered a familiar voice, loudly.

I brought up the lights a little so we could see Lorette as she continued. "We are not here to do nonsense and I am not putting up with it!" I could hear someone grumble. She heard it too. "I am not having any of that. Don't come here to grumble. You came here to sing, but some of you ain't singing. You think I can't tell that! Some of you are not making an effort. I don't want to call any names, but you know you ain't doing right!" Somebody moaned. "So you're tired. You think I ain't tired too. Who could be more tired than me? Listen, we have to perform tomorrow for the public. People have heard that we have an excellent choir, so they have high expectations. I don't intend to let them down. But it's up to you. So make up your minds to practice tonight and get it right!" I dimmed the lights. The music started again and the choir sang. I mean really sang, as they would in performance the next night.

I fished a handkerchief out of my pocket to dab at my eyes. Lorette's fire and smoke had gotten to me, and like the song says, "SMOKE GETS IN YOUR EYES." But I've been in Lorette's position often enough to be able to afford a few tears of empathy. This group has great potential but they often lack discipline or fail to stay focused. So it takes a lot of work to bring out what's in them. At Tuesday night's performance I shed more tears, but of joy and pride as this group lived up to expectations in performance. It has been a very great privilege and a rewarding experience for me to be associated with them. I've seen some of what goes on "behind the scenes" and know how hard everybody must have worked to reach where they have. I cannot say anything to praise this group too highly.

With so many other distractions, especially TV, it seems something like a miracle that this group of close to thirty young people would make the time to come together night after night, to put their energies into an effort such as this. While many other young people are spending their spare time idling, creating noise, mischief, or wasting their precious lives in other ways, this group was slowly, lovingly creating something of inestimable, inspirational value for this community.

Some people who read my column often feel I am overly critical about some things. But in reality, like Lorette Brand, I believe the people in this community can make beautiful music together. But we need to be more disciplined and focused. We need to understand that we are not here to do nonsense. We should not be lackadaisical in our approach to things or our performance will be lacking. The public should have high expectations and we should make every effort to achieve high standards. I'm always ready, willing and able to praise whatever is praiseworthy. And I'll point out the flaws whenever I see them. But I cannot be inspired by things lacking in quality or excellence.

After witnessing the example of Lorette Brand and the Charlestown Methodist Youth Choir and what they have accomplished, I don't think that any of us should want to settle for less. Their programme "KING OF KINGS" is in celebration of Christmas. So in keeping with tone, spirit and quality of their performances, I want to wish all of my readers an excellent Christmas and an inspiring New Year!

St. Kitts-Nevis Observer, **December 24, 1995**

Resolutions And Absolutions

I've never been very good at keeping resolutions so I've decided not to make any for 1996. After all, what's the point of making 'em if you're only going to turn around and break 'em at the first opportunity? It's not that I ever set out consciously to break a resolution mind you, but I am somewhat forgetful and usually by the time I remember my resolutions, I've either broken them, or it's too late to keep them for the year gone by. Resolutions, like promises it seems are made to be broken.

I know I made several resolutions that I wanted to keep last year, but I'll be dashed if I can remember any of them now. Oh, well. I'm sure at the time I made them I had every intention of keeping them. I think I can even recall writing them down on a piece of paper, which I put somewhere for safekeeping and promptly forgot. It's probably still tucked away safe and secure somewhere, wherever that is.

It suddenly occurs to me that if you have something you want to get rid of, you should simply give it to me for safekeeping. Chances are you'll never see or hear of it again. So it is with my resolutions. Once made, twice forgotten. Or something like that.

One year I resolved to reply religiously to all correspondence I received. People stopped writing to me after that. I suspect they thought I was going to expound on my theological theories and wished to avoid any challenges to their faiths. I remember this only because the cut-off was so sudden. Prior to that I was accustomed to receiving three or four letters in the mail every week. Mostly junk mail, it's true, but mail nonetheless.

Needless to say, that resolution never had the opportunity to be properly observed, but since the fault was not really mine, I have no feelings of guilt or embarrassment about it. In fact, I seldom feel guilt or embarrassment over any of my un-kept resolutions. There isn't any point since I can't even remember what the forgotten resolutions were. The way I figure it, if they're so easily forgotten, they couldn't have been of much importance in the first place. So why worry?

My life is filled with plenty of other things to feel guilty or embarrassed about. I don't need any more, thank you. My cup runneth over as it is! So if any readers happen to remember any of my old un-kept resolutions, don't bother to tell me about them. It's too late to embarrass me. There's a statue of limitations, you know. Or there ought to be, just like the Statue of Liberty. And under the

Statue of Limitations there is sure to be an expiry date of December 31st. So I'm absolved of all my un-kept resolutions up to then – phew!

This year I'm going to play it safe. I hereby resolve not to make any New Year's resolutions for 1996. That should take care of everything. Shouldn't it?

St. Kitts-Nevis Observer, **January 7, 1996**

A Sense Of History

Negro Builders and Heroes by Benjamin Brawley, one of the few possessions I've managed to hang onto over the years, is a book given to me in 1946 by close family friends, Glen and Sylvia Warner of Montreal, Quebec. The book is well worn, but by no means falling apart; its pages, although browning with age, are unmarked by pencil or pen and not one dog-ear can be found. Not even termites or bookworms have marred its appearance, and the only faults worth mentioning are some flecks of paint and a few scratches on the cover. For fifty years it has been a source of inspiration for me and except for old family letters and photographs, no other possession of mine is more cherished. It has been well loved, well used, and well cared for.

In the preface of this book, copyrighted 1937, the author states that the work is intended as an introduction to Negro biography. It became much more than that to me, for the description of the efforts and accomplishments of people who were then called Negroes, were like a beacon to my life. And though other factors have certainly also influenced me, this modest volume of three hundred pages has been a good companion and in recent years, fondly remembered and reviewed during Black History Month.

The first few pages succinctly describe Africa as a vast continent between three and four times as large as the U.S., containing over eleven and a half million square miles, and four thousand, six-hundred and fifty miles separating the farthest points East and West from each other. Only the great lakes of North America can equal the lake system of central Africa, and four mighty rivers, the Nile, the Zambesi, the Niger and the Congo, each rival the great Mississippi of the U.S. Also described in the opening pages, are mighty African kingdoms that existed for hundreds of years until the Europeans came.

The old Western Sudan in the eleventh century, had a kingdom of Ghana with a capitol built partly of stone and an army of two hundred thousand men. A student and organiser called Askia, built up the empire of Sanghay, which was nearly as large as Europe. But when Europeans came, they developed the slave trade and traffic in human lives, which continued into the nineteenth century. Then they discovered the riches of 'The Dark Continent' and engaged in a mad scramble for territory. Africans resisted as best they could, especially outstanding Zulu chiefs whose surprising tactics cost the invaders dearly, but were no match for superior modern weaponry.

In 1935, Italy invaded Ethiopia with chemical warfare as well as conventional bullets and bombs. At that time, my parents were executive members and organisers of the Montreal (Canada) Chapter of the U.N.I.A. (Universal Negro Improvement Association) and had personal contact with Marcus Garvey, the Black leader from Jamaica, founder of the organisation. My father was also editor of the *Free Lance*, one of the few Black newspapers being published in Canada at that time. I was eight years old then. Old enough to sell and deliver the papers at two cents a copy, and to read and understand that atrocities were being committed against Black people thousands of miles away.

The U.N.I.A. and the *Free Lance* were supporting Garvey's call for Negroes everywhere to form a volunteer brigade to go to Africa and help Ethiopians in their fight against the aggressors. I can remember the men were to board a train at Montreal and embark on a ship at Halifax. The plans for the ship never materialised and Mussolini's forces might still have crushed Ethiopia anyway. But young as I was, I could feel a sense of history, and that somehow, I was part of it, or at least, very close to it.

Negroes in my community were trying to assist others thousands of miles away. I knew my parents were involved as leaders in this effort, and I felt very proud. I felt a sense of history and pride on other occasions too, when my parents brought us into close contact with outstanding U.S. Black activists of the time; Paul Robeson, Mary Mcleod Bethune, Philip Randolph and also Senator Marryshow of Grenada.

Growing up in this family didn't mean my sisters and I enjoyed any special privileges. On the contrary, because the main efforts of our parents went towards improving conditions of the Negro community. They were remarkable Black people who made superior efforts to improve their condition and that of their fellows, under conditions far more difficult than those facing us today. When we grew up and went off into the world on our own, to a large extent our efforts were the same as our parents'. Trying to improve the community where we live, the best way we could. Trying to see what needs to be done, getting involved and adding our bit to the effort.

Here in Nevis in 1996, I feel a sense of history again. So much seems to be happening, yet so much is being neglected. While physical (and fiscal) development is taking place, basic human development is largely being ignored. Many young people who were not kept in school and given a basic education or training are now roaming the streets, unable to read, write, or communicate properly or find employment. In a few years the situation will be much worse as the flood of juveniles will become mature (or immature) adults, with no way to participate constructively in this community. They will be unable to go elsewhere to seek ways to improve their situation, so they will stay in our midst, most likely drifting into negative behaviour and activities adversely affecting our society, our image as a friendly people and our country as a place of tranquillity and beauty.

The danger signals are all around us. We ignore them at our peril. There is need for more of us to be seriously involved in efforts to improve our community today. Our young people should be able to look to their elders for direction, guidance, inspiration. If we don't supply it, we leave them a sad legacy. As we celebrate Black History Month, we should recognise that we are part of a continuum. We are creating our own little chapter in Black History now. Will our heirs and future generations find our efforts and actions inspiring? The answer to that question lies in you.

St. Kitts-Nevis Observer, **February 10, 1996**

On Being Black

I've always tried to get along with my fellow man by assuming that he wants to get along with me, thereby adopting an open mind and a friendly attitude towards all those with whom I come into contact. Religion, nationality, academic qualifications, financial status, never enter the picture – a man's a man for all that, as far as I'm concerned. Unless a person is known to me to be morally degenerate, criminal, bigot, or insane, I usually have no trouble developing friendly relations with others. I have been troubled however, by several locals who display hostility towards me for no apparent reason.

Some people always glare at me rudely and scornfully. Some narrow their eyes and push out their mouths with an "if looks could kill" expression. Some suck their teeth, or curse, as I pass by. I have never done anything to these people. In fact, never had any dealings with them, know nothing about them, not even the name of any one of them. At times when I've tried to find out what the problem is, I've met with stony silence. Occasionally I've been abused with inappropriate language. And a couple of times I simply couldn't understand the lingo. Only once have I heard clearly and distinctly what was troubling somebody. I didn't like it.

I was down by the market trying to sell newspapers one Saturday morning, when a vehicle approached, slowly inching towards me. The driver's window was lowered, so I held up a copy of the newspaper and asked if he wanted to buy one. He scowled and growled something, which I didn't hear distinctly because of other sounds. He repeated when I asked him to, and this time I clearly understood the words that he angrily barked out; "You don't love Black People!" He drove away before I could think of anything to say, leaving me with a lot of unpleasant thoughts on my mind. All of those other people who glare, scowl, or are generally rude to me, might be thinking and saying the same things about me. It is not pleasant to encounter that sort of negative attitude in the community.

In my column I am often purposely critical about many things that I believe need improvement in this community. So I try to help bring a focus on the things that I feel need attention. While I certainly don't expect everybody to see things my way, I don't think it's asking too much from those who differ, that they at least behave in a civil manner. I will not accept that being rude, crude, nasty and narrow-minded, are the hallmarks of being Black.

In last week's column, I told how a book about Negro Builders and Heroes, which I have owned for fifty years, is still an inspiration and one of my most cherished possessions. I told of my parents' involvement in the U.N.I.A. in Canada and of their efforts to improve the condition of Black communities, an effort their heirs still carry on. I've always tried to conduct myself with honour and dignity, to do the best I could in any undertaking, to be reasonable, fair, and respectful of others.

I don't glare, stare, scowl, cuss, fuss, or make improper remarks to others because they're not as "Black" as I think they ought to be. I don't think that's an appropriate way for anyone to show love for Black people. Maybe I'm wrong, but I doubt it.

St. Kitts-Nevis Observer, **February 17, 1996**

Changing Standards

In trying to transact some business the other day, I went to a local establishment to inquire about their services. A woman, well dressed, well groomed and attractive, who was chatting on the telephone, indicated with a gesture that she would attend to me when she was finished. Her manner of speaking to the party on the phone seemed rather slack, so I assumed it could not have been a business call. She was soon finished and turned her attention to me again. "I could help you?" she asked. I told her I hoped so and made some inquiries.

She did not have the information I needed and did not seem to be a very resourceful person. I asked if she could contact someone else who might be able to assist me. She picked up the telephone rather grudgingly I thought, and spoke to another party. She told the other person that "Missa Trott" wanted certain information and paused for a reply. After a few moments she resumed speaking. "I tell um me ain't know", she said, "but he say I mus' call an' ax yuh".

I left the establishment moments later, unsatisfied. I would have to return or call again when someone with more authority might be more helpful. I felt uncomfortable about the prospects of having to deal with that establishment again. There seemed to be a lack of professional conduct and the communication skills appeared to me to be less than satisfactory. I was not favourably impressed with the attitude or competence of the staff and decided to see if I could obtain better service elsewhere.

The next place I went to completely won me over. An attractive young woman greeted me here also, and although she apparently knew no more than the other girl, she seemed eager to get the information I needed as quickly as possible. She first tried leafing through several file folders she thought might be helpful. Then she made a couple of telephone calls, identifying herself and saying that "Mister Trott is requesting" certain information that she was unfamiliar with. After making the calls, she apologised for taking so long, but explained she was trying to contact the person who could best handle my unusual request. She was unsuccessful but said he would return to the office at 2 p.m. and I could call again after that or, that if I would leave my phone number, she would make sure that he contacted me.

I left impressed with the competence exhibited by the young woman and feeling confident that my business would best be handled by this firm. I didn't know for a fact whether this establishment could handle things any better than the other; it was just the impression I got from the attitude of attentiveness, eagerness to be helpful and command and use of good grammar and standard English.

Many times I have heard the use of "local English" being stoutly defended by persons with more knowledge and education than I possess. Their strongest case is; that it is a part of our cultural heritage and identity, which should be treasured and preserved. I have no such romantic notions. While I can admit that at some point there may have been merit to that argument, in my opinion "local English" has now become so debased and vulgar that its cultural value has drastically diminished. Its validity and respectability has also been so undermined that it is generally accompanied by lackadaisical attitudes of wantonness. It certainly has no current value as a tool in major business, education, or social development. I would strongly recommend that business establishments urge their employees to use proper English on their premises, that civil servants be required to use standard English in the workplace, that teachers and students use only standard English at school, and that the public at large generally strive to use better English to communicate with one another.

In these fast-changing times, I think it is imperative that we change those parts of our speech and language habits, which have become sloppy, outmoded, and unattractive. Let us change and upgrade our standards for the better.

St. Kitts Nevis Observer, **February 25, 1996**

GIVE ME THAT OLD TIME RELIGION

Although I don't consider myself a religious person and am not a regular churchgoer, I have always felt that the church has played the most important part in my life, aside from the nurturing of my parents. Of course I learned to read and write in the public schools and must admit that without those skills I would probably be nothing. And it is true that I have been strongly influenced by several individuals and role models. But I feel who I am and what I have become, was shaped and informed mostly by experiences with the church.

My mother was an avid churchgoer and Bible reader who saw to it that all of her offspring got the message very early. As children, my older sister and I used to sing duets in church every Sunday. Mother was our music-teacher and would train us to learn a new piece every week. We also attended Sunday school where we often were expected to recite scriptures. I didn't mind the singing, but I used to find a lot of the other stuff boring. Sunday school was worst of all because that was in addition to the regular church service. I know now however, that the discipline was good for us, and the early training and appreciation for music has enriched my life immeasurably. But those early years in the church in Montreal also gave us so much more.

The Reverend Charles Este, who was the pastor of the Union United Church for many years, is indelibly etched in my memory. Not only because he officiated at the wedding of my parents, and at my own marriage forty years later, but he was also the most eloquent and powerful speaker I have ever heard. He seemed a mild-mannered man when you met him on the street, but in the pulpit on Sunday mornings, a sudden transformation would occur in his personality.

The timber of his voice and the expression on his face would make every sinner in the room feel exposed, as if he'd found them out and was preaching this sermon as a lesson to them, with the whole congregation listening in! I used to wonder how he knew so much about me. Then later as I grew older, I would marvel at his eloquence and his technique.

What an act! What a performance! What an inspiration! When I was very young, Reverend Este would put his hand on my head to acknowledge my presence. Then as I grew a little, he would place his hand on my shoulder. Finally the day came when he grasped my hand in a manly shake, and I knew I'd reached adulthood.

Through the years I'd been involved in many activities on that old church property that had nothing to do with the church, per se. The Negro Community

Centre was housed and ran its programmes there. The Negro Theatre Guild mounted many productions in the church basement. Art classes, dance classes, glee clubs, debating clubs, and social clubs as well as church groups, performed, met, or practised there. And although I eased myself out of church orientation vis-a-vis religion, I was spending more and more time on church premises developing social and vocational skills for use in the wider world. I never regretted the time I'd spent growing up in the church, reciting scriptures, singing duets, or listening to the passionate sermons of Reverend Este.

I also never felt pressured or an obligation to stay. My growing interest in developing both my obvious and latent talent was approved by all that knew me, including church members. So as I journeyed out into the world and tried to find a place in the theatre, I did not feel that I was leaving the church, but rather establishing myself in a new ministry. I don't think I became any less religious, but I certainly felt I became more spiritual. And during two winter seasons, I even made myself available as an actor in travelling productions for Ontario's Religion and Theatre Council.

When I came to stay in Nevis over ten years ago, I was surprised by the scarcity of activity involving the performing arts. I did meet a few promising actors, but became really excited about several singers with marvellous voices I heard in various churches. I began to think about the possibility of creating a new indigenous folk-opera, and invited those singers to meet with me to discuss the idea. I was shocked and disappointed when they all turned me down. The reason they all gave, was that they could not be involved in secular activity. It was like a slap in the face, to me. It was as if I'd asked them to do something degrading, something unworthy and shameful. Something that would compromise their religious integrity and cause them to fall from grace.

My true intention was however, to bring something uplifting to the community. Something to help fill the spiritual void I felt existed in many places and many persons on this island at the time. I pointed out earlier that the direction of my life had been shaped and formed by my involvement with the church. Something impelled me towards a career in the arts. I answered the call. Secular impulses are not what brought me to Nevis, or caused me to turn the family home into a community centre for the arts, or even to start a column for this newspaper.

Good plays, concerts, poetry, dance recitals, literary evenings or art works can provide valuable spiritual communion for people in need. It should be recognised that the church will reach by traditional means, mainly other churchgoers. Church members who are gifted with artistic talent and ability should be encouraged to broaden their ministry beyond the ambit of the church whenever possible. That doesn't mean giving it up. But it may lead to new ways to reach and spiritually inspire many young people who don't go to church and may otherwise be led astray.

When I was a kid, music and theatricals inspired me. The people involved in those efforts were well loved and respected in our community. Some were avid churchgoers and some I knew, didn't go to church at all. But they all got together to produce something of value for the community. I don't recall anybody from church ever opting out because of secular activity. In fact, I believe the community was even closer because we were all drawn together, church and non-church-goer in the same effort. I know we all got a spiritual charge out of it. I think churchgoers in St. Kitts and Nevis need to try some of that OLD TIME RELIGION, it was good enough for me!

St. Kitts-Nevis Observer, **March 3, 1996**

The Quality Of Life

I'm not so sure that I want to live to be a hundred anymore. Once upon a time that was one of my goals, but several years ago I decided to take that off the list of things I intend to do before I check out. Not that I intend to die before I reached a hundred, it's just that the longer I live, the more I appreciate the uncertainty of life, and the more determined I become to live until I die. So I threw a big party at Hamilton House and invited a hundred people to celebrate my hundredth birthday in advance.

Not everyone I invited was able to come of course, but I had a wonderful time anyway. So many people commented on how young I looked, and how fit and spry I seemed for my age. I danced with all the gals, joked with all the guys, stuffed myself with barbecued chicken, shishkebab, salad, cakes, beer, wine, and probably collected more kisses, hugs and handshakes in one night than in my whole life up to then. It certainly was a night to remember, and I remember it well, because it was one of the few things I've planned that worked out the way it was supposed to.

Some people asked me at the time, why I was celebrating my one-hundredth birthday so far in advance. I explained to them that I wasn't sure I'd be able to kick up my heels, down a few beers and kiss all the gals in 2027, and I just wanted to make sure I had a roaring good time at my hundredth birthday party. So it made a lot of sense to me to do it and enjoy myself while I was still able. I did it and don't regret a minute of it. It was a wonderful once in a lifetime event that actually happened. So, no matter whatever else may or may not happen, like the song says, "They can't take that away from me!"

Life is not made up, however, so much of birthday parties as the times between. Much as I might like to, I can't invite a hundred people over every day to share and celebrate the other moments of my life. It is not difficult to recognise the impracticalities of that scenario. But I see and interact with a lot of people every day anyway, and even though I don't kiss, dance, or exhibit my 'party mode' flagrantly, I try to celebrate this human contact with a warm hello, a friendly smile or gesture, an open mind, and an attitude of congeniality and sincerity. Generally this pays rich dividends, as the majority of the people I have daily contact with respond in kind.

When people in any community exhibit respect and concern for each other, it helps to enhance "the quality of life" for all. Some people however, find I quibble, question and complain about too many things openly. Although they say that they understand and appreciate my motives, they don't care much for my method. I think about this every once in awhile, because I would really like to find a better, more effective way of doing things. But because a better way hasn't occurred or been suggested to me yet, I'll continue in my usual mode.

After dining at Mem's Pizzeria with some friends on Tuesday, I started driving them home towards town. Another car overtook and passed us, and before we turned off at Pump Road, we were amazed that its occupants three times tossed trash out the windows onto the roadside. These reckless actions underscore elements of some of the topics we discussed at dinner. We were concerned about the trash, the junk, and the litter that marred some of the beauty of Nevis and spoiled the environment. The incident we had just witnessed, revealed thoughtless actions and reckless behaviour that could lead to environmental, aesthetic, health, and economic problems if left unchecked.

We discussed among things, the large numbers of schoolchildren begging strangers to "sponsor" them. In most cases the purpose is obscure; the child seldom adequately articulates things and the consensus was, that it is not generally a good exercise for the youngsters. Some children risk hazardous traffic situations in their eagerness to reach possible "sponsors." And quite frankly, I don't appreciate being mobbed, or stopped half-a-dozen times in quick succession with cries of "sponsor me, sponsor me…!"

We explored alternative fund-raising methods for schoolchildren, and agreed that an "ADOPT A SPACE' programme properly organised, would be something where children's energies could be used more positively and productively. Children purposely involved in keeping an area clean and tidy should certainly have a better learning experience and understanding of environmental and conservation issues through this "hands on" approach, than those who merely run around with cards begging for "sponsors."

We believe it is a more positive exercise if children are offering "something of value" in exchange for sponsorships or contributions, and that the whole approach could be managed so that it is less disturbing than it now is in many cases.

We also talked about the negative impact of the massive amounts of trash being generated on such a small island, and searched for remedial ideas and suggestions. We wondered if anybody else out there is interested in doing something meaningful before this island is swamped in debris from rusting auto hulks, refrigerators, weird contraptions, old tires, glass bottles, plastics of all descriptions, and other items and materials creating unsightly vistas, and growing health hazards. Ultimately, the quantity of our trash, if not properly managed and disposed of, can have overwhelmingly negative effects! Especially on our tourist industry upon which, our economy is so dependent.

We discussed these things because we love this island and want to help protect the environment. We'd also like people to become more aware that each of us plays a role, no matter how small, that affects us all. Those who litter our sidewalks and roadways, not only help give tourists negative impressions which might drive them away, but also show a lack of pride in our country, or respect for others. I may not live to be a hundred, and I don't intend to throw another big bash anyway, but I'd like to invite everybody to celebrate life each day with respect and concern for how we live it. If we can clean up our act, believe me, we will improve THE QUALITY OF LIFE.

St. Kitts-Nevis Observer, **March 17, 1996**

A Spade Is A Spade

In its editorial of Wednesday, March 13ᵗʰ, titled "Call a Spade by its Name", *The Labour Spokesman* complained bitterly that a minister of religion in a well-established church had accused both the *Spokesman* and the *Democrat* newspapers of "...a low level of journalism."

The Labour Spokesman claimed, "...this accusation is unfair, unreasonable and unfounded," and reflects "...an element of dishonesty in the face of the facts." The editorial says, "As a newspaper which has dedicated itself to the enlightenment of our people and to the raising of their level of consciousness, we cannot accept this umbrellalike, generalised accusation when we are innocent and not at fault. We detest very strongly any categorisation of this newspaper as one which indulges in gutter-level journalism and personal abuse." At this point I had to put down the paper for awhile and walk around a bit to wipe my eyes and catch my breath. I wasn't even halfway through the editorial and was laughing so hard I was crying!

In October 1985, I rushed home to Nevis to take up permanent residence and be with my ailing parents after living abroad since I was born. I had lived in Montreal, Toronto, New York and Los Angeles, and was an avid reader of a variety of daily and weekly newspapers that were published in those large metropolitan areas. Long before I took up residence in Nevis, I had learned to distinguish responsible journalism from trash.

It became my opinion after settling here, that there were no local publications worth reading. *The Labour Spokesman* and the *Democrat*, the only regular publications in the Federation at the time, were engaged in a senseless vendetta, a war of words and warped ideas, conducted wantonly, viciously and ruthlessly, without regard to the damage being done to the social, spiritual, intellectual and emotional climate of the community. Damage, which because it has been conducted so viciously, over such a long period of time, cannot be easily or quickly repaired.

"Gutter-journalism" in my opinion, is too mild a term to describe the collective output of these papers since I have been here, and I don't know how long it had been going on before I arrived. The last two pages of the *Democrat* of Sunday, March 2ⁿᵈ might even be too much for a modern sewage plant to handle. The disgusting cartoon of the Prime Minister on the back page, the language and tone of the caption, the offensive column and verse on page 11 accurately fit the *Spokesman*'s characterisation of "The depraved level of print and journalism practised by that newspaper." But the *Spokesman* cannot hide behind its claims that it has "…been making a gallant effort to raise the level of print journalism in the country."

As I pointed out earlier, ever since I came here in 1985, I have been appalled at the product *The Labour Spokesman* and the *Democrat* have jointly been producing. It takes two to tango and insofar as both papers have been publishing for many years, I suspect they must have been involved in their mad dance long before I arrived on the scene. I have been witness to this nonsense for only a little over ten years, but others have been subjected to it for much longer. the *Spokesman* claims that "Long ago, in deference to certain professedly moral voices in the community and in keeping with our own high standard of public discussion, we stopped the publication of the 'Dem Say' column in this newspaper. Even in times of heightened political campaign activities, we suspended the 'Talk of de Tung' column. Our efforts to lift the standard of print journalism in the country have been evidenced. We therefore find unacceptable, allegations of our involvement in gutter journalism." The editorial goes on to say, "It is about time that those who would demand a high level of journalism, have the honesty and forthrightness to directly confront those who are responsible for the journalistic depravity in our society."

In that light I have to state right here, that I believe the "Minister of religion" to be absolutely correct in accusing both *The Labour Spokesman* and the *Democrat* of a low level of journalism. A little over a year ago, I complained about these papers in my column. While it is true that the *Spokesman* has stopped publication of two of its most offensive columns, this only happened sometime after the election of June 3rd last year, an event that cannot yet be classified as "long ago." The dismal fact is that both newspapers have been involved in demeaning, destructive practices for decades. For one of them to suddenly claim to be the paragon of virtue on the basis of a few, fairly recent cosmetic changes, is ludicrous.

I am not blind to the changes the *Spokesman* has made, but enough time has not yet passed to be assured of consistency or permanence. And a lot still remains to be done if they are sincere about raising the standard or level of journalism in this country. Old attitudes die hard and though the most offensive columns may have disappeared, too often the *Spokesman*'s pages still contain inflammatory references such as, "This modern day Hitler and his heartless PAM regime" or, "…political nitwits and rejects…" I can't find that this raises the level of journalism at all. To the contrary, I find that this feeds the flames of fanaticism and ill will. This only perpetuates the problems generated by decades of internecine verbal warfare between the two major political parties in the Federation, and their mouthpieces.

Because of what has gone on in the past, and despite the recent slight improvements by the *Spokesman*, and is still going on in the present - if I am to be honest and forthright as the *Spokesman* urges, I must say that I find both the *Spokesman* and the *Democrat* equally responsible for the "journalistic depravity" which still exists in our community. I find the efforts of the *Spokesman* to masquerade as an innocent in this regard, less than forthright and honest. Though some may not like it, I have no difficulty recognising that "A spade is a spade!"

St. Kitts-Nevis Observer, **March 31, 1996**

My Word

As I was passing Vic's Bar last Saturday, a fellow hailed me and said that he read my column in the *Observer* every week. He always looked forward to reading and enjoying my column, he said, even though I sometimes used big words that he didn't understand. I began to apologise for my lack of consideration, but he insisted it was not a defect with my writing, and that he actually benefits from the opportunity to learn the meaning of unfamiliar words. I felt immediate gratification for two reasons. First, it is not my intention to discombobulate my readers with a style of writing that is beyond comprehension. Second, my own understanding and appreciation of the written word increased immeasurably after I discovered writers who wrote in a fashion that held my attention, even though I had to consult a dictionary every once in a while.

In fact, I still consult a dictionary and a thesaurus regularly and not just when I am reading or writing. I often find them a source of pleasure, and agreeable pastime that can actually help me to relax, or add point and pith to my many musings. I also love crossword puzzles, am an avid Scrabble player and although I am usually gracious when losing, I know my chances of winning (which I enjoy immensely), are increased by being a good wordsmith. My interest in and love of words, has led me to develop some skills useful for writing plays, poetry, short stories, and a certain type of journalism, all of which I've dabbled in at one time or another with mixed results. Oddly enough, I've never been much of a letter-writer, much to the disappointment of family and friends.

My stint as a columnist for the *Observer* came about mostly because I felt there was a need in this community for writing, which served a variety of purposes instead of just the political agenda. I also felt that most writing of any sort being done here had a very narrow appeal, and that I could help enliven the local literary scene with my somewhat iconoclastic and freewheeling approach to things. So here I am, working with words and trying to make words work to benefit the community. This verse by Anna Hempstead Branch, best mirrors my feeling about words and motivation for writing:

> God wove a web of loveliness
> Of clouds and stars and birds,
> But made not anything at all
> So beautiful as words.

I once made a feeble attempt to put my own feeling about words into verse, and came up with this:

> I write a word, and then another word
> And soon, I have a start
> To what I hope will be (it's so absurd
> I swoon), a work of art.

I know that doesn't really make the grade, but I have fun doing things like that anyway. I love to dabble with poetry and light verse, because I derive so much pleasure from rhythm and rhyme. But I believe my real métier to be playwriting. It is extremely disappointing to me though, that few Nevisians are seriously interested in participating in or supporting the dramatic arts. The last time I enjoyed seeing one of my plays in production here was in 1991, when *Nonsense in Nevis* had a short run. I am really not hopeful of ever having another play produced here, which is really such a pity, because I believe that first-class drama productions could make a valuable contribution to the cultural life of the community. But most of the arrangements of words I've invested in playwriting here will probably never be realised in action. It seems therefore, that this column will continue to be the only outlet for my wordage. I'll try not to use too many "big words." I'll try to keep things interesting. And of course, I'll always try to write to the best of my ability. On that, you have my word!

St. Kitts-Nevis Observer, **April 7, 1996**

ANGLE IRONY

On Main Street just outside of Scotiabank, a steel post is bent from about two feet up, at what seems to me to be a forty-degree angle towards the building. The sidewalk is narrow, so persons of average height must walk close to the building at this point, or duck as they pass to avoid a bump on the head or worse. The end of a rusty nut and bolt protrudes from the post at just about the height of my brow. An unwary person could receive a nasty gash. Several times I've had close calls when my attention was diverted elsewhere. Often schoolchildren or other persons waiting for a bus, line the wall at that point, leaving little room to pass safely. Sometimes I'm forced to step out into the street. The thing is not only an eyesore; it's a danger to pedestrian traffic!

What bothers me is that it's been bent, been an eyesore and an obstacle for many months without anybody doing anything about it. I know I'm not the only one aware of it, but this community is too lethargic about too many things. I've seen students, local pedestrians, and visitors dodging their way past that pesky post. Dozens, if not hundreds of people must pass it every day. I've witnessed high-profile businessmen and women, teachers, lawyers, a nurse, hoteliers, and clergy at various times, dipsy-doodling around that point. Most amazingly, I've frequently spotted public servants, including officials from the Public Works Department and police officers, ducking past that spot too. But nobody does or says anything. Where is our sense of national pride, or our sense of civic duty? Some people say I complain too much about too many things. They may be right, but to me that bent post is symptomatic of many things gone awry in our community that too many people are ignoring.

TROTT TALK

Too many of us have become accustomed to, and adept at ducking things instead of confronting problems and dealing with them sensibly and fairly. We are dipsy-doodling our way around important social, economic, environmental, legal, criminal, constitutional, educational, political and cultural issues, and we are doing so at our peril. If that post were bent in the opposite direction towards the street, it would have been straightened or removed a long time ago. Commercial trucks, police vehicles, buses, taxis and ambulances would be endangered otherwise. But don't pedestrians matter too?

In recent weeks I have witnessed thoughtless youths, apparently with nothing better to do, testing their strength in an effort to bend the post further with brute-force. The people who are dipsy-doodling now, may be forced to do the limbo when the bend reaches a ninety-degree angle. Sad to say, some are doing that already; those who know the drug-dealers, dog-poisoners and other criminals, but refuse to say or do anything, fall into that category. Those who bend the rules at Culturama, and those who can, but refuse to straighten things out, are dancing to the same tune. While we proudly build up our self-esteem with projects for so-called "development," we unconsciously lower our posture by constantly ducking many other issues.

That bent post, those bent rules, and other bent areas of our community have got to be straightened out. We can't keep ducking, dipsy-doodling, or limboing lower and lower and pretend we're walking tall. Let's get real folks! Sure I complain about a lot of things. But don't you think somebody should? Regardless of what others think, my angle is not for personal aggrandisement, but for community improvement. What's wrong with that? Some people it seems, expect community improvement to come about by being quiet. How warped. How twisted. How spineless. Because I choose to take a different angle, some excoriate me. How ironic!

St. Kitts-Nevis Observer, April 21, 1996

I wish to open my comments this week by offering my congratulations to Premier Vance Amory and his bride, Verni Lee, of Montserrat, on their recent wedding. I sincerely hope they enjoy a long and happy union, and extend my very best wishes to them in this regard.

The tardiness of this felicitation was due to a lack of information, and uncertainty on my part, about the propriety of using this column for that purpose. Certain factors now lead me to conclude that this method is not only appropriate, but also necessary.

In my column I have sometimes been critical of certain policies, actions, or inaction of Mr. Amory's administration. I have taken a mild approach on some things and a harsher attack on others. But even in my most passionate writings I have employed restraint and respect. I often use a little humour, irony, or other device to cushion the effect of my words. Nevertheless, many people erroneously assume that I am anti-government, or opposed to this current administration for personal reasons.

It has always been my practise to criticise poor government policies, decisions, actions or practices. It doesn't matter to me who is in power. Personal friendships notwithstanding, if in my opinion the administration's performances are flawed in some way, I'm going to say so, hoping for some improvement. Certainly not with the intention of destroying the government. Unfortunately, this does not seem to be well understood or appreciated, and I feel I've been maligned at times.

On April 14, the *Observer* published a satirical article by "Vigilante." Many people didn't like it and have spoken to me about their displeasure. Some have said that they will stop buying the paper and warned that some businesses may stop advertising in it. They point out that the *Observer* should respect the "office of the Premier", and so on. I believe these people to be sincere, yet I can't help wondering why nobody raised a fuss over the obscene manner in which the Prime Minister was lampooned in the *Democrat* on March 2nd, which I believe was far worse. The back page cartoon shows the Prime Minister "pooping" on St. Kitts and Nevis. The caption reads, "Lawd, Douglas a poop pon arwe now!" And on page 11, part of a verse reads:

> "... 'Just cock you foot', he shout out loud,
> 'Leh it come out', he yell to de crowd...."

I was shocked and extremely offended and said so in my column "A spade is a spade" on March 31st. But I heard very few comments about that affair, and to the best of my knowledge, I was the only person to complain in writing.

It seems to me that everyone who really is concerned about "..respect for the office..." should have publicly condemned the *Democrat* on that occasion. Every educator, housewife, minister of government or religion, professional person, or individual with a sense of decency, should have swamped the *Democrat* with their outrage. Strangely, not even *The Labour Spokesman* responded at the time. I'm not trying to get the *Observer* off the hook here. I made my feelings about the matter known last week. But I am trying to show a little perspective. Is not the office of the Prime Minister as important and worthy of respect as the Premier's? Was not the crude attack on Douglas at least as bad, if not worse than Vigilante's piece?

I would like the *Observer* to be more classy and professional, but it is still fairly new, still trying to find its legs, still experiencing 'growing pains'. Vigilante may be one of them. As a writer contributing to the *Observer*, I realise that it has problems and challenges similar to the government, in that it is never going to be able to please all of the people all of the time. I do feel however, that the publisher's instincts are generally valid, and strongly supportive of any efforts to generate goodwill in this community. That is why I opened my remarks the way that I did. I feel all men and women of good will, will want to show their respect to the Premier and his bride, with warm expressions of welcome and best wishes.

St. Kitts-Nevis Observer, **May 5, 1996**

THE BENDS

About a month ago – April 21st to be exact - a piece I wrote titled Angle Irony appeared in this column. It was a short piece calling attention to a bent post on Main Street, just outside of Scotia Bank. I pointed out that not only was it unsightly, but also hazardous to pedestrian traffic. A number of people who read what I had to say in that column, agreed with my assessment and have told me so. Furthermore, some have pointed out to me recently, that nothing has been done about it yet.

I wish they wouldn't do this. I wish they would alert the proper authorities to the fact that something needs to be done. If I'm the only one to raise a fuss about such things, why should they bother? I'm not all that important. But if seventy-five other citizens raised a chorus and said "hey what's going on here, what are we paying you guys for?" something might get done. Somebody in authority somewhere might pick up a telephone and tell somebody else to see that a certain situation gets straightened out pronto! It seems to me that it should be as simple as that.

I don't see the need for a feasibility study for something like this. I don't think it requires the Attorney General's fiat. Or a loan from the World Bank, or a grant from UNESCO. Or a meeting with the OAS, consultations with CARICOM, help from the CDB, or a majority vote from the UN Security Council. Dis is "We Own Ting" man! You mean we can't do better than this? I'm sure if you loaned "Jam Dem" a hacksaw and gave him five bucks, he'd have that post down in less than ten minutes! But probably, taking care of things like this is not on anybody's job description. So nobody's going to take care of it? I don't know. I haven't the foggiest notion about what's going on. I'm completely confused about the way things are done around here.

For instance, the Culturama Queen thing from last year still puzzles me. They said they were going to settle it. They didn't. Then they established a Culturama Task Force – but not to deal with "the Queen thing!" Well, not only have we not heard about any sensible resolution to last year's Miss Culture controversy, but the Culturama Task Force and their mandate seems to have faded into obscurity as well. Mind you, Culturama '96 ain't too far away. Something is going to have to come to the surface pretty soon.

Any experienced deep-sea diver can tell you, if you stay down too long and come up too fast, you get "the bends." I understand it can be pretty serious. I think we'd best be prepared with all sorts of emergency procedures and strategies. In my opinion they've been down far too long already. They're going to have to come up pretty fast and when they do, we're likely to witness the worst case of the bends seen around here in a long, long time. They're likely to find it pretty painful. It won't be pretty.

Tell you what – I really feel for these guys and to show you that my heart is in the right place, I'm going to help some of them out a little. This Wednesday coming, I have a little free time in the morning. And I know a fellow who has a hacksaw. I'm going to see if I can line him up to give me a hand on Wednesday morning. Between the two of us, we should be able to take care of that bent post outside Scotia Bank. That'll be one less thing for those other guys to worry about. One less bend. I won't even send them a bill. They'll be strictly on their own with that other stuff though. I know my limits and I won't venture beyond certain depths. If there's one thing I'm scared of, it's "the bends". No kidding!

St. Kitts-Nevis Observer, May 21, 1996

IGNORAMA

Stupidity, ignorance and intolerance are still sad to say, alive and well in Nevis. On Monday June 24th I attended the opening ceremonies for the Federal Office in Nevis. I arrived just as things were starting and stood at the rear some distance behind the last row of seated guests, but in front of other people who were lolling about further behind me. I had a pen and paper and began to take notes so that I could write a report for the *Observer*. Things started off reasonably well, although I found some of the chattering going on behind me somewhat distracting. When the Prime Minister began his address, the chattering began to disturb me more, and by the time he got into the meat of his speech, had reached the point of rude heckling, causing me to lose my composure and my patience as I struggled to capture and crystallise the Prime Minister's presentation on paper, while dumb comments by thoughtless, insensitive people were being shouted in my ear.

I turned to face the hecklers holding up my hands, gesturing and asking them to tone it down. A torrent of rudeness was then unleashed upon me. Soon afterwards, I left the scene in disgust and went home, feeling that if I stayed, I might become the focus of an unpleasant incident. I find the best way to deal with ignorance is to walk away from it, you can't reason with it and it is best not to get drawn into an argument.

Unfortunately ignorance and stupidity are expressed in many ways. The new Federal Office was vandalised sometime between Wednesday night June 26th and Thursday morning June 27th. If it was intended to be an act of protest, it is a misguided act, which succeeds only in damaging the image of Nevisians. It is an act that ought to be condemned by every sensible person in the community. If the perpetrators are known they should be identified and prosecuted. Make no mistake about it, this is a very serious criminal act which can in no way serve the interests of the people of Nevis. I would be inclined to believe the damage was done by thoughtless, misguided persons, but also recognise the possibility of provocateurs.

The opening of the Federal Office in Nevis was either a very serious miscalculation by the Labour Government, or a deliberate, carefully orchestrated provocation. Whichever it was, it was up to our leaders to respond, and they did so in no uncertain terms. They told the country and the world that Nevis intends to separate from St. Kitts and have started the legal process to do so. They have asked for the prayers and support of the people of Nevis to help encourage and sustain them through this difficult period.

The eyes of the world are on us, and we need to conduct ourselves intelligently and responsibly. Smashing federal property only shows ignorance and irresponsibility since our tax dollars have to pay for it. Why should investors take us seriously if we mash up what we have to pay for? Think about that. We cannot support the cause of autonomy for Nevis by projecting a negative image to the world. Instead, our thoughts and our energies must be directed in positive ways.

These are challenging times and we can only successfully deal with these challenges by using our God-given intelligence. Ignorant behaviour is counter-productive and should certainly not be the way sensible and loyal Nevisians want to be characterised.

St. Kitts-Nevis Observer, July 7, 1996

For Honest Debate

Last week I listed several points to support my view that Nevis was in a very favourable position to secede from the Federation. A reader quickly pointed out to me that I had neglected to list the Nevis Historical and Conservation Society among the assets. The NHCS is not only one of the most important NGOs in the Federation, but is also the most highly rated organisation of its kind in the Caribbean, which others are attempting to use as a model, and for consultations. Nevis has many other assets too, but the NHCS obviously should have been included in my primary listing. My focus this week though, is on comments made by some other writers opposed to the idea of secession for Nevis.

In the *Observer* last week, Desmond Herbert raised the question of whether Premier Vance Amory played the "secession card" to gain popularity and win another term in office. I seriously doubt this, believing if that were the case, he and his administration would have been much better prepared. It seems to me that the Premier was more surprised at having to play his "secession card" than some of us at a distance who were following events and could clearly see it coming.

Mr. Herbert also spoke about history, and how successful generals always drew up plans with clearly defined military and political objectives before going into battle. For those who can accept that sort of analogy, how about this: While Hitler was creating his war machine, building up his mighty armies and making his intention of dominating Europe very clear, the British Prime Minister, Neville Chamberlain, was pursuing a policy of appeasement, friendly relations and all that. England was completely unprepared for battle when she finally declared war on Germany. Yet who can deny that she had to do it, unprepared though she was? I'm not suggesting that we approve Amory's lack of preparing proper plans for secession. I am just saying that it is not unusual that leaders of nations are sometimes compelled to embark upon a serious course of action with little or no preparation.

Mr. Edward Herbert, in his letter, gives us examples of "divided peoples around the world, and the pain and suffering caused." Then he points out that "England and 14 other European countries are joining together, and so too are Mexico, Canada and America." So why, he asks, are we divorcing? He neglects to point out that the countries he mentions are striving to form economic unions. Political union is not on their agenda and is not likely to be at anytime in the foreseeable future. Anyone, who has been following developments here, should be aware that those of us who support secession, want the same sort of arrangement for Nevis, political independence and economic unity within our region. Surely that is not so difficult to understand. Should that be denied us merely because of our small size and population?

The Labour Spokesman last week reprinted an article from "the *Vincentian* Newspaper", by Caspar London. In it Mr. London says, "Caribbean peoples should not give Vance Amory and his group of "madmen" any support in their efforts to destroy the Federation of Nevis and St. Kitts". (That's the only time I can recall seeing the name of Nevis preceding that of St. Kitts when the title of our Federation is mentioned in print.) The *Democrat* of August 10th, published a "Letter From Oxford" by Rolston E. Williams, in which he states, "The only people pushing for DISUNITY, DISHARMONY, FRATERNAL HATRED, SECESSION, are a few so-called 'POLITICAL LEADERS' eager for personal power and self aggrandisement..."

I find these statements by the last two writers to be intemperate in the extreme. I know of no one in either St. Kitts or Nevis who is "pushing for disunity, disharmony, or fraternal hatred", and I doubt that Mr. Williams sincerely believes that himself. I would certainly publicly condemn them if I believed such a thing, and would also oppose any "madmen" trying to destroy our Federation. Strangely enough, while Rolston E. Williams, now residing in England, and Caspar London in St. Vincent are calling for unity for St. Kitts and Nevis, they resort to harsh, intemperate, inflammatory statements in an effort to show that they apparently know more about the issue, and can speak with more wisdom, truth, and authority than any secessionist living in Nevis.

I am strongly in favour of secession, as readers of last week's issue must realise. Yet my mother was actually born in St. Kitts. My uncle, a shoemaker, practised his trade there. Other relatives and friends had businesses and homes there. And for many years before I came to live permanently in Nevis, I would spend an equal amount of time in St. Kitts whenever I visited from Canada. My support for secession is not in order to mash up family and other relationships, but to gain for Nevis, the freedom to manage her own affairs.

I feel it is of the utmost importance for all Nevisians to hear all sides of the issue and to be involved in the discussion. But the type of outrageous remarks which I've quoted from Rolston Williams and Caspar London, add nothing of value to the debate by mis-characterising either the issues or the people involved. In this debate, let us all strive to be civil, honest and reasonable. Let us truly debate, rather than debase and demean each other.

St. Kitts-Nevis Observer, **August 25, 1996**

Mea Culpa

My comment this week is simply to apologise for an action, which some people consider offensive. At the close of the panel discussion held by the Nevis Lions Club on Wednesday, September 18th, I rose and started to leave the conference hall. Before I completed my exit, the gathering started to sing the national anthem, which the moderator had earlier invited us to do at the closing of the evening. I however, did not stop to join them, but ambled my way outside and down the street towards home.

Someone standing with a group of people just outside the door, remarked about my leaving during the national anthem, but I just smiled and blithely continued past them. When I was about halfway down Chapel Street, a gentleman caught up with me and released a torrential rebuke condemning my action. I did not try to defend myself because by then, I had independently reached the conclusion that I had committed a serious *faux pas*.

I tried to apologise, but he wasn't interested, preferring instead to heap scorn and contumely upon me from his vantage point of self-righteousness. I chanced upon him the following day, and hoping that he was in a better mood, tried to let him know that I understood his annoyance with me, that I realised I had set a bad example and deserved his criticisms, that I accepted his chastisement and would honestly strive to do better in future. My genuine remorse did not ease the situation one whit as he continued to bombard me with angry, stinging comments.

I hope he and others can get over the need to excoriate me. I am after all, admitting that I was in error. I am not proud of my momentary lapse of good judgment, my moment of stupidity, if you will. It did happen and I can't change that. But I think that my failure to stand at attention for the national anthem in this one instance belies my true character and intentions, my sense of civic responsibility, social justice, and love of country. I can and do apologise for my transgression, and hope my offense can be weighed against the positive contributions I've made and will continue to try to make in this community.

St. Kitts-Nevis Observer, **September 29, 1996**

DREADED THOUGHTS

I am offended that a child in Nevis has recently been refused admittance to primary school because he has dreadlocks. His father is a Rasta and is bringing his child up in his image. Surely he has a right to do this, just as every Catholic, Methodist, Seventh-Day Adventist, Jehovah's Witness or person of other religious persuasion does.

The state has an obligation to provide education for its citizens. As a member of the U.N. and signatory to the United Nations Charter, it is supposed to abide by the codes guaranteeing certain basic human rights to its citizens, certain freedoms and specific sections relating to children, equal education, and protection from abuse. By what stretch of the imagination can the authorities justify requiring the Rasta parent to cut his child's hair before providing the education every citizen is entitled to?

It seems to me that this could be a violation of human rights, religious freedom, and quite possibly, a form of child abuse. What do you tell a child who idolises his father and wants to be like daddy? Sorry kid, but you can't be like your dad if you want to go to school. You have to be like somebody else! In my opinion, something's wrong there.

I know that Rastas are not the most admired group in this society. They all smoke marijuana, which is illegal. They commit all sorts of crimes and offences. They have strange, false, religious beliefs. They have long dirty hair, and they talk crazy. Those are some of the widespread perceptions that I'm aware of in this community. These prejudiced views affect the way Rastas are treated in relations with the general public, with employment situations, the business community, public officials and police authorities. Haven't we as a people been discriminated against enough already? Why should we now discriminate against our own?

As a group, Rastas are probably no better or worse than the rest of society. Most of the Rastas I know in Nevis and associate with from time to time, are highly intelligent, articulate and skilled workers, mechanics, tradesmen, farmers and musicians, all of whom I respect in the same way as I respect others. There are a few I don't like and try to avoid, but that's not because they are Rastas. There are lots of other people I avoid the same way. If the vibes aren't right, or they're coarse, crude, aggressive or drunk, it doesn't matter what they are, I try to stay away from them.

It should be noted that across the Caribbean as well as the United States and Canada, many Rastas have risen to prominence or distinguished themselves in the professions; Educators, lawyers, technicians, financial experts, government officials, entertainers. What would happen if one of them would locate here for a while and tried to enrol his child with dreads in the primary schools? I don't think we should wait for it to happen before we make changes. We are far behind the times in too many areas already. Fogbound attitudes are not a luxury we can afford at this stage in our development. It is not acceptable to me that authorities promote prejudice and ignorance in the school system or anywhere else. It should not be acceptable to anyone in this day and age.

That child should not have had to miss a day of school. That was unwarranted punishment. In any dispute of this sort between the parents and officials, I firmly believe that the rights of the child to an education should come first, and the child be allowed in school with dreads while things are getting sorted out. In the process, valuable lessons might be learned. Tolerance perhaps? To deny a child equal access to schooling because of his hair is a dreadful thing.

St. Kitts-Nevis Observer, October 6, 1996

THE SPIRIT OF CHRISTMAS

I'm not sure I understand what is meant by "the Christmas Spirit" anymore. I'm not sure that I ever did. But at least, once upon a time I thought I did. I used to look forward to Christmas holidays with much anticipation when I was a child, and "getting into the Christmas spirit," meant trying to be on my best behaviour, usually starting a few weeks before Christmas if I expected to get any Christmas gifts.

It meant doing my chores without complaining, in fact, even without being told to do them. It also meant doing an extremely good job, so that everybody would be forced to remark what a good job I had done, and I could justifiably expect to be well rewarded on Christmas Day. It meant being extra nice and polite to my uncles and aunts and older family friends, so that they could see what a lovely and deserving child I was, and put in a good word for me with Santa.

During my adolescence I though I caught "the Christmas Spirit" when I went shopping for gifts for my sisters and my parents, and postcards for other relatives and friends. I didn't have much money to spend but knew that wasn't as important as "the spirit" in which the gifts were given. "It's the thought that counts", is a phrase I'd heard often, and so choosing the right words on a card for each individual began to be important to me then. If the cards actually had the words "the spirit of Christmas" in the text, I was sure this was thoughtful and felt confident that this would be proof of my sincerity.

When I was a young adult working and living on my own, office parties and other friendly social gatherings among friends and acquaintances as Christmas approached, practically guaranteed if not dictated, that "Christmas Spirit" came in liquid form as everyone was asked to "bring your own bottle" to a party. But I'm older now, and as I reflect on the spirit of Christmases past, I can't say that I ever got things right. Mind you, I don't believe that I ever did any harm. But it has occurred to me off and on that my concept of the Christmas Spirit may not even have jibed with what was on everybody else's agenda at the time.

Because of long and strong involvement with dramatics, I've been involved in more staged presentations of the Nativity than I can remember. Yet, in only a very few cases did I sense a "Spirit of Christmas" permeating, motivating and guiding things along. In most cases, personal egos seemed to be motivating things and hindering the fullness of expression and understanding.

What each individual actually feels as he or she celebrates Christmas is really known only to that person. I'll be celebrating this Christmas in my own inimitable style, and if others want to believe it is not in the best "Spirit of Christmas", that's not my problem. I don't do cards anymore, so don't be disappointed if you don't get one from me. I've bought only a few gifts and hand-delivered them already. And I sincerely hope that those recipients don't feel strongly obliged to reciprocate. That was not the object of the exercise.

I am involved peripherally in several Christmas presentations at churches and elsewhere. I will enjoy a festive dinner with a large group of friends and family. And over the holidays I will spend time and share what I can with friends, acquaintances, and whoever else I can. This is really the way I spend the larger part of my life, to tell the truth. Maybe that's why I'm not sure what others mean by "the Christmas Spirit".

If they mean something that only infuses one's thoughts, and actions, and feelings, during the Christmas season, well then, I guess I haven't got it yet. But if it can be something motivating thoughts and guiding one's actions day by day, which we officially recognise when we celebrate at Christmas time, well then, Season's Greetings, Best Wishes, and Merry Christmas to you all!

St. Kitts-Nevis Observer, December 22, 1996

Why Worry?

When 1995 was ending, I resolved not to make any New Year's Resolutions for 1996. The reason was that in previous years, not only was I troubled by my inability to keep my resolutions, but all too often, couldn't even remember what I had resolved and spent an inordinate amount of time worrying about it.

Worry, as you know, is not a good way to spend time. In most cases it is non-productive, un-enjoyable, unrewarding, incapacitating, self-destructive and stressful. Stress, as most people are aware, is related to any number of illnesses, ranging from heart attacks to headaches. Since this is such a well-known and well-documented fact, I am prompted to ask the well-known question: "why worry?"

Why worry if it leads to melancholia, mental anguish, or some other form of malaise? Why worry if the pay-off is so noxious and negative? Surely sensible people should not be investing in health-threatening exercises. And, since I had come to believe that I'm a sensible person, it seemed senseless for me to keep worrying about resolutions, if the effort to keep them was going to make me sick.

But even though I managed to stop worrying about New Year's Resolutions by not making any, I've been worrying about scores of other things all year. The resulting stress I'm sure has contributed to most of my health complaints: pains in the neck in January, shortness of breath in February, gas problems in March, twitching eyelid in April, sneezing fits in May, sprained ankle in June, hiccups in July, diahorrea in August, lethargy in September, ringing ears in October, nervousness in November and depression in December.

So I've had a hell of a year, even though I didn't worry about breaking any resolutions. This has led me to adopt a different approach for 1997. Since most of my discomfort during 1996 was caused by my tendency to worry about too many different things, I've decided to eliminate worry entirely from my agenda for 1997. That ought to reduce a great deal of stress in my life and allow me to become more serene and happier.

So here goes: In order to enjoy peace of mind, better health and a positive outlook, I hereby resolve not to worry about anything at anytime during the year 1997. If you check with me next December, I'll let you know how things worked out. Till then, don't worry, be happy, and have a Happy New Year!

St. Kitts-Nevis Observer, **December 29, 1996**

Woman Of The Year

Last week I wrote a feature article that was titled "MAN OF THE YEAR". Some people have subsequently suggested that women were left out of the picture and I may be guilty of gender-bias. I reminded them that in the article I used the phrase "PERSON OF THE YEAR" three times and never referred to "MAN OF THE YEAR" at all. This is because my selection was made after considering both men and women, and could have gone either way irrespective of gender. Among several women high on my list was Lorette Brand who, along with her brother Franklin, runs the Nevis Bakery, the very successful family business started by their father, Hubert, over thirty-five years ago.

That Nevis Bakery owes its high standing in the local business community to the interest, hard work and dedication of this brother and sister team is well known to many people. And Nevisians can justifiably and proudly strive to emulate the Brand family as role models in our community. If every Nevisian family had children who were as industrious and dedicated as Lorette and Franklin, Nevis would undoubtedly rise to a position of pre-eminence in the Caribbean. For such attributes as high quality and excellence would then permeate every aspect of Nevisian character, bringing us to the fore and justifying the term that once identified Nevis as 'Queen of the Caribees'.

Franklin's reputation for excellence in business, drama and public speaking, may have tended to overshadow Lorette's efforts, but her contributions to business, family, and community have been no less, and in some respects, are even more remarkable. In 1995 Lorette had asked me to assist her with the Easter Presentation of "ALONE ON THE ALTAR" at the Methodist Church. Lorette was the Director of the Charlestown Methodist Youth Choir and she wanted me to provide stage lighting for this performance which incorporated drama as well as music. I agreed to do the lighting, but frankly, wasn't expecting much from the group.

Although I had heard from others that this group was "good", my experiences during ten years of residence in Nevis had solidified my belief that Nevisians generally have very low standards. Too often what I had been told was "good", "great", or "excellent", were far below standards I was accustomed to and expected. Too often in Nevis I had witnessed high praises and rewards being accorded to mediocrity. So although I intended to do my best as always, I believed at the time, that my best efforts would be supporting mediocrity.

The first few rehearsals I attended did nothing to dispel that belief. Very few members showed up on time. Some didn't show up at all. It was not uncommon for rehearsals to begin two hours later than the appointed time. And also not uncommon at any rehearsal for a variety of members to be hungry, sleepy, or preoccupied with a number of other things. These are not the conditions conducive to producing first-class results. These behaviours are best utilised if the intention is to induce apoplexy or a nervous breakdown in the director.

That I expected the worst, I believe is understandable. That Lorette was able to bring out the best in these people is surely some kind of miracle. For in the few weeks that transpired, I witnessed Lorette transform a ragtag, undisciplined, unruly, disorganised, disinterested and disappointing bunch of individuals, into a first-class concert choral group. The transformation was all the more remarkable considering that except for Raymonde Rohan, there was not one outstanding or trained voice in the group. Yet these ordinary voices belonging to quite ordinary people, were brought together and coaxed, wheedled, threatened, coerced, moulded and fashioned into something quite extraordinary by Lorette Brand.

Later that year, Lorette asked me to do the lighting for the group's Christmas concert, "KING OF KINGS". I could not have been more willing, in fact, ever since my first experience with her group; I anxiously await her call. And call she did, for me to do the lighting again for this season's concert, "THE WONDERS OF HIS LOVE". I have been as proud to have been involved with Lorette and her group as with anything I have done in the performing arts anywhere. Lorette consistently demands and strives for excellence. Many in this community pay 'lip service' to the idea of excellence, but few are able or willing to work as hard as Lorette does to produce it.

At the Christmas concert in '95, I was troubled that some members of the audience tried to "chisel" their way in to the performance without paying. This season I was troubled that some people who came late to the first performance wanted to be admitted free to the second. That sort of thing contributes to the low standards that I spoke about earlier.

In the three years that Lorette Brand has been Director of the Methodist Youth Choir, she has established an unblemished track record for excellence. Those who come late to her concerts are exhibiting disrespect. Her intention is to always start on time. Those who want to get in free for whatever reason, show a lack of class.

Because of my many years of involvement in theatre, as both performer and director, I know what it takes to put a show together. I know the preparation that must be undertaken even before rehearsals begin. I know the commitment one must make to time and energy that others will never really appreciate. And the many personal sacrifices that others never know or understand. In these days when so much trash is served up to our youth as entertainment, when crude, rude and lewd is the message too many are receiving and adopting, it seems to me that anyone who can offer wholesome alternatives can help to restore a balance and should be respected, honoured and valued by the community.

I thought I worked hard when I was actively involved in directing stage performances. But after seeing what Lorette Brand goes through and puts up with in her efforts to produce something of quality – that all Nevisians can be proud of – I can't help thinking that she is twice the man that I used to be.

Just so there's no doubt in anybody's mind, for the YEAR 1996, Lorette Brand is my choice for WOMAN OF THE YEAR!

St. Kitts-Nevis Observer, **January 4, 1997**

SOMETHING TO SING...
OR WRITE ABOUT

It had been a frustrating afternoon.

Three hours after starting to write for my TROTT TALK column, I had produced a page and a half of unsatisfactory text, and five crumpled pages of false starts. I had been nervous, edgy, and unfocused. I can't do my best work under these conditions. I need to be relaxed, quiet and calm. I like to work without interruptions.

So, most often I do my writing assignments away from the busy Observer Newspaper offices, where the noisy presses, the jangling telephones, the sporadic flow of clients, and the frenetic chattering of employees, provide constant interruptions and distractions which interfere with my attempts to concentrate on my work.

There is a spot in the Hamilton House Arts Centre, an antique round table and comfortable armchair by the window, which I find, creates the right milieu and helps to get my creative juices flowing. The only trouble is that sometimes the sounds of traffic or of noisy neighbours becomes too intrusive and completely destroys my sense of tranquillity.

This particular afternoon, quarrelling neighbours had kept a running verbal battle going for hours. The best I could do was to try to write a line or two during lulls in the hostilities. But a sudden barrage of bad words would incapacitate my ability to hold my trend of thought, so my writings were disjointed, disorganised and disappointing. My mind kept spinning around with the question - why do people carry on like that in public?

Indeed, why do they carry on like that at all? It seems to me that they are out there three or four times a week, viciously bad-mouthing each other in the street. Since it seems that they can't resolve their differences amicably, why don't they just stay away from each other? And if they happen to cross each other's paths, why can't they just keep their mouths shut instead of erupting with vicious verbal pyrotechnics that contaminate the atmosphere.

Scenes of discord and disturbance are all too frequently encountered in our small community, and in my opinion, the increasing display of bad language, bad manners, bad attitudes and bad behaviour by so many of our young people, is because our society in general puts up with it. Our tolerance can only be taken as a sign of approval and encouragement.

Every day except Sunday, I walk a route between Hamilton House Arts Centre on Main Street and Nevis Printing, which houses the *Observer*, on

Government Road. For the past several weeks, I cannot recall once walking that route without hearing somebody along the way using foul language. Too many of those were young and ignorant. And a goodly number were not so young, but just as ignorant. Some seemed to want to intimidate others by the use of foul language. And some seemed to use foul language because of the company they keep. They were afraid to be different from the others, I guess. How sad.

Anyway, since I couldn't get any satisfactory work done, I decided to stroll up the street to Tony's for a soda. There were no more in my fridge. Dusk was falling fast and except for the noisy neighbours, I like this time of day. As I approached Chapel Street, I saw a familiar figure, Llewellyn Parris, sitting on the ledge in front of the Longstone Building. He seemed engrossed with some sort of manuscript, which I recognised as a music score as I drew closer.

"Hi there," I said, stopping in front of him for a moment. "Getting ready for an Easter Concert or something?"

He looked up and smiled, "No, just getting ready for choir practice for Sunday services."

I told him I hoped it went well, and to keep up the good work. I felt pleased with this brief encounter and continued on my errand. Later, when I had settled down to write again, my mind wandered back to Llewellyn sitting on the ledge studying his music. I thought of the tremendous contrast between what he was doing and how it affected me, and the way my noisy neighbours had affected me.

The loud and foul-mouthed neighbours had completely disrupted my trend of thought, had so befouled the atmosphere that it interfered with my productiveness. On the other hand, the moment with Llewellyn had buoyed my spirits, had filled me with positive feelings and helped renew my energy. Llewellyn is a member of the Charlestown Methodist Youth Choir, a group that I have lauded several times before in my column. When I saw Llewellyn sitting in front of the Longstone building with his music, I was reminded of the times that I've seen him in concerts, and how thrilled I was with his performances.

Llewellyn does not have a great voice, far from it. But he makes the most of what he's got. He can carry a tune and he loves to sing. He is quite competent and blends in naturally, smoothly and comfortably, singing in the chorus. But when he does a solo number, he brings a special quality to the rendition, animating it with his personality. Enriching it with earnestness. Filling it with joyousness and enveloping the audience with an infectious spirit.

There are about thirty other young people who sing with the Charlestown Methodist Youth Choir, and it is not my intention to single out anybody to elevate over the others, because they all make beautiful music together. And each of them adds some special quality to the group. But because of meeting Llewellyn after a particularly frustrating and annoying afternoon with noisy people befouling the air, I was able to rid myself of the poisonous atmosphere, enter a mode of peace and tranquillity, get my productive juices flowing again, and sit down to write this.

Thanks, Llewellyn.

St. Kitts-Nevis Observer, **February 8, 1997**

A CHANGE OF PACE

(A post-election commentary)

I thought I'd try a change of pace today
And let my column speak with wit and rhyme
And give my restless mind a chance to play
With words and lead my readers on a climb
To heights of fancy far above the din
And roar that we most recently did bear
Hoping that we can now perhaps begin
To free our hearts and minds and clear the air
Of rancorous thoughts that only can debase
I think what's called for is *A change of pace.*

I urge Nevisians to be civil now
Regarding neighbours not as 'friend or foe'
Showing respect to each one will allow
The healthy healing processes to grow
This country needs us all to help to build
A nation strong and free and filled with pride
That notion though, can only be fulfilled
With selflessness and friendship as our guide
We must our former opponents embrace
And work together with *A change of pace.*

I call for every person, high and low
To make a solemn pledge to do his part
True patriot's love must be allowed to grow
And flourish within each Nevisian heart
Rise then above the petty narrow schemes
Which only can obstruct and block our way
We truly can realise our fondest dreams
And live to see that newer brighter day
When this fair land is free and full of grace
What's needed first though is *A change of pace.*

St. Kitts-Nevis Observer, **March 8, 1997**

SIMPLY SPEAKING

I'm not very good at public speaking, so you can thank your lucky stars that I'm seldom asked to do so. I tend to lose my trend of thought very quickly in front of an audience and often have great difficulty getting back on track. I'm sure this either bores an audience or confuses them. Sometimes it may do both. I do have one saving grace however, which affords me a small measure of redemption. I tend to be brief. Mercifully brief, in fact. And I'm sure that this is why I've even drawn polite applause on a few occasions.

My main technique for brevity is to skip all the usual fol-de-rol at the opening of my remarks before I begin my talk. That's the part you might call the salutation, or some such thing. Most speakers around these parts are in the habit of acknowledging too many people before they begin their speech. On a panel with several speakers for instance, it seems redundant if not downright ridiculous – for each speaker to acknowledge all of the other speakers, chairperson, foreign dignitaries, visitors from abroad, and so on down the line before finally getting around to saying "ladies and gentlemen." Some will even add "boys and girls" if young people are present.

I fail to see the necessity for this since the chairperson always acknowledges people to preface the opening welcome remarks. That should be quite enough. On too many occasions even the chairpersons tend to overdo the acknowledgements. Official ceremonies are the worst, since there are large numbers of government ministers, department heads, visiting dignitaries and their wives or entourages. Such lengthy acknowledgements can severely test a person's patience.

Why can't public speakers be more simple and direct like Shakespeare's Mark Anthony? "Friends, Romans, Countrymen – lend me your ears…" Can anything be more simple, direct, sensible and riveting? Could anybody really be offended, feeling that they weren't properly recognised? Well, how about this: "Dear Friends and Distinguished Visitors - it is my pleasure tonight to…" Wouldn't that cover just about everybody? If you really insist on more distinct categories, how about "Gracious hosts, distinguished guests, ladies and gentlemen…"

Of course if the entire gathering is made up of society's elite, we should be able to get by with "Esteemed guests, it gives me the greatest pleasure to address you this evening…" And if the audience is merely the hoi-polloi, I can't imagine them kicking up a fuss if the speaker started off with, "Folks – I'm here to tell you about something you may not have thought of before." The fact that they actually may have thought about it before is of little importance. At least they haven't been bored to death with a litany of names, titles, degrees, and so on before the speaker has even begun his topic.

Of course if the speaker is dynamic, forceful, charismatic, the audience soon forgets a boring opening. But if the speaker is anything like me, it's best to take my advice: Keep things simple!

St. Kitts-Nevis Observer, **March 29, 1997**

Don't Clone Me!

"This heart of mine, goes on and on
Though life is empty, since you have gone..."

Those lyrics are from a song, which, if I remember correctly, was popular in the 1940's. A couple of decades later, a South African physician successfully performed the first human heart transplant. It's interesting to realise that some of the popular lyrics from the "Tin Pan Alley" era of song writing and music making, were actually predictors of some of the greatest advances of 20th century science and medicine.

In my opinion, old songs like *"You belong to my heart"* and *"I've got you under my skin"*, were light-years ahead of their time. Nowadays surgeons routinely transplant human hearts, kidneys, livers, and though I'm not up-to-date on what other body parts can be transplanted, I'm aware that modern brain surgeons may have been inspired by that old love song; *"You go to my head."*

Another interesting old love song contains the words...

"Fly me to the moon and let me drift among the stars,
Let me see what life is like on Jupiter and Mars...."

I don't remember if that song was popular before NASA embarked on its ambitious space programme. But even though there haven't been any recent lunar landings, reports of astronauts or cosmonauts spending weeks or months aloft in spacecraft circling the earth have become routine. The Hubble telescope and various space probes thousands of miles away, are instruments that have sent back valuable information, not only about our own solar system, but also about the star stuff out there in deep space.

Can there be any doubt that the lyrics of *"Fly me to the moon"* have spurred some space scientists on? Nevertheless, old-timers like me can fondly remember a time when "Lift-off" was achieved not from launch-pads at Cape Canaveral, but at our favourite dance halls when we were young and danced and romanced to songs like *"Blue Moon"*, *"It must have been Moonglow"*, and *"How high the Moon."* The U.S. Federal Air Administration ought to ban any airline that does not heed the message of *"Straighten up and fly right."* And even LIAT's services might improve if all of their employees learned that tune.

People today are travelling around the world for all sorts of reasons. Princess Di once travelled from London to Nevis to get away from Prince Charles, or something like that. Nevisians customarily travel abroad for serious medical operations. Israeli and Palestinian leaders have travelled to Washington D.C. searching for peace. The UN has sent "peacekeeping" forces all over the place, but found it necessary to allow a bunch of countries from all over the world to make war against Iraq in order to bring peace to its neighbours.

Canadians flock to Florida or nip down to Nevis to escape cold winters. And Nevisians who had travelled on steamships to England forty odd years ago in search of employment, are returning by jet planes to their roots in their retirement years. All this feverish activity was surely predicted in the lyrics:

"Around the world I've searched for you
I travelled on, though hope was gone, to keep a rendezvous..."

One of my old favourites was the song *"There will never be another you."* It expressed exactly, my feelings about a certain girl I fell hopelessly in love with in my teens, and remained hopelessly in love with for an awfully long time, even after she married and raised a family with another fellow. She was, to my mind at the time, *"The most beautiful girl in the world"*, and I couldn't imagine anyone else like her.

At the same time, the intense feelings I had for this girl were also succinctly expressed in the lyrics of another song:

"I can't love you any more – any more than I do,
For if I loved you any more, I would have to be two..."

Recent advances in biological science have proved to me that one of those songwriters was out of tune with reality: Scientists in a laboratory in the U.K. have taken a bit of matter from one sheep and using a process called cloning, have produced another ewe. They say the process can be used with humans too, which is a bit unsettling to me. While the idea of having two identical versions of the *"Girl of my dreams"* is not repugnant to me, the thought of having a clone out there competing with me certainly is.

I don't mean to split hairs, but it seems to me that if scientists managed to create two identical versions of *"My Ideal"* from one sample, I wouldn't be able to tell them apart, and being the selfish, jealous person I am, I wouldn't be comfortable with the thought of another man making time with the carbon copy of *"My funny valentine."* I couldn't help but echo the lyrics from the song Frank Sinatra used to sing:

"All, or nothing at all – half a love never appealed to me."

But don't get me wrong, I really don't mind those scientists getting some of their ideas from old "pop" tunes. A lot of great songs were created in the '40's and '50's. But there were a lot of weird ones too, so these scientists had better be careful about what tunes they're singing or they might create a lot of problems. At any rate, I have no intention of leading a double life so cloning is not an option that I would seriously consider. Besides, I have grown too accustomed to thinking of myself in the singular, which reminds me of another old song:

" I'll go my way by myself..."

***St. Kitts-Nevis Observer*, May 5, 1997**

175

Mango Skins

My mango tree is currently doing its thing, and the results are very fruitful. This makes me quite happy because the tree had not done well the past couple of years, probably due to the several hurricanes, which had visited us. The tree had been grafted by Vernon Hendrickson, a family friend who was employed by the Agricultural Department before he migrated to Canada about thirty-five years ago. If he reads this, I'd like him to know that his work was well done and the tree is still going strong.

The ripened fruit from this tree is especially tasty this year, with a unique, tantalising flavour, difficult to describe, but which brings pure joy to one's palpitating taste buds. I've been sharing this largesse with a visitor from abroad who is enthralled with the exquisiteness, the piquancy, and the ambrosial character of this delectable edible.

I prepared a couple of bowls of sliced mangoes for us to feast on after lunch the other day. But no matter how you slice 'em, there is always mouthwatering material left on the skin and on the seed, which I am loath to waste. So I brought the platter of mango skins and seeds to the table and did a number on them.

While the visitor would gently spear a slice of mango with her fork and nibble away with murmurs of approval and delight, I'd be working the flesh off the mango skins and seeds with my teeth and tongue and sucking the juices with great gusto.

I know of no graceful way of doing this without appearing affected and foolish, so I let my hair down, so to speak, and gorged myself with orgiastic fervour and delight. Needless to say, I wasn't quiet about it. I nibbled, sucked, moaned, groaned, and slurped with pleasure. I licked the juices from my fingers and my lips and expirated loudly with ecstatic satisfaction.

My visitor inquired about the noises I was making. I hastened to assure her that the sounds were quite in keeping with what I was doing and the pleasure I was experiencing. "But they are only mangoes," she said. I told her that when mangoes are this succulent, sweet, flavourful and delicious, it would be a sin to withhold the appropriate feelings and sounds of pleasure.

I started to expound on some of the sensuous qualities of a good mango, but she began looking at me with alarm and I sensed she was getting the wrong idea. "Don't worry," I said, "I'm not going to bite you." Then I explained that in my opinion, sensuous is not necessarily sensual, although both have something to do with the pleasures of sensation.

She asked me about a certain house she frequently passes, where she hears strange sounds at odd hours of the day. I cautioned against passing so close to someone's house that she could hear what's going on inside, but she insisted that she wasn't very close and couldn't help hearing. I told her that I think I know the house she spoke of. There is a nice large mango tree in the back yard, which is heavily laden with delicious-looking fruit. It's a safe bet that what she heard were local people enjoying a plate of mango skins and seeds. "Everybody does it," I said. "It's a national pastime, at least during the mango season."

After that my visitor asked if she could sample a plate of the mango skins and seeds, so I obliged her. It didn't take her long to get the hang of it. She dispensed with the fork and the delicate air and worked her way through that platter like a well-seasoned veteran. The only trouble is, I think she enjoys mangoes even more than I do. I'm sure I don't make that much noise when I am eating mangoes. Sure I smack my lips, moan, sigh, whimper and carry on depending upon the intensity of the moment, but I'm surely not that loud about it. She really enjoys those mango skins and is much more expressive about it than I ever was. I only hope anyone passing close to my house doesn't get the wrong idea. Oh, well...

St. Kitts-Nevis Observer, **May 10, 1997**

THE STRANGERS AMONG US

There are a number of recent business ventures and other operations in our community which would not have been successful without the involvement, commitment, employment, or association of people from other places, other islands, other countries, other nations. I believe most people will recognise this when they think about the Four Seasons Resort in Nevis and the important role it plays in our economy.

Without foreign capital, that project would never have started. Without foreign designers, contractors, machinery, material and labour, the place would not have been constructed. Without foreign owners, trainers, and managers, it may have been able to function, but I very much doubt that it would have achieved the high international status it has acquired and consistently maintained.

The St. Kitts/Nevis Observer wobbled onto the local scene in late '94 in competition with well-established journals, which have been publishing for decades. Can anyone seriously deny that the *Observer* now holds the pre-eminent position among newspapers published in this Federation? Yet in order to attain and maintain this stature, it has relied heavily on members of its staff who are originally from other places.

In its Nevis office where the paper is actually printed for instance, those most responsible for putting the paper together and getting it out every week come from Nevis, Dominican Republic, Canada, Montserrat, Trinidad, U.S., and Jamaica.

This healthy mix of nationalities I feel, actually serves to sharpen the collective intellect as we strive to understand and accommodate each other in order to work together effectively. This diverse group of individuals work in rather tight quarters where space is at a premium. Yet, although it is sometimes difficult to keep from tripping over each other, the differences in accents, language and lingo, do not appear to get in the way of proper communication.

Each of us has a high regard for the skills and knowledge the others possess and contribute to the overall effort. The differences in culture and background offer wonderful opportunities for us to explore, understand and appreciate other people and to some degree, expand our knowledge of the world around us. The differences enrich the total contribution we are able to make as a team.

It should be clear that the infusion of foreigners has not been a bane, but a boon to Nevis. Unfortunately, it is painfully evident that some locals do not welcome or appreciate the strangers among us. All too often I hear some Nevisians making negative remarks about "de Guyanese" or, "de Santo Domingans" or, "de white people dem." I am appalled by the ignorance and prejudice displayed at such times. Not only because of our continued need and acceptance of whatever benefits we get on so many different levels through donations of money, equipment, or various volunteer efforts from "de white people dem", but also because of the failure to recognise that almost every Nevisian family has had relatives living abroad, making contributions in other lands. Why should we not accept people from other lands making contributions here?

Some immigrants from the Dominican Republic have surnames common to the people of this Federation. This should not be surprising since some locals sought work and stayed in Santo Domingo many decades ago. In my family, my uncle Bruce Mills died in Cuba in the 1970's after spending more than thirty years of his life there. My aunt Una Mills died in Montreal Canada about ten years ago, after living there for fifty years or so. Dennis Mills, son of Julia and nephew of Una, went to St. Thomas to live about thirty years ago. All of these Mills who went abroad, are from Craddock Road and my mother's side of the family. And I have other relatives from Nevis residing in the U.K., the U.S., and in other countries of the Caribbean.

Most Nevisians I'm sure, can say similar things about their families. Nevisians have lived and are living and making their contributions all over this planet. If we can spread out over this world, going to strange places with different cultures to find "a place in the sun," how on earth can we deny similar opportunities to strangers coming to our shores? Certainly, it seems to me, if we make things difficult and unpleasant enough for "de white people dem," they will grow weary of our attitude, stop coming here, and spread the word about the hostile reception foreigners can expect if they go to Nevis. And if we continue treating "de Guyanese, de Santo Domingans" and our own returning nationals with disdain, we may ultimately find ourselves alienated from those we need the most.

I regard all Caribbean people as my brothers or, part of my extended family. Most of us came from the same Diaspora and our blood has been mingling with others for generations. Don't tell me that any Guyanese, Trinidadian, Santo Domingan, or other Caribbean nationals should be looked upon with suspicion and disdain because of his place of origin. Only sheer idiocy will support that kind of thinking. Neither can I accept the kind of racist stupidity inherent in mouthings against "de white people dem," or the mind-boggling attitude of resentment towards Nevisians who after living abroad for many years, have come home with new skills, broad experience, and fresh ideas to share. In my opinion, these "strangers" among us, should not be viewed or treated as strangers, but invited to take a place at the table of our developing nation.

Those who have no family or regional ties here, should be considered our honoured guests and friends. Those who come from other areas of the Caribbean or are returning after years abroad, are our family. Our message to each of them must be either "Welcome" or, "Welcome home." If we indeed are to have any pride in ourselves as a people or as a nation, and if we are serious about meaningful social, economic cultural and human resource development in this land of ours, nothing else makes sense!

St. Kitts-Nevis Observer, May 23, 1997

BON MOTS

While entertaining some friends at home the other day, one of them remarked that I was a born actor. Meaning of course, that I possessed an abundance of natural talent for performing. Although I was pleased by this remark, which I considered a compliment, I've had to work very hard to develop whatever talent I am now able to occasionally display. So the phrase "born actor" really doesn't characterise me properly at all. When I told my friends this, a lively discussion ensued.

During the few hours that we spent together, a number of other phrases cropped up that set me thinking about certain anomalies and provided further grist for the mill. Having "eye-contact" with someone for instance, doesn't necessarily mean that you see "eye-to-eye" with them.

And of course, it is possible to see "eye-to-eye" with someone without actually having "eye-contact" with them. In some cases that's even preferable, as with two enemies who vow to never see each other again. By so vowing, they reach agreement. And since they agree, it could be said that they see "eye-to-eye." Yet, if they remain faithful to the agreement, they will never have eye contact again.

We bandied thoughts like that about in a rambling discussion. When somebody said something he didn't mean, he apologised for "a slip of the tongue." It was quickly pointed out to him, that although his tongue was involved in the utterance, his lungs, larynx and vocal chords certainly played a greater role. This led to a pretty lively debate with lots of back-and-forthing and a few more "slip of the tongues." Ultimately we sorted things out by deciding that the brain was to blame.

The person who first reached that conclusion was a young woman whose contributions to the conversation had generally been sound. One of the fellows undertook to thank "the member of the fair sex" for so adroitly leading us in the right direction. But another fellow promptly questioned the use of the phrase "the fair sex" as the lady in question was exceedingly dark. I said that I felt he was being a little unfair, but by then the tone of our light-hearted conversation had *changed complexion completely.*

The young lady took serious umbrage with the young fellow's remark and decided to *put him in his place.* Too many men, she said, tend to belittle women's contributions. She was livid. The poor fellow *hemmed and hawed* but try as he would, he *couldn't get a word in edgeways.* The lady was *firing with both barrels* and all he could do was duck for cover. And at close range, you must realise that's pretty hard to do.

Somebody suggested he might have merely suffered a "slip of the tongue," but she wasn't having any of that. Sparks flew as she let her new target have it *up one side and down the other.* I didn't know what to do. I don't have any talent for dealing with situations like that. I like peace and quiet, but somehow, things had gotten *completely out of hand.* I was confused, embarrassed, desperate.

I reached swiftly under the table with my fist and gave a few quick knocks. "What was that?" One of the fellows asked. "Opportunity" I said, giving him a knowing nod toward the door. Mercifully, he got the message. "Oh my gosh" he said, "I didn't realise it was this late. Look fellahs, I got to go!" Things quieted down pretty rapidly after that, and in a few minutes everybody had gone and I was alone.

I reflected on the afternoon and the discussions we had about certain words and phrases. I had never put much stock in the phrase "opportunity knocks" before, but I'm a firm believer now. It is also my firm opinion that whether you are a "born actor" or not, it's not a very good idea to make a "slip of the tongue" while a certain member of "the fair sex" is around. Even though you may have established "eye-contact" and you think "opportunity knocks," you could be making a big mistake unless it's fairly obvious that you both see "eye-to-eye."

St. Kitts-Nevis Observer, **May 24, 1997**

"Gɪ' Me A Dollah!"

Some people seem to have the erroneous impression that I have a lot of money. I don't know where they get this strange notion. It certainly can't be because of my lifestyle. I'm not a fancy dresser. I don't own a flashy late model car. Don't have a swimming pool in my yard. Don't own a yacht or an aeroplane.

I also don't make frequent trips to anywhere. Don't employ any hired help such as cook, maid, or gardener. Don't throw frequent parties. And am seldom seen in bars and restaurants simply because that's too expensive for me. So I find it amazing if not amusing, when people approach me for financial support for some venture or the other.

I don't mind buying a ticket to a Red Cross tea, or a Lions Club raffle, or a church dinner once in a while. Those things are affordable and within my budget as long as they don't happen too frequently or all at the same time. But like most semiretired persons, I have to watch the pennies carefully.

Yet some people actually expect me to make serious investments in business projects. This is probably because they mistakenly believe that the high profile I maintain through my column in the *Observer* is reflected dollar-wise in my bank account. Sorry to disappoint you folks, but it ain't necessarily so. If I really did have any money, I would invest in arts and cultural projects – but the way things are, are the way things are. Anyone who's trying to raise some venture capital should look elsewhere. Please spread the word.

But those aren't the only ones pursuing me for financial largesse. Anytime I venture down Main Street through Charlestown, I am likely to encounter a number of individuals who approach me with the demand "Gi'me a dollah!" Sometimes the demand is for more than a dollar and can even be quite specific as the amount necessary to purchase desired items. Sometimes there is merely a request for "some change."

At one time I used to give more freely and with a more charitable attitude. But I have become more reluctant and selective as the numbers of those making demands have increased. Some are surprisingly aggressive and offensive in their manner, and at times have received more than they bargained for in the form of a richly deserved lecture from me.

I sometimes feel that I am unfairly singled out as a "soft touch" by some of these people. For instance, as I came out of a shop one day, I saw one of these fellows a short distance away. A bank manager, a big name lawyer, and two heavy-duty politicians walked by him and all he did was smile pleasantly. He didn't stick out his hand, or his foot. He didn't open his mouth and demand a dollar, or even fifty cents.

While I stood there pondering this – wondering why it was that he didn't solicit funds from those who obviously had access to more money than I did, a stranger came out of the shop and spoke to me. "Oh Mr. Trott – I read the *Observer* every week. And your column is so well endowed with such a richness of expression…"

Before I could respond, I felt a tug at my elbow, I turned and there he was – the fellow who had ignored the bank manager, the big-name lawyer and the two heavy-duty politicians. His upturned palm stretched out to me. "Gi'me a dollah!" he said.

St. Kitts-Nevis Observer, **May 21, 1997**

Ouch!

Some people are unhappy that I find so much to criticise in Nevis. So am I. It does not fill me with joy to frequent my column with as much faultfinding and disapprobation as I do. I get no pleasure from dredging up negative views of our community. In fact, sensitive readers would be correct if they assessed my outbursts as reactions to pain. If one sits on a pin, gets stung by a bee, or jilted by one's lover, it hurts. The normal response is to cry out or express pain in some way. I do a lot of that in my column.

Now certainly, Nevis is a wonderful place to be; a tropic isle with a beautiful mountain, sandy beaches, warm, clear waters and gorgeous sunsets - that is very pleasurable to be sure. Nevis is also the land of my mother's birth and in being here, I am not only fulfilling a family wish, but a longtime personal desire to try to make some kind of meaningful contribution to this land and its people before I die. Unable to sustain my efforts in the field of drama, I feel fortunate that the *Observer* provides an outlet for me to express at least some of my ideas for publication. But a great deal of my writing for this column has been critical of many things in Nevis and St. Kitts and predictably, a number of people don't like it. They don't want me expressing pain over things that hurt about this beautiful country. They call it "negativity."

Awhile back, one reader called me a curmudgeon in his letter to the editor. Others have called me less flattering things in the press and on the street. I've been called "traitor" and "madman" for my views on secession, and "scaremonger" and "troublemaker" for pointing out what I considered a health hazard. I have weathered a storm of other epithets and sobriquets for merely presenting my observations and opinions about things in these islands. But the dictates of common sense and conscience keeps me putting a focus on things that some would rather hide or deny, finding my comments too harsh or serious.

Sure I'm capable of seeing the lighter side of things. I'm basically a humorist and know that my best writings are light, funny, and whimsical. Every now and then, I do such a piece for my column. But unfortunately, at such times I usually feel that I'm merely supplying a little comic relief from some of the serious issues of the day which not enough people are paying attention to. In my opinion, tragic consequences will surely result if people fail to react appropriately to injuries to our society, our environment, and our country.

Every day things take place that undermine efforts for the proper advancement of this country and its people. In the rush for development, prosperity and progress for example, expediency seems to have outweighed environmental considerations. Some builders and contractors have savaged our beaches to get sand for their construction projects. Shouldn't sensible people recognise that is a destructive rather than a constructive approach to things? Despite legislation and monitoring designed to prevent such plunder, sand mining has occurred at such an alarming pace that environmental specialists are now saying that within five years, Nevis could lose the beaches that helped make the island such an attractive spot for tourists.

That's just one of many things that disturb me. And like I said before, it gives me no joy to write about that. But I think we ought to do something before it's too late. I know that my voice alone is not going to change the tide. Many more people will have to speak up in order to save, protect and develop Nevis and its inhabitants in a responsible way. I remember a time years ago, when an unbroken stretch of beach existed from Pinney's to Charlestown. But no more. Sand mining may not have done the damage then, but it is known beyond the shadow of a doubt, that it is a serious problem now.

Other people may wish me to keep quiet about this and a lot of other things I consider detrimental to the well being of Nevis and its people. So I suppose I'll continue to be called "Scaremonger, traitor, curmudgeon, madman" and a whole raft of other things. But I know that indiscriminate mining of our beach sand hurts Nevis. Somebody's got to say it - ouch!

St. Kitts-Nevis Observer, July 12, 1997

CONCATENATION

In last week's *Observer*, fellow columnist Washington Archibald raised the issue of constructing a bridge between the islands of St. Kitts and Nevis. I have found this to be a fascinating idea ever since Dr. Kennedy Simmonds proposed it a while back, seemingly with the intention of boosting his public image as a "visionary" and increasing the chances of lengthening his tenure in public office.

Dr. Simmonds may not have benefited from the effort, but the idea itself has had sufficient appeal to be brought up again and again by others whom I imagine are less motivated by personal political considerations than by the many benefits they honestly believe the construction of such a bridge will bring to both islands and their inhabitants.

Initially, I was not in favour of the bridge. Although I have never before aired my opinions about it in the press, I have told many individuals just where I stand on the matter whenever the subject arose in conversations. Lately though, I have been wavering. Not because any new arguments have been offered which may cause me to reconsider. But rather because much cogitation over a period of time, has caused me to consider that the expected benefits of a bridge may actually outweigh the perceived disadvantages.

Aside from Dr. Simmonds, Desmond Herbert, Washington Archibald and others whose names I don't recall at the moment, have in recent times been recommending that the idea of a bridge between St. Kitts and Nevis be given serious consideration. Washie himself claims the idea has been floating around for decades.

I have never had any problem with the economic growth and expansion they predict will take place. And the social and other linkages that will be enhanced are naturally, greatly desired. I know that many real benefits can be expected to accrue from such a project, and of course I'm always in favour of meaningful benefits. So why then have I been less than enthusiastic about the construction of a bridge between the two islands?

The ease with which people will be able to travel between the two islands at practically any time they feel like it, will I am sure, bring a rapid increase in the traffic of drugs, assorted crimes, the spread of AIDS, traffic accidents, noise, litter, and other pollutants. Since people still insist on tossing trash out of car windows, increasing amounts of plastics, tinfoil, glass bottles, and other debris will despoil our waters and endanger marine life in the area, as motorists jettison their rubbish while crossing the bridge.

Who can predict the direct impact the construction of such a structure will have on the environment? In what ways will the normal and natural movement of the waters be altered? Will marine life and coral reefs be seriously affected? And what about our beaches which have already been savaged by builders intent only on "progress and prosperity?" What is the prognosis for the environment which is such an important part of what attracts visitors to our islands? Sure, I'm all in favour of closer links between Nevis and St. Kitts. But not linkages that will create irreparable damage to the country and the people.

On June 14 *The Labour Spokesman* published an article by C.A. Beach, a civil engineer who very impressively propounded the feasibility of a bridge link between the two islands. Washie's piece last week was very informative and persuasive, as was Desmond Herbert's proposal last year.

But despite the apparent desirability of the project, despite Simmonds, Herbert, Washie and others who paint such a pretty picture of the upside of the bridge project, it seems to me that nobody has properly examined the downside. That's what continues to give me pause. Besides the negatives I've already mentioned, the *MV Caribe Queen* will probably reduce operations as more people will go to St. Kitts by car, bus, and motorcycle. Nevis Express will probably feel the pinch too and reduce its quick air hops across the channel. And believe me, there are other things we haven't even begun to look at yet.

So I'm not rushing to judgement over the bridge. I'll take my time and cogitate a bit more. And if I eventually reach the conclusion that the advantages of constructing a bridge between the two islands reasonably outweigh the disadvantages, well then, I don't suppose I'll have too much difficulty crossing over.

St. Kitts-Nevis Observer, July 19, 1997

GONE ARE THE DAYS

Several times during the past couple of weeks I've been accosted by people whose views about secession differ from mine. Drastically. I've listened to diatribes which were delivered with such emphasis and vehemence that I thought it would be prudent to refrain from anything more than the mildest of responses. "Everyone is entitled to his own opinion," is a phrase I've been using very frequently. I even used it as a form of salutation the other day when approached by someone who usually misses no opportunity to browbeat me with his special perspective on things.

He did not seem amused and after brusquely brushing aside my droll attempt at levity, proceeded to instruct me about the futility of Nevis separating from St. Kitts at this time. None of his arguments were new and some of them in fact, revealed ideas that are extremely outdated. And to compound the situation, not only had I heard them from him before, but a number of other people had already expressed the same views in the pages of the *Observer* as well as other newspapers during the past year.

His main argument used to be that Nevis was too small to go on its own and lacked sufficient population, resources, or industry. Other countries were joining together, not breaking up. And according to him the larger countries or political and economic unions which are being forged, would not take a new tiny country of Nevis very seriously.

They would not bother to deal with us and so we would be left to drift perilously alone, at the mercy of unscrupulous international economic predators, financial sharks and powerful drug barons. Lately though, he and many others seem to rely on the more spurious idea that we should wait until the country is built up more before opting for secession.

They point out that the roads, the schools, the hospital, the electricity supply are inadequate. They fuss about land, housing, jobs, high prices and victimisation. They want improved education, price controls, police, health and consumer services. And they say we shouldn't have little boys doing big men's jobs. They say all these things and more should be remedied before we talk about secession. They say that to talk about secession first is "putting the cart before the horse." Balderdash!

The fact is; if Nevis had fine roads, schools, hospitals, electricity supply, affordable land and housing for everybody, good jobs, topnotch education system, price-controls, good police, health and consumer services and no victimisation, we would be foolish to cry for secession. Why would anyone want to secede if things were that good?

People only secede when they reach the conclusion that they aren't getting a fair shake under the established scheme of things and believe they can do better on their own. They don't say "Let's secede after we get everything we want and need."

What would be the point then? In my opinion, the people of Nevis have never gotten a fair shake. Not ever! And they have allowed themselves to be sidetracked from the idea of secession for far too long. Don't try to convince me that it's better to wait until things get better.

The USA would not exist today except for those who took the bold steps to chart a new course for their own land around two hundred years ago. Taiwan would probably not have emerged as one of the wealthiest Asian nations had its people not decided to go their own way separate from mainland China barely fifty years ago. Those countries have succeeded to forge an envious place in the world for themselves, not by waiting to be built up before they pulled away, but by rejecting old established arrangements under which they were constrained and frustrated and devising new formulas under which they were able to flourish. Am I to believe that Nevisians lack the intellect and courage to do the same?

Nevis may be small, but like a tiny seed, has great potential. This land of Nevis is not barren. Fertile minds and willing hearts ought to be able to nurture and nourish the seed of secession until it reaches full bloom. Only then will we be able to savour the sweetness of its fruits.

Mankind has been making a serious effort to explore beyond the boundaries of this planet for half a century. Man first ventured into space and actually set foot on the moon in the 1960's.

The Hubble telescope, two hundred miles above the earth's surface, is studying different stars of the universe around us. The surface of Mars is being examined up close and in detail by devices sent there by modern scientists. To do all this, new modes of transportation had to be developed. We had to find new ways of looking at things to meet the challenges that awaited us. And no matter which way you arrange them, horses and cart could never take us to the moon. So jets and rockets were developed. Propulsion and thrust describe the action needed to deliver a payload these days.

So when people come trying to persuade me that I'm "backing the wrong horse," or that calling for secession now is "putting the cart before the horse," you'll understand why I tell them "Balderdash!" This is 1997, the eve of the new millennium. In this day and age, how seriously can I be expected to take anyone whose vision is rooted in the days of horse and buggy. Those days are long gone, we now must focus on the future! We must not lose our thrust for secession!

Let us propel the nation of Nevis into the 21st century.

St. Kitts-Nevis Observer, **August 2, 1997**

REPRISE

When the *Observer* made its debut in 1994, it carried an article I had written titled "The State of The Arts in Nevis". The piece was actually written in 1990 when I had plans to produce an arts magazine. Unfortunately, those plans evaporated that same year after I suffered a breakdown caused by overwork and stress. But the arrival of the *Observer* in '94 allowed me finally to dust off that article and present it for publication (see page 69).

Although I have covered a wide range of topics since then, the major interests and influences in my life have been in the creative and performing arts, especially the field of drama, where I have gathered much practical experience as an actor, a writer and a director. It was perhaps only natural then, that the first article I submitted to this newspaper for publication and which I keep revisiting from time to time, is about the arts.

"A healthy, vibrant, cultural situation is critical to the proper development of our country. It is the artists who define a country's culture and character. A country's poets and singers, dancers and sculptors, playwrights and painters, musicians and actors, tell its stories, sing its songs, write its histories, folklore and fable, giving colour, shape, form and meaning to a national identity."

When I wrote that years ago I was hoping that others would take notice and a serious attempt be made to rectify the declining state of arts and culture in this community. I suggested that the government put more emphasis on the arts through the departments of education and tourism. I pointed out that in most countries where tourism plays an important role, arts and cultural activities are assisted to ensure that visitors are exposed to the richness and depth of the national character. And of course, to extract more of those tourist dollars before the visitor departs. Hence literature, visual and performing arts are often subsidised to ensure quantity, quality and variety during the tourist season".

During the height of the tourist season, there is very little of the performing arts available to most of the tourists who visit Nevis. And except for Culturama time, there isn't much for visitors to see and spend their money on at any other time of the year either. What has emerged with an overpowering presence in recent years is a D J and boom box industry, which in my opinion, is devoid of any meaningful cultural value. Most of what they project is unnecessarily loud and crude, and seemingly exalt images of debasement rather than refinement. Nothing is being done to combat this trend.

This is not the cultural image Nevis needs to project. This is not the kind of attraction that will draw tourists to our shores. I had pointed out that a healthy entertainment industry is good for the business sector. "The more interesting things there are for a visitor to see, do or experience, the likelier he is to stay a little longer, spend a little more and visit more frequently."

I suggested too that the government and business sectors might commission (financially) appropriate entities to produce special works of art, drama, literature and music. This would help struggling artists to survive, provide incentives for those who take their craft seriously, add to the tourists' experience and enjoyment of his visit, and because the money he spends for this added enjoyment eventually circulates throughout the community, the business sector reaps dividends on its investment.

But no one seems to have taken these ideas seriously. Despite a policy to develop a national policy for arts and culture for St. Kitts/Nevis, plus another meeting to develop a local policy for Nevis, precious little has changed with the sorry state of the arts in Nevis since 1990. Despite a few music and drama workshops, Nevis has not done enough to nurture and develop creative artists or its potentially rich cultural resources. It has not sought to provide opportunities for expansion beyond the narrow boundaries of Culturama.

Recently it has been announced that St. Kitts and Nevis will be hosting the next CARIFESTA, which will be held in August 1999. I don't doubt our ability to be gracious hosts, but what calibre of presentation can we expect from our artists if we do not provide them with enough support on a regular basis so that they can develop the knowledge, the skills, the experience and the confidence to match their talents against the best from other countries.

CARIFESTA is only two years away. If Nevis is going to seriously participate, our artists should start training now, just as if for the Olympics. They will have to know the requirements for gaining a place on the local or national teams. They will need advice and assistance for sponsorship and coaching. They should have to demonstrate discipline and dedication besides talent. They will require constant scrutiny, review and evaluation as part of the selection process. They will need more instruction, attention, exposure and support during this period than they ever had before.

The administration and the business sector must initially provide the bulk of that attention and support. Then the general public must show increased support through the box office. If our artists cannot count on that kind of support to participate in CARIFESTA, then we might as well throw up our hands and forget it. We'll just be spectators watching the parade. At least that's my opinion.

St. Kitts-Nevis Observer, **August 9, 1997**

Etalage

Some people are convinced that the "Cultural Parade" which took place in Charlestown on Tuesday, August 5th, was the biggest and best seen in Nevis in many years. Some have even told me it was the best ever and that I should acknowledge this through my comments in the newspaper. My viewpoint is a little different from others however, still, the annual Cultural Parade is an important institution in this community and my observations may be of some interest.

I've always viewed this parade from the vantage point of the windows at Hamilton House Arts Centre. Every year a few friends gather with me here, bringing their own refreshments to help while away the time as we chitchat waiting for the parade to begin. This is an ideal situation for me since I don't have to prepare to go out for it. The parade comes to me, passing practically beneath my windows.

This year we did the usual yakkety-yakking about what time the parade was going to start. It usually starts much later than announced, which is one of the things we criticised while waiting. Some of us were under the impression that it was scheduled to begin at 1pm. Others said they heard it was 2pm. Another person said he was sure it was supposed to start at 3pm. And somebody else said that in that case we shouldn't expect it to start before 4pm!

In my opinion, the public shouldn't be kept waiting in limbo for two or three hours for any event. Except when caused by rain or other unavoidable conditions, delays of longer than ten or fifteen minutes duration reflect poorly on organisers and participants. Especially when the end product consumes less actual time than the time spent "waiting in limbo."

The parade eventually passed my window and most of it was lovely. The creative ideas depicting history, folklore, and environment through colourful costumes, props, staging, and dozens and dozens of enthusiastic adults and children were applauded again and again by me and my friends. I had to withdraw in discomfort from the windows several times though, as the shock waves from the high-powered sound systems of the electronic bands, not only threatened to shatter my eardrums, but actually seemed to interfere with my heartbeat.

I admit that I am probably much more sensitive than the average person in this regard, but I was not the only one who had to recoil from the acoustic assault and was unhappy with this part of the pageantry. I feel that this kind of electrically generated and over-amplified sound is completely out of place in this type of parade which I believe is supposed to primarily project culture, history, folklore, tradition and lately, environmental awareness.

The output of the electronic bands is completely at variance with any of these themes. The volume of sound is far in excess of normal traditional instrumental output. Far in excess of the natural level for human perception, understanding and enjoyment. It doesn't blend in, supplement, complement, or support anything in our environment or our culture. Instead, it is as invasive, overpowering, and destructive as a raging beast.

How many traditional bands were in this year's parade? How many traditional musicians with fife, kettledrum, big drum, quatro, and other old-time, traditional, un-amplified instruments? Not very many at all! Why were we bombarded with the excessive and aggressive sounds of these electronic gangs instead of being treated to the artistry, skill, charm and romance of the cultural, traditional or old-time bands? What kind of values were the organisers encouraging by allowing the few traditional players to be drowned out by ear-splitting banality? What an insult to those who are heroically trying to preserve some of the old traditional forms of music and merrymaking. What a slap in the face to the old-timers!

In my opinion, there isn't much artistry involved in blasting a parade route with mind-numbing electronic sound. There may be some minimal amount of skill involved, but I'll be dashed if there's any charm or romance in it. As far as I'm concerned, these electronic bands should not be dominating the "cultural" parades. One or two should be more than enough for any parade, and if they played at half the volume it would probably still be too loud.

If the Department of Culture can't find enough performers for local traditional bands, they might try bringing some in from other places just for the occasion. After all, this electronic "culture" is imported from other places isn't it?

While it is clear to me that the vicissitudes of modern times will naturally force our culture to change, it is also clear that through the inappropriate deployment of these overpowering electronic bands in our cultural parades, we may be sounding the death-knell of some of our most cherished traditions and carelessly hastening the destruction of an important part of our heritage. Though it may have been the biggest and the best, that was the sad message I heard loud and clear during this year's passing parade.

St. Kitts-Nevis Observer, **August 16, 1997**

WHEN IN ROME?

A letter to the editor from my good friend and cousin Irving Liburd was published in the August 9 issue of the *Observer*. He mentioned the Dominican Republic Association's troupe, which participated in this year's cultural parade and said that their meringue music and their national flag "really get the culture mixed up." He claimed he had no problem with them participating in Culturama, "but if they want to take part, please let them do it Nevis style, for when you go to Rome you do as the Romans do."

I believe that Irving's remarks were motivated by a strong sense of pride for things Nevisian and a desire to protect our familiar and traditional cultural features from being overshadowed or degraded by foreign characteristics. While Irving's heart is in the right place, his remedy is a harmful, unnecessary and futile solution.

The different nationals of the Caribbean are all of the same Diaspora, national flags not withstanding. Check the names and the features of some of the new arrivals among us. You may recognise familiar features. There may be family connections through a relative who went abroad years ago. Should we not find better ways to welcome some of our own than to tell them they must do exactly as we do?

We should also recognise that the constant flow of people, goods and ideas, enhances economic and intellectual development. Our development is just beginning. We can hold back if we insist, but I think we've been held back for far too long already. Previously we were held back by circumstances and lack of opportunity. But a restrictive outlook must not now be allowed to block our vision.

The ascendancy of many of the countries of the modern world is the result of borrowing, stealing, integrating or assimilating parts of other cultures. *A little spice in the soup improves the flavour. Mix thoroughly for best results.* In the old days, conquests by exploration or waging wars facilitated a variety of cultural exchanges. Today the preferred method is through trade, immigration, travel and of course, the arts.

For many years many of our most able people had to go abroad in order to survive and prosper. Our labours abroad have helped to enrich other countries. Now others who have come to our shores, may help to enrich us. Some of our culture, West Indian culture and Black Man's culture, has enriched the world. This has been most evident through our music and dance.

Calypso and reggae have long ceased to be purely regional. Steel pan orchestras flourish in high schools in the U.S., Canada and the U.K. Jazz clubs abound all over the globe from Alaska to Argentina, from New Orleans to the Netherlands, from Russia to Rimouski, to Rome. Black and West Indian culture is rubbing shoulders with and enriching other cultures all over the place. You mean to say other cultures can't rub up a little with us here?

Our culture is not threatened so much by outside influences as from internal neglect. This is something that has been pointed out many times before, but it seems that no one pays attention. Our culture will certainly not be enhanced by suppressing others. We can only strengthen our own culture by understanding and identifying it, refining and treasuring it, supporting, projecting and capitalising on it.

In my opinion, the cultural focus in Nevis is generally too narrow and ephemeral. This diminishes our cultural vitality and security and fosters a fearful protectionist outlook. A strong culture is its own protection and will absorb elements of other cultures from time to time, molding them to suit its own image. Our failure to do this results in such absurdities as seen and heard around here at Christmas time. Santa in warm, red winter suit to protect him from the icy cold out there. Plastic Christmas trees and fake snow. "Jingle Bells" and "White Christmas" played over and over on local radio stations. But meringues from Santo Domingo mustn't be played at Culturama time?

Trying to keep other Caribbean nationals from projecting their culture when they come to live here is unfair and does nothing to enhance our own. It merely exposes our weakness. Incidentally, if you do happen to go to Rome, don't bother speaking Latin there. They don't use it anymore. It has long been a *dead language.* Romans speak a different language now. One more vibrant and in keeping with the times. *Perhaps they were influenced by other cultures.*

St. Kitts-Nevis Observer, August 23, 1997

WATCH YOUR LANGUAGE!

For most of my life, my primary means of communication has been through language, and more specifically, the spoken rather than the written word. And although some people are under the impression that I'm good with words, that's only because for the most part their contact with me is this column in the newspaper. Almost anybody can look good in print if they take a little time, like I do.

For instance, I think about what I'm going to write before I write it down. Then after I've written it, I read and edit it, making additions or changes, and rewriting until I've finally shaped it into something that I think I really want to say and that most people will understand. It usually takes me several hours to produce something that readers will consume in a few minutes. But if I don't take the time to do this, my words would probably never be found in print.

The other day I exchanged greetings with someone on the street. He inquired pleasantly, "How are you?"

"Not too bad", I replied without thinking about what I was saying.

"Then you must be one bad or three bad since you're not two bad" he said, "so which is it?"

We laughed at his jollity as we parted, but that little jest bugged me for the rest of the day.

For various reasons I often use the phrase "Not too bad" when people ask, "How are you?" or "How are you doing?" As I grow older I am visited by a variety of ills not troublesome enough to drive me to see a doctor. At these times I'm certainly not going to say that I feel great when people ask how I am. On the other hand, I sometimes don't want to let anybody know what really ails me either. Too many people in Nevis seem to have a ready remedy for whatever ails you and to tell the truth, sometimes I prefer to suffer the illness than to try the cure.

I made the mistake once of telling a little old lady about some really minor symptom I was experiencing and the next thing I knew, she was at my house with a bag of bush which she insisted on brewing and administering before she would leave. There was nothing I could do to dissuade her. I simply had to take the medicine. Did it cure me? Well, as my father used to say, "I ain't dead yet". But it is not an experience I would wish to go through again.

Sometimes I've used the term "so-so" to describe how I felt or how I was doing. It surprised me to learn that certain people feel that this is a more serious condition than "not too bad". So I don't use "so-so" nearly as much as I used to. No point in being an alarmist. What could be alarmist about "so-so"? Well, I once received a long distance call from my sister in Quebec the day after I told somebody in Nevis that things were only "so-so" with me. It took me the best part of an hour to convince my sister that she needn't rush down here on the first available flight. I wasn't dying. I wasn't going through an emotional or financial crisis. And I wasn't about to slit my wrists in despair. Things had merely been "so-so" with me, not great and not lousy.

Occasionally I use phrases from different languages in my writings as well as in ordinary conversations. Mind you, I can't speak any language other than English, but I do know a few foreign phrases. A perky young lady greeted me pleasantly one bright day with a big smile and a big "Hi there Mr. Trott, how're you doing?" I responded with my best impression of the continental manner, "Comme ci, comme ca".

"Come and see what!" She backed away with shock and amazement. I had the devil of a time explaining that I wasn't inviting her to come and see anything. I was merely using a French phrase, which was the equivalent of "so-so".

Such are the perils of prose. Whether written or spoken and in whatever language you choose, you have to be careful what you say and how you say it. I'm not such a good conversationalist because I spend so much time thinking about what I want to say and how to say it, that by the time I say it, the topic may have changed and I wind up with a nonsequitur. When it comes to writing however, taking the time to think, edit and rewrite, is time well spent. At least in my opinion.

St. Kitts-Nevis Observer, **September 13, 1997**

NOT QUALIFIED

Amba is "…not qualified to lead the secession struggle…" This quote is from no less an authority than HURT NEVISIAN in the pages of the *Democrat* on September 13th. It comes near the end of his diatribe and is one of the few things he has written about me which is absolutely true and has my complete concurrence. But he wastes a considerable amount of time and space leading up to this less than earthshaking pronouncement. The place of my birth and other factors, which he presents as reasons to disqualify me, are completely irrelevant. I didn't just land in Nevis the other day and begin to tell people that we ought to secede from St. Kitts.

"The secession struggle" as Hurt Nevisian puts it, has been going on for over thirty years. Others started and led the struggle at various times in the past, and when Premier Vance Amory raised the secession call again last year, I publicly proclaimed my unqualified support and that is where things still stand at this moment. I can't imagine where Hurt Nevisian gets his information or his whacky ideas.

But more to the point; my mother and youngest sister moved from Montreal back to Nevis in 1948 and my father followed a little over a year later. Nevis had been my emotional and spiritual home long before that because of the stories my mother would tell when I was a child and the songs she would sing, and the parcels and packages filled with coconut, sugar cane, cassava bread, and such that would come for us on the "lady boats" every so often.

It was my cousin Grace Herbert and her sister Blanche who would send parcels, or sometimes Aunt Julia, or her sister Ida Mills, or Granny Edgehill, my mother's mother. My uncles Harry Knight and Bruce Mills, Captain Fred Weekes our cousin, and Dennis Mills, the Drews, the Liburds, the Webbes and so many others in both St. Kitts and Nevis, I had to get to know better through letters and pictures rather than the infrequent visits.

Still, I managed to get my first donkey ride in Nevis when I was four years old. And our immediate and extended family has always kept close tabs on each other even when we were oceans apart. So it may hurt Hurt Nevisian even more to find out that I am not the stranger to Nevis that he tries to make me out to be.

When my parents lived in Canada, our home became a meeting place for many West Indians away from home. We always had a good idea of what was happening all over the Caribbean. When my parents moved back to Nevis, our home here was again frequented by all and sundry in the community and my father who was an inveterate letter writer, kept those of us abroad well informed of the goings on down here. We visited whenever we could afford it, and offered whatever we were able to the community.

In January 1957 I willingly acceded when asked to give some advice to students at the high school who were rehearsing a play about Alexander Hamilton. I didn't realise at the time that it was going to be almost thirty years before I was again involved with drama in Nevis. But during other visits in subsequent years, I assisted my parents in the preparations and promoting the Annual Tea Party held on our property to raise money for the Alexander Hamilton Scholarship Fund, which benefited needy local schoolchildren.

I am also proud of the role of the Trott family in spearheading the drive which led to the restoration of the Alexander Hamilton House, which now houses the museum and the Nevis House of Assembly, and the creation of what is now the Nevis Historical and Conservation Society. I can proudly and honestly state that the Trott family (including me) has played a meaningful role in this community during the past forty years.

No I wasn't living here during the difficult times of the seventies, but I was never so far away or out of touch that I couldn't feel the trauma and grieve along with other Nevisians over the Christena tragedy. Hurt Nevisian can't realise how much I know about and empathise with the severe hardships in Nevis that he describes. Nor would he be likely to understand or believe the saga of hunger and cold and deprivation I endured in my sojourn abroad. Hard times and hardship are universal experiences and part of the human condition, which believe it or not, is not uniquely Nevisian.

No, I wasn't actually born on the soil of Nevis, but the emotional and spiritual connection is indisputable, and I've always played a role through my family. My love of this land is no less than any other Nevisian and I have as much right as any son-of-the-soil, to speak my mind and play my part according to my conscience and the laws of the land.

A dozen years ago, I came back to Nevis to stay and be with my parents in their declining years. I didn't have the piles of money I had hoped to amass when I was young, but I had piles of experience and expertise that I was willing to share whenever the opportunity arose. I have shared my talent, my skills, my ideas and my energy with others in this community – I have little else.

Many people know of my efforts here as a dramatist, and of my attempt to convert our family residence into an arts centre. It is perhaps not well understood that a lack of sufficient commitment and support from the community has caused that dream to fade. But I am still able to offer something of value through my writing. Over the years I've learned that in order to be a good writer, you must write about what you know.

A dramatist, a novelist, a columnist or a poet can't really write effectively or realistically about people, or situations, or things without knowledge gained through study, observation or experience. Everything that I write about including the *Democrat*, *The Labour Spokesman*, the political relationship between St. Kitts and Nevis, the secession issue and the Hurt Nevisian goes through this process. That's what qualifies me as a writer.

Hurt Nevisian on the other hand, tries to hide the fact that the two St. Kitts newspapers, which have been publishing for four decades and more, accurately reflect the political relationship between our two islands by largely ignoring coverage of Nevis. And it seems that because he doesn't know enough about me to be able to give an accurate, honest rendering, he resorts to blithely claim, "My instinct tells me that Amba is once again doing his secession masquerade number…" while he himself masquerades in anonymity, characterising me as hypocritical. I have subsequently come to the opinion that as a writer of anything more than sheer fantasy, Hurt Nevisian is simply not qualified.

St. Kitts-Nevis Observer, **September 27, 1997**

PERCEPTIONS

As I was crossing Memorial Square on my way to the library the other day, I noticed a young workman pounding away with a mallet and chisel at a hole in the concrete curb on the south side. I stopped to watch awhile with interest, then asked what he was doing. He explained that he was enlarging the holes in order to install some posts. "Oh – and then will heavy chains be installed from post to post?" "Yes," he replied, that was the idea. "That's wonderful," I said with much enthusiasm.

He asked why I thought it was so wonderful. I told him it would help to beautify the area. I said that I had some old photographs of this very spot and remarked how attractive it appeared in the old photos. Much better than it looks today. It would be nice to see the area restored to its former glory. I could sense something going on in his mind. He spoke again and told me that a young man who had passed by earlier, didn't feel it would be wonderful to restore those old posts and chains. I wondered why not. "Because they'd remind him of slavery days," the workman said.

I smiled grimly and tried to marshal my thoughts. I'd heard this sort of thing before – or variations of it over the years; at other times, in other places. But I'm the sort of person who isn't afraid to be reminded of slavery days. In fact, I think it is a great pity that so few artifacts or structures built by, used by, or imposed on African slaves in Nevis, remain in good enough shape for this generation to use, appreciate, or derive any benefit.

The Great Wall of China, the pyramids of Egypt, the coliseum of Rome, and a number of castles in Europe, were all largely built with slave labour. Scholars, archeologists, and historians from around the world are now busy studying and learning from these structures today. Novelists, musicians, painters and filmmakers use them as sources of inspiration or even as the main theme in some of their works. Tourists crisscross the globe in ever increasing numbers, boosting these countries' economies in their efforts to see first-hand, to take snapshots, to touch, to purchase souvenirs, to thrill at the opportunity to experience for themselves in any way they can, something of human historic relevance.

Nevis has an interesting history. So do most other countries on this planet. When we examine almost any of them, we find bloodshed, pain, slavery and man's inhumanity to man were major features in their evolution. I think it is important for a people to be able to look back and see where they have come from in order to properly assess where they are in the present and where they are heading for the future. If a few posts and chains can help remind us of our past, that's a very valuable function which should not be dismissed. They will also help to improve the appearance of the square, which in recent years has become quite rundown, bedraggled and unattractive.

It seems to me that the descendants of slaves should not forget the past, but should use whatever reminders still exist as one of the means to help better our condition. I smiled my assurance at the young man and told him I was pleased with the work he was doing and that I wished more of this sort of thing would take place in Nevis. I said that he should be proud of his labours and do the best job he possibly could, so that everyone could enjoy it. I told him that people may say whatever they want about what he does, but it's the end result that counts. Others of course may have a different view, but at least, that is my perception.

A Hamilton House Studio Publication, February 3, 1998

HISTORICALLY SPEAKING

An unknown white man and a black slave woman were the parents of Frederick Douglass who was born into slavery in the U.S. in 1817. Frederick escaped when he was twenty-one years old and became one of the most powerful spokesmen in the U.S. against slavery and for the freedom of Black people. His prowess as an orator was so impressive that he was deemed to be among the greatest orators of the nineteenth century.

In one of his most powerful addresses titled "What the Black Man Wants," he insisted that Negroes be given full measure of American citizenship – "not benevolence, not sympathy, but simple justice." Although his life was devoted to the freedom and elevation of black people, he was subjected to much criticism for marrying a white woman after his first wife died.

Black astronomer, Benjamin Banneker, obtained his early education from his grandmother, a white Englishwoman who was an indentured servant in Maryland until the end of her term in 1692. With her "Freedom dues" she had purchased a small farm and two Africans to help her run it. She soon liberated both and married one of them, Banaky, who was said to be a prince in his own country.

Banneker was not only an astronomer, but also an original thinker concerned with the welfare of all mankind. In 1791 he sent a letter to Thomas Jefferson, who was Secretary of State at the time. The heart of Banneker's letter pointed out the inconsistency of slavery with the ideals of the Declaration of Independence. Other thoughts and ideas that he put on paper included "A Plan Of Peace-Office for the United States," and visions for such things as a Department of the Interior and a League of Nations.

Harriet Tubman is sometimes referred to as "The Moses of her people." She earned this title by leading over three hundred slaves to freedom during the many perilous trips she made from the Southern States to Canada. Harriet had to put her trust not only in God, but also in many white abolitionists who risked all they had to help her "Underground Railroad," providing food, money, transportation, and of course that priceless commodity – human compassion.

Blanche K. Bruce was the first black ever to be elected and serve a full term in the senate of the United States. Born a slave in Virginia in 1841, he made rapid progress under instruction from his master's son. He learned to read books and newspapers while very young, worked in a printing office, then served as a teacher. Politics interested him and he was drawn to the Republican Party.

On March 4, 1875, he was called to take his seat as a new senator. It was customary for the senior member from a state to accompany a new member to his desk when his name was called. But the senior member who had been a brigadier general in the Confederate Army, then the first Governor of Mississippi under the reconstruction plan, was busy reading a newspaper, obviously with no intention of paying this tribute to the former slave.

As Bruce started to the desk alone, Roscoe Conkling of New York, one of the most prominent men in the senate came forward and asked Bruce's permission to escort him to his seat. Later, when he saw that no one else was looking out for his interests, Conkling maneuvred to have Bruce placed on several important committees.

John Mercer Langston born in 1829, was the son of Ralph Quarles, estate owner in Virginia, and Lucy Langston, who was of African and Indian descent. Quarles had voluntarily emancipated his slaves but was legally stopped from giving his name to the four children he fathered with Lucy Langston. Ralph Quarles and Lucy Langston both died in 1834 when John was only five years old. But following his father's wishes, the boy was put under the care of a special friend, Colonel William D. Gooch, of Chillicothe, Ohio, who raised him as he would have done his own son.

The family became very attached to John and Virginia, one of Gooch's three daughters, laid the foundations of his education. When John was about ten years old, the Gooch family had to move to Missouri, which was a slave state. So the Gooch family sorrowfully passed him into the care of Richard Long who was an elder in the Presbyterian Church of Chillicothe, and a staunch abolitionist.

Long sent John to a private school in Cincinnati, and in 1844 John Mercer Langston was proudly enrolled in Oberlin College. Oberlin had offered the presidency of the college to Professor Asa Mahan of Lane Seminary in 1835. Mahan, a white man, had accepted only on condition that Negroes be admitted on the same terms as other students. This institution then became known as one founded on abolitionist principles. By the start of the Civil War, more than 30% of its students were Negroes.

Langston graduated from Oberlin in 1849, then took a theological course, studied law privately, and was admitted to the bar in Ohio in 1854. In 1855 he was elected for the position of clerk of Brownhelm Township, after being nominated by the Liberty Party. This is believed to be the first time that a Negro was ever chosen for an elective office in the U.S.

These few stories are meant to show relationships between some blacks and some whites during one of the most sordid periods of mankind's history. We are all only too familiar with the stories of black people being captured in Africa, clapped in chains, packed in slave ships like canned sardines. Sold to the highest bidders at slave markets in the American colonies and the West Indies. Beaten and brutalised with whips and clubs while being forced to labour under the most terrible conditions. Shot, maimed, or murdered when they tried to resist or escape. And debased and dehumanised in the most incredible fashion. Surely all that must not be forgotten.

But at the same time, there were men and women in different places playing roles which are seldom mentioned but which should not be forgotten either. These stories only mention a few of them. And these short extracts cannot possibly do them justice. But that is not my purpose here. My intention is to try to remind the descendants of both slaves and masters that we have a common bond – our humanity.

Other races, other peoples have endured periods of darkness and anguish too. Black people did not have the monopoly as slaves. Nor do white people own the monopoly for cruelty and oppression. Yet, because of the will to survive, we exist. All of us. Because someone was there to nurture and care for us, we survived. We have the power and the responsibility to nurture and care for each other wherever we are and whoever we are.

This is Black History Month. But Black History should be seen as part of the continuum of the Human Condition. We are not alone.

(Source: Negro Builders And Heroes by Benjamin Brawley, The University of North Carolina Press, 1937)

A Hamilton House Studio Publication, February 10, 1998

FREEDOM'S CAUSE

My father was born in the U.S. in 1898, and although that was a hundred years ago, at the time it was only thirty-five years after the emancipation proclamation which ended slavery.

It was only thirty-three years after the terrible civil war ended in 1865. The war in which whites from the Northern states fought whites from the South who were determined to keep their way of life which depended on the forced labour of African slaves and their descendants.

My father was born and grew up during a period in which many of the older Negroes he knew, had either first-hand experience of slavery, or had close relatives who did. It seems to me that my father was only a heartbeat away from slavery himself.

In the Caribbean where my mother was born, the slaves had been emancipated in 1834. But even though the institution of slavery had ended one or two generations before my parents were born, the aftereffects were very potent, severe, long-lasting, and impacted almost every area of their lives.

The subjugation, bigotry and discrimination that most Negroes had to face after emancipation, was in some cases, almost as bad as being enslaved. For a person cannot truly be free without equal rights, equal access to housing, education, employment, health care, justice, and voting privileges.

Today, some five generations after slavery ended, the wrangling is still going on over who is entitled to what in "the land of the free." The sickening residue from African slavery is still with us. It infects the politics of the U.S., the Caribbean, England, Africa, and other large areas of the world. It infects the psyche of many people of African descent including those in our little corner of the world.

The problem is a huge one and of course, there are no simple solutions – no easy answers. But I have become quite concerned over the number of diatribes against white people recently published in our Federation. I'm disturbed too, by the verbal hostile comments and accusations I've been hearing, and disappointed with the people making them.

I'm disappointed that descendants of Africans who were treated so cruelly in the past, and who themselves may have suffered unjust injury from bigotry and discrimination, seem to have learned so little as to stoop to such levels of contumely and intolerance. In fact, I'm more than disappointed; I'm deeply annoyed.

Two of my sisters and one of my sons are married to white persons. There is also white ancestry on my father's side of the family. And I am not alone in this regard, other blacks in this community are of mixed background, and some are mixing right now. I can't imagine that they feel comfortable with these anti-white attacks.

My white brothers-in-law and my white daughter-in-law are not part of any white conspiracy to dominate blacks. Nor do I believe are any of the other whites I normally see and associate with. And I sincerely doubt that the increasing number of interracial marriages taking place in our Federation is part of any conspiracy for white domination.

I know very well that there are some individuals in our midst who are trying to take unfair advantage of others. It grieves me to have to say this, but there are more blacks in that category than whites. That should not be surprising though, since blacks in this country far outnumber whites.

Black and whites and others are living, loving and doing business in this country – that's a fact. And that's how it should be. It ill behoves any of us to try to scare the bejeebers out of the rest of us with racist sentiments.

That's no way to build a country. That's no way to boost the economy. It's going to take all of us working together to keep this country moving forward. If blacks and whites are able to live together peacefully and raise families together, they should be able to build a country together.

The big shots, the little shots, and everybody in between have a stake in this place, white or black. And everybody who has a stake in this place has a right to be heard – black or white, make no mistake about that.

What some whites were doing to blacks prior to emancipation was horrendous, no doubt about it. It was a terrible crime and a blot on human history, which should never be forgotten. But it will not be rectified now by some blacks saying that freedom of speech should not extend to whites, or that whites are intent on taking over the country and returning blacks to slavery.

The proclamation that freed the slaves did not provide our ancestors with much more than the right to breathe free air. Sure they were short-changed, and nobody should be happy about that.

But today we enjoy such freedoms our ancestors could never even dream about. They would be happy for us, even though our freedom was paid for dearly with their blood. What sense can it possibly make for us to excoriate and vilify the whites that live among us now?

We should be doing positive things with our freedom instead of stirring up racial animosity. The proper authorities should prosecute individuals, black or white, who are guilty of wrongdoing in our country. But blacks that unjustly persecute whites in the press, do injury to the cause, insult people's intelligence, and cheapen our claim on freedom.

A Hamilton House Studio Publication, February 17, 1998

FOREIGN INFLUENCES

It grieves me sorely that many locals are openly complaining about "foreigners" in our midst. Most of those doing the complaining are poorly educated, non-skilled, poorly trained, marginally employed or unemployed and unemployable. It seems they are taking their cue from some of the narrow-minded opinions that are expressed through the local media from time to time.

These commentaries often raise warnings against "takeovers" by foreign investors, personnel, or ideas. Because they seem to offer a convenient scapegoat to account for the lowly position they find themselves in, these opinions which are authored by a few more literate and better educated locals, find ready currency among their less fortunate brethren.

Thus it is that expatriates (whites), Santo Domingans (blacks), Returnees (Nationals who've been away for many years), and citizens like me (not born here), become targets of derision and suspicion by those who see us all as foreigners who will exploit them in some way. Unfortunately, the false rumours, half-baked theories, twisted logic, and outright lies which spring up to support this perception, has done incalculable harm and seriously retards the proper growth and development of our community.

For instance, there is an enormous untapped human resource pool that has been languishing away in our very midst. This pool is made up largely of returnees and expatriates who live here. People who have had successful careers abroad in the arts and sciences; professionals of all sorts as well as tradesmen and journeymen.

Many of these people find it very difficult trying to integrate or reintegrate with the local community. They are often met with suspicion and sometimes even open hostility when they offer themselves, their skills, training, expertise and different approach to things. Some have given up trying and withdrawn to live as privately as they can. Some have suffered from "burnout" or "breakdown" as I have, and consequently are forced to do as little as possible in order to preserve their health and sanity. Some have given up altogether after a few years and left the island in disappointment, after selling their homes and property. Even returnees who had expected to spend the rest of their years "at home," have faced this predicament.

Although I don't believe I will ever "give up" and leave Nevis, too often I am still treated as an outsider. In 1985 I "came home" to Nevis to stay. Some locals don't appreciate my critical comments in the press because "you ain't bawn here." There are even a couple of people who don't speak to me and have angrily told me "Don't call me name," when I bid them good morning on the street. "This is Nevis" I've been told, meaning I suppose that since I was not born in Nevis, I'm not entitled to express a view which differs from the local mind-set.

My father was a resident of Nevis from 1950 until his dying day in 1985. He wasn't born in Nevis, but I am proud to say that he made a sterling contribution to this country. He and my mother who had been away from Nevis for twenty years worked with others like Mary Byron who was born in Belize, and her husband Spencer who was born in Nevis, to lay the groundwork for what is now the Nevis Historical and Conservation Society.

The influence of foreigners or residents born in foreign countries is of greater importance than most people seem to realise, because contacts and access links to many foreign institutions, business associations, cultural and other entities can be enhanced or cultivated through the so-called foreigners among us.

There is a local chap who loudly brays that foreigners are "mashing up de place" every time he sees me. His goats in the meantime are straying untended, mashing up somebody else's property. Apparently, if you're born here you can do that. It seems to be good for some sort of development in the country, although because of my foreign way of looking at things, I can't imagine what.

If being foreign born is the worst that people find to say about me, I'd consider myself truly blessed. They can't say I beat my wife, abuse my children, rob my neighbours, or consort with the devil – because I live a pretty transparent life and it is fairy simple to see that none of that could be true.

But to call someone who lives here, works here, does as much and gives as much to this community as he possibly can – a foreigner merely because he was born somewhere else, is ridiculous, stupid and shabby. I know I'm no foreigner, and if the guy down the street doesn't know that yet, shame on him. Perhaps he's under the influence of alcohol, or one of those other "foreign" substances.

A Hamilton House Studio Publication, March 10, 1998

IMAGES

As Nevis rushes slowly towards the referendum in which its voters will decide whether or not to remain within the Federation of St. Kitts and Nevis, its citizens will be exposed to an ever increasing barrage of self-serving rhetoric by leaders, spokesmen, dilettantes and pundits of every political stripe and persuasion.

Every conceivable means to disparage and embarrass the other will be used by opposing forces, and clarity and truth is more likely to be eclipsed by fiction and fable. Silly beyond belief are some of the rumours, which are currently making the rounds, about the private lives of certain individuals. These rumours are ridiculous attempts to tarnish someone's image. Yet I'm sure they will find currency and be repeated again and again by those with limited intelligence among us, or to satisfy certain political agendas.

Almost, if not just as bad, is the recent spectacle of officials of the Nevis Island Administration, ripping into Prime Minister Douglas's comments on Voice Of America and his appointment of the Constitutional Commission. Mind you, I'm 100% in favour of secession for Nevis, but I realise that Douglas as our Prime Minister has to at least give the impression to the rest of the world that he's trying to keep the Federation together. Would anyone seriously expect him to say otherwise on Voice Of America? I can't begrudge him that at all.

So he says the constitution is flawed. Let him point out the flaws he sees, and the Nevis Island Administration can point out the flaws they see. Should anyone have a problem with that? And he appointed a commission to weed out the flaws and to consult with the public for ideas to improve the flawed situation. Should he be lambasted for that? I prefer to give him high marks for effort, regardless of what I might feel about his sincerity. And furthermore, if I were the Premier, I'd lead a delegation of the best minds at my disposal, to meet with the PM's Constitutional Commission to tell them point blank what's wrong with the present Constitution, and how it could best be improved.

I'd tell the commission that regardless of any improvements to the Constitution, it would still be best for Nevis to be a separate entity, and that we will continue on the course that we have started that will allow the people of Nevis to decide for themselves. I would stress to the members of the commission, that Section 113 is the best thing in the Constitution as far as Nevis is concerned. Then I'd lead my delegation back to the task of preparing for the referendum in Nevis. I would certainly not have any people who may be needed in negotiations after the referendum, engaged in attacks through the media against the Prime

Minister or the Constitutional Commission. I would certainly not have any Cabinet Ministers engaged in that sort of thing.

Regardless of which way the referendum goes, selected teams of Nevisians and Kittitians are going to have to sit down and negotiate a new arrangement. Both sides need to admit, recognise and prepare for the coming change. It is certainly not too early to practice the art of diplomacy. It may pay big dividends later.

The Prime Minister has on a number of occasions since Vance Amory's call for secession in '96, indicated that he would respect the outcome of the referendum in Nevis. And he has indicated that if the people of Nevis vote "YES" to secession by a two-thirds majority, the St. Kitts Government would negotiate with us, the terms of a new arrangement. That's diplomacy, which should be respected. He didn't say, "Nevis can secede only over my dead body."

The Nevis Island Administration has to be concerned that its public image has been tarnished somewhat, by the negative publicity in the media regarding the airport, the Delta/Shell brouhaha, stray animals, theft by government employees, and various other problems. It has to deal with these problems head-on in an open, honest, and convincing fashion. And if a few heads have to roll – so be it.

We cannot afford to keep sweeping things under the rug. The troubling problems, which bedevil us, now, are surely not insurmountable. Surely sensible remedies and solutions can be found which will improve the situation. The manner and speed with which this is done can redound to the benefit of both the administration and the community, and can certainly help restore the confidence of the questioning public.

Our quest for secession is a noble and honest one, one that as I've said before, I fully support. But I don't want to see this quest used as a convenient smokescreen, camouflaging problems we haven't the guts to deal with properly. Let us prove ourselves and show to the world now, that we are fully capable of standing up and dealing expeditiously and judiciously with our troublesome domestic problems.

If we can do that, we are likely to improve our image at home and abroad. And we are more likely to be taken seriously when the time comes for us to negotiate the terms of a new arrangement with St. Kitts. In the meantime, when we have reason to talk about Prime Minister Denzil Douglas, it wouldn't harm our image one whit to demonstrate our ability to employ the tactics and language of diplomacy.

A Hamilton House Studio Publication, March 24, 1998

BRIEF ENCOUNTERS

Wicklyn Hanley is one of my favourite people in Nevis, although we're not close friends or anything like that. Regrettably, I don't have many close friends in Nevis, but there are some people I'm always glad to see and Wicklyn Hanley is one of them.

I guess I see Wicklyn several times a week, usually on Craddock Road or Main Street, but sometimes on Chapel Street or Government Road. Always when I see him, he is with a push broom, a shovel and a wheelbarrow, busily working cleaning the street. As we approach, we hail each other with a "Good morning," "Good afternoon," or whatever the case may be. Once in a while I may stop for a little chitchat, but we seldom say very much to each other. A smile speaks volumes though, and Wicklyn always greets me with a magnificent smile.

The brief exchanges that I've had with Wicklyn have meant much more to me than I can ever adequately explain. I've had many brief exchanges with other people, which have not left any noticeable impression, or had any meaningful effect on me, except for exchanges with rude or inconsiderate people with characters, which are generally very annoying, often inducing stress and sometimes leading to bouts of depression. But something about Wicklyn Hanley has had a most profound effect upon me.

Wicklyn has a very open, honest expressive face. Whenever we meet, the look in his eyes, the expression on his face, his warm smile, tells me that he recognises and respects me as a worthwhile human being. His countenance tells me that he likes me, he trusts me, and that he will treat me as a friend.

I look forward to the brief encounters that I have with him, because they help to sustain me; help to dispel the anger, annoyance and depression I regularly experience as a result of unpleasantness from other elements in this community.

I've never discussed my problems with Wicklyn, and I probably never will. I never said very much to him at all, until one day last week when I inquired a little about his personal life, and asked if I could write something about him and publish it in the newspaper. He acquiesced and so I found out his age, and that he had three sisters and a brother all living abroad, although all were born in Nevis.

Wicklyn lives in Taylor's Pasture, and has been employed as a labourer with the Health Department for the past two years. He is also a self–employed handyman, does odd jobs here and there, and a little gardening and crop farming for himself.

"If somebody wants me, they call me," he says, "I always helping somebody do something."

He likes to read books, newspapers, and watch TV. He attends the Gingerland Methodist Church and although he doesn't sing in the choir, possess a powerful bass voice.

When I asked about his politics, he demurred saying that he supports only good policies. About development, he said things were "looking okay." About secession, he said that since Nevisians have been talking about it for a long time, he is "ready to vote and get it over with." I didn't press him about which way he would vote. But I wanted to dig a little deeper and find out a little more about the character of this man about whom I knew so little, and yet felt was my friend.

I asked about his job as a labourer, and how he could do it with such a cheery disposition, a job which many look down on as demeaning. He smiled his big generous smile and told me he was happy to be doing honest labour, it was something that needed to be done. He told me to consider what Nevis would be like if nobody cleaned the streets. He told me that he knew some people would prefer to "sit down all day and do nothing", rather than do this type of work. He assured me that he was glad to be able to do something useful, and understood the importance of keeping Nevis clean for health reasons as well as for personal and national pride.

Far from being demeaned, he saw what he was doing as a meaningful job and said, "I try to do it to the best of my ability." He said that whenever he is responsible for doing something, he wants to see that it is well done, whatever it is. I knew then what it was in all those brief encounters that drew me to him, that made me recognise him as an equal, which made me see him with admiration that commanded my respect, and the realisation that he is my friend. I tip my hat to Wicklyn Hanley.

The Leewards Times, July 17, 1998

Stop The Yakking

Probably at no other time in the history of the movement of secession for Nevis has there been so much opposition against it in this island.

Even more remarkable is the fact that those in Nevis now leading the charge against the movement for secession are the leaders and officials of the political party whose very existence was predicated on the objective of "Secession at all costs" for Nevis.

In the debate in the Nevis House of Assembly on July 14th, contributions from the three members on the opposition bench included the following statements: (1) "All over the world economic forces control governments. It is a fallacy to think that if Nevis separates, things will get cheaper". (2) "Secession is only going to cost us more and nobody can tell us where the money is going to come from". (3) "There will be sacrifices and the people should make their decision knowing that if we choose secession, sacrifices will have to be made".

My purpose is not to dispute these statements, but to point out that they were just as applicable to our situation thirty years ago as they are today. Haven't Nevisians had to make sacrifices all along the way, even without secession? Did things get cheaper between now and then? Did anybody tell us in advance where the money was going to come from to meet the increasingly higher costs that we've been paying?

The situation, which for decades has given rise to the longing for separation from St. Kitts, has not changed. But the philosophy of the party that once reflected the hopes and dreams, the heart and soul of the people of Nevis, has been radically altered.

The party that was once the darling of the vast majority of Nevisians because of its bold cry "Secession at all costs", is now boldly instructing the people of this island to "vote NO to secession".

They are now saying that the costs are too great – that we haven't been given all the facts – that the present administration is incompetent and corrupt – that we aren't sufficiently developed and hence, "not ready yet" – that the rest of the world will not accept or deal with such a tiny nation and that constitutional reform is a much better option.

But the fact is, the imagined or projected costs have always been very great, even when they were leading the cause for secession. We certainly didn't have all the facts then either. Every country that has ever broken away from another knew that it had to pay the costs. Nobody gets a free ride. We can't expect Nevis to be an exception. And if the previous administration had been viewed by the voters as being competent and incorruptible, they would probably still be in power.

We are much more developed now than when they were screaming for "Secession at all costs!" In modern times the world more readily accepts and deals more fairly with smaller states than in the past, and up until the moment the Premier decided to seek separation from St. Kitts, I supported the idea of constitutional reform.

But the Constitution of St. Kitts and Nevis is like an ill-fitting set of hand-me-downs from somebody else's family. Altering, cutting and patching up somebody else's worn-out suit is not nearly as attractive as choosing to have something tailor made to one's own specifications. After that, whenever the garment needs alteration or modification because of an expanding waistline or a receding chest, it will probably still suit the original owner.

About negotiations: The classic position has always been to hold negotiations after the people have indicated their determination to become an independent separate country. To negotiate anything before the people have spoken, would give the secessionists an enormous advantage. If the Federal Government agreed in advance to everything the secessionists wanted, the people would vote in a landslide to leave, leaders in the Caribbean would be angry and distressed, and those of the international community would be shocked and appalled.

On the other hand, if under the guise of advance negotiations the Federal Government refused to recognise what we are clearly entitled to and offer little or nothing, it could be seen as mean and authoritarian and drive more converts into the secessionist camp. Only after the people have clearly expressed their will, can the proper atmosphere be established for meaningful negotiations.

If the referendum goes against secession, it is obvious we will have to be satisfied with striving to make substantial and creative alterations to an ill-fitting constitution. That may satisfy certain entities in the short run, just like the present patched-together Constitution did. But I don't see it doing much for the confidence and self-esteem of a people who for far too long have sensed a lack of equity in the constitutional, political, and administrative relationship with their sister island.

Finally, those who say there hasn't been enough discussion on the matter know very well that that is not the case at all. Like in Canada where Quebec wants to become a separate nation, the debate has been going on for decades. And even though the secession forces have lost two referendums in Quebec in recent years, the Canadian Federal Government at no time negotiated anything in advance. The debate rages on because the constitutional reforms the Federal

Government had offered, fall far short of what the Quebecois can comfortably live with.

Nevisians have a choice to make on August 10th, and a chance to escape that trap. A "NO" vote will likely mean we go on for decades "yakking about the pros and cons of secession. A "YES" vote means we stop the "Yakking", roll up our sleeves, and get busy to make it work.

The Leewards Times, **August 7, 1998**

PILLOW PRATTLE

A pillow may not seem like much of a substitute for a lover, and indeed for those who are lucky enough to have a spouse or a sweetheart to snuggle up with from time to time, I would certainly not recommend a pillow for anything more than resting one's weary head upon, or indulging in playful pillow-fights with the kiddies. But for those who spend long, lonely nights yearning for the warmth and contact of an inamorata, or inamorato as the case may be, a good sized pillow may at least help to fill the void and provide a certain measure of comfort.

That I have come to appreciate this more and more in my latter years than when I was younger, is perhaps due to the fact that the type of pillow being produced these days, more closely resembles the feel of the woman I love or would like to love, when I wrap my arms around it. I remember when I was a young man, living in a rooming-house in a strange city far away from home, the pillows on my bed were kapok-filled and were not much comfort for me. I did not enjoy wrapping my arms around them at night, because the kapok filling was lumpy and tended to bunch up at one end of the pillow or the other.

Sometimes there would be kapok at both ends but nothing in the middle. That was totally unsatisfactory when I was trying to imagine that I was with a woman. I have never been attracted to women who were configured that way. A few lumps in the right places is fine, and in fact, extremely desirable. But it was impossible to get the lumps in the right places with those old kapok pillows.

At various times I've tried hugging up with feather pillows, but I must say that while they kept a better shape and feel than kapok pillows, sharp quill ends of the feathers would sometimes work through the pillow coverings and prick me. Although the results were not fatal, they would quickly destroy my nocturnal reveries.

Thank goodness though, that modern scientific advances and technological developments have allowed manufacturers to produce substances for pillows which are more compatible with my requirements. At present I possess two pillows which if I didn't know better, I might say were heaven-sent.

These pillows are shaped like generous sized, full-bodied pillows, and that is in fact, exactly what they are and exactly what they look like on a properly made bed. But on nights when I am lonesome, if I wrap my arms around one of these pillows and snuggle up close, the pillow accommodates me, yielding to the gentle pressure of my hands, like a woman, yet firm and resilient without bunching up and becoming lumpy like kapok, or pricking me through the covering like feathers. I am transported then, on flights of fancy until I drop blissfully off to sleep.

The beauty part is; if I wake up in the middle of the night, I don't have to disturb anyone whose weight may have caused my arm to go numb. The pillows don't weigh that much. And there are lots of other benefits too. I'm not a very big talker, especially not in bed. And a pillow which makes no demands, does not keep me struggling, trying to find the right things to say. I don't have to listen to comments about my snoring. And if I decide I want to sleep on the other side of the bed, I just roll over there – no problem.

And speaking about no problem, I can bury my head in my pillow and have a good cry anytime I want without having to explain what's wrong. It doesn't give me a lot of well-meaning advice which we both know I'm not going to use anyway. A pillow will listen without commenting. Sometimes that's very comforting.

Still, a pillow proxy is no proper stand-in for the real thing and I'd rather hold a real woman in my arms any day, or night for that matter. Lately I've found that holding the pillow in my arms and snuggling up, comforting though it has been, hasn't been enough. So I've been talking more intimately to the pillow – whispering little endearments. Sort of practicing for when I can hold a real woman in my arms again.

One thing has me concerned though, and that is; what to do if the pillow whispers back! But don't you worry. I'll probably have a more satisfactory arrangement going before that situation arises. At least I hope so.

P.S. I'll let you know.

The Leewards Times, **August 28, 1998**

TROTT TALKS TO TROTT
A SELF INTERVIEW

Q: I hear a lot of rumours about you. Is it true that you're worth a lot of money?

A: Absolutely. I'm worth a lot more than people seem to realise. A heck of a lot more. Especially in this day and age when everything costs so much!

Q: What do you mean?

A: Somebody asked me the other day to do a job for him. I agreed, but when I said I would charge 500 dollars, he looked at me as if I was crazy. He expected me to do the job for nothing.

Q: Was this a writing job?

A: It was. When I explained that I needed money like everybody else to pay my phone bill, buy a new pair of shoes and have a few beers, he sucked his teeth as if he thought I was lying. He said he thought I was asking a lot. I said I'm worth a lot and I guaranteed to give him his money's worth. People always tell me I'm so good at what I do. But nobody wants to pay me for it. That's why I'm worth so much but have so little money.

Q: How do you survive?

A: I've actually asked myself the same question, many a time. The only conclusion I can come to is that the age of miracles is not over yet. It ain't easy. But luckily, I have relatives who help me out.

Q: Why do you write?

A: Do you mean why didn't I go in for banking, or shop keeping, or garbage collection, or some other such more dignified and lucrative profession? Well, basically I don't have the brains to be a banker, the temperament of a shopkeeper, or the stamina to be a garbage-man. On top of all that, I'm a terribly lazy person and a regular slob. I didn't have much choice except to become a writer.

Q: Are you saying that writers are lazy slobs?

A: Well, maybe not all of them. Writing gives me an excuse to cop out on other things. I don't really know why other writers write. Why don't you ask them?

Q: But doesn't writing take effort?

A: Everything takes effort, even breathing. That's why they whack babies' bottoms when they're born – to motivate them to make that first effort.

Q: Where do you get the ideas for all of the things you write about?

A: They're all around all the time. Even a lazy writer like me doesn't have to go far for ideas. Just pick one out and grab it.

Q: What's your favourite subject?

A: Women. But I don't write about them much.

Q: Why not?

A: I like people to think I'm a decent fellow, which I basically am. But the fantasies I have about women might change peoples' opinion about me. I wouldn't dare put any of those fantasies into print.

Q: What was your greatest writing achievement?

A: A letter to the IRS when I was living in the States, explaining why I shouldn't have to pay what they said I owed. They never bothered me again. That was great!

Q: What was your greatest disappointment?

A: A love letter that didn't generate the desired response. Actually there've been more than one – in fact several. I put a lot into them, but they just didn't do what they were intended to.

Q: Are you still writing love letters?

A: Not at the moment, but that doesn't mean that I won't try again sometime.

Q: Are you currently in love?

A: Who isn't? Unless they're dead. But let's not pursue that line of questioning any further.

Q: What would you like to talk about?

A: Science, Art, Religion…

Q: I didn't know you were religious.

A: I'm not really. But that doesn't mean that I can't talk about it.

Q: I know just what you mean. There are a lot of people around here who talk a lot of religion but don't practice much.

A: That wasn't exactly what I meant. I was thinking more like how people tend to make a religion out of things like money, for instance. A lot of people here actually worship money. They will do more for a dollar than they will for their church. Money actually replaces God in their scheme of things.

Q: I think you're right. But why do you think that is?

A: Greed is the obvious answer where money is concerned, but then you also have people who have replaced God with politics.

Q: You're saying that politics is their religion?

A: Precisely. Mind you, they still go to church on Sunday. They'll drop a few coins in the collection plate. They sing hymns with the congregation, recite scriptures, and often will quote the Bible backwards, forwards and sideways too. But nothing gets them body and soul like their political beliefs. Especially when they're on the campaign trail for their political party. Jesus Christ couldn't ask for better disciples. Talk about religious fervour, spirit, and zeal. God Himself couldn't expect more passion, more dedication, more love, and more devotion.

Q: I see what you're saying. Do you think that's something you might write about sometime?

A: Do you think I'm crazy! Do you want me to lose my readership? Things are tough enough for me already. I need this job. I need the money!

Q: But weren't you just saying something about money and religion?

A: Don't you get smart with me, fellow!

Q: I'm not trying to be smart – I'm just trying to understand what you were saying – trying to get the proper perspective. Can't we talk about this a little more?

A: That's it Buster – I've got nothing more to say!

The Leewards Times, September 4, 1998

Pillow Frazzle

An irate lady called me on the telephone the other night and told me she was going to sue me for alienating her husband's affections. I told her she must have dialled the wrong number. "Is that Trott talking?" she barked. I cautiously admitted that it was. She said that ever since she read my Pillow Prattle article a few weeks ago, her husband prefers sleeping with a pillow and is paying no attention to her.

I offered the lady my condolences and informed her that my article was specifically directed towards those persons who had no inomorata or inomorato to cuddle up with. "I'm no inomorata, I'm his wife" she exploded, "and I resent being replaced by a pillow!" I told her I sympathised with her completely and would probably feel the same way if I were in her place. I suggested she broach the subject gently to her husband and ask him for a little more consideration.

"He won't listen to me" she sighed, "he just whispers sweet nothings to the pillow as if I'm not there." She paused as if waiting for me to say something. "Have you tried pulling the pillow over your head?" I ventured. "I'm going to make you pay" she screeched, "you put him up to this!" I quietly hung up the phone and wondered if somebody was just trying to pull my leg or whether I should really be concerned.

About an hour later, a guy calls me on the phone. He wants to know if I'd consider swapping pillows with him. I told him I wasn't interested. He said he would make it worth my while. I said I didn't want to part with my pillow, that I'd become quite attached to it. He offered to throw in a mattress as part of the deal. He said it was barely used, and what's more, it was a Posturepedic.

I told him my posture was fine and that I had no use for an extra mattress. I asked what was wrong with the pillow he had. He said he didn't know, but that it wasn't doing anything for him. I told him that my pillow might not do anything for him either. He asked if he could just borrow the pillow for a few nights to see how it worked. I said that was out of the question. I wasn't going to let the pillow out of my sight.

I suggested that he shop around for a new pillow – check out the stores in town. I assured him he could find the right pillow if he just looked around. He asked me what brand I used. I didn't know, so I went to the bed, took off the pillowslip and searched for a label, but there was none. When I got back to the phone, the chap had hung up. He's probably still laughing at me. And I bet that lady who had called earlier was his wife – or his inomorata. I don't really mind. I got a chuckle out of it too.

In fact, when I write a piece like this, it's an attempt to provide a little levity. Lord knows there's enough sombre, seriousness in the world. I was kinda serious about the pillow though. It really worked wonders for me, cuddling up on lonely nights. And I really have become somewhat attached to it. Which brings up a little problem; it really isn't my pillow after all.

I've been staying at my sister's house while she's away. The pillows I've been raving about belong to her. I don't know if she'll let me keep them when she gets back. Perhaps I'd better start looking around now. There are a few shops in town that might have what I need. You might see me in one of them this weekend checking out the pillows. Nightie night!

The Leewards Times, **October 2, 1998**

CURRENT THOUGHTS

I was thinking about the "mainstream" the other day and wondering whether I should seriously consider becoming a part of it. What would the benefits be and what are the pitfalls? I'd never given it much thought before, but in recent times on radio, TV, in magazines and in newspapers, so much has been said about the mainstream that it cannot be ignored.

Mainstream religion, music, art, and politics have all undergone substantial changes in the last couple of decades according to reliable sources, and so has science, medicine, education, and just about anything else you can think of, mainstream or otherwise. All the changes or "advances" are supposedly for the betterment of mankind, but when I think about it, I'm not so sure.

Mainstream scientists for instance, claim that the results of the latest experiments show that it is possible to duplicate people through a process called cloning. There is even serious speculation that they will do so in the not too distant future. But since in so many areas of the world, conflicts and crisis are caused by overpopulation, and unemployment, I wonder about the wisdom of this. Why not simply put people to work transporting others from overpopulated areas to under-populated areas where they are needed, why bother cloning?

And isn't mainstream economics the cause of the collapse of the monetary system in Russia and Asia and the resulting global financial crisis? Still, mainstream is where it's at these days and changes have been taking place all around without the slightest effort on my part. So I began to feel a little guilty and decided to study the situation to see what I could do to become a mainstream type of person and help affect the course of events.

One of the first things I learned is that a good mainstream person around here has at least two jobs – not all of course, but some, and some even manage to have three. One person with three incomes is good mainstream material. Especially in purchasing power. Banks and business places adore them.

Most mainstream people are also regular churchgoers and very likely are members of the church they go to. Some in fact, seem to know more about religion than their church pastors, although in daily practice there may be little actual evidence of their professed Christian faith. A goodly number of mainstreamers are members in good standing of several clubs and organisations in our community, and often hold key positions such as President, Treasurer, or Executive Board Member.

In the main though, mainstream persons are made up of quite ordinary people who are the backbone of our community. Policemen, shop clerks, carpenters, fishermen, taxi drivers, schoolteachers, bakers, and so on. I tried to picture myself to see if I fit in there somewhere, but couldn't quite get the picture so I asked an acquaintance for help.

He seemed surprised that I asked for his advice. He said that he had always assumed that I was part of the mainstream even though he thought some of my ideas were cockeyed. He said it was important to be part of the mainstream because that is what defines "who you are". When I said I wasn't sure I could agree with that, he told me that those who are not a part of the mainstream could not make a positive contribution and therefore were of no real value to society.

Before I could object, he asked what church I belong to. I told him I was not a belonger but that I've tried to follow basic Christian principles throughout my adult life, and that I am also a member of a couple of well known community organisations. He said that was nice, but then wanted to know how much I had paid for my car. I explained that it wasn't really my car at all, that I just had the use of it from time to time.

He focused awhile on how much I spent as a consumer on clothing, food, entertainment, appliances, and the like, suggesting that my place in the mainstream was to be largely determined by the amount of conspicuous consumption I was accustomed to. He wasn't pleased with the meagre figures I reported.

He asked how much I earned from writing and other sources of income such as stocks and bonds. I told him the amount I received from writing and my old age pension – my only sources of income. He insisted that my total income was insufficient for anyone to live on for any length of time. When I pointed out to him that I wasn't dead yet, he smiled and said that was a matter of opinion. He said that at my age, I really shouldn't be too concerned about becoming mainstream anyway. I thanked him for his advice and we parted amicably although I most likely will never seek his advice again.

The picture of the current mainstream that my friend revealed to me is not one in which I particularly want to find myself. Although it may be futile to swim against the current, I don't think it would make me happier to just "go with the flow". I guess I'll continue stay out of the mainstream, but still try to contribute whatever I can in the current situation.

The Leewards Times, **November 6, 1998**

PASS THE DUMPLINGS

I adored many nursery rhymes and Mother Goose tales when I was a little tyke. I guess everybody did. I thought they were lots of fun then. I didn't realise I was learning anything in particular, it was just a way to have fun. When I grew up though and revisited some of those nursery rhymes, I began to realise how important they were to the learning process in my childhood. When I had children of my own, they learned those funny rhymes and stories too. The one I liked best went something like this:

> Diddle diddle dumpling, my son John…
> Went to bed with his stockings on…
> One shoe off and the other shoe on…
> Diddle diddle dumpling, my son John!

I suppose the reason why I liked that one so much, is because although it is obviously a little nonsense rhyme, it is one that I could relate to completely. For instance, Mother used to call me her little dumpling sometimes. And many a time I would flop on my bed for a nap without removing my shoes and socks. In fact, way back then I actually did wear stockings. Lots of little boys did. So that particular nursery rhyme articulated some of my own, personal, real-life experience, even though my name wasn't John.

Another one I liked was the Humpty-Dumpty rhyme. It was a neat way to learn to be careful in the handling of fragile things, which couldn't be repaired once broken. Valuable information can thus be painlessly imbedded in a person's memory at a very early age through nursery rhymes. "Three Blind Mice" though, and "Hickory Dickory Dock" just tend to tick me off. It makes no sense to me to teach kids that three blind mice were running after anyone. I mean like, one blind mouse is bad enough – but three…? Come on…!

In Hickory Dickory Dock why didn't the mouse simply get a seeing eye dog? Then it wouldn't have had to run up the clock for the time. It could have saved its energy for other things. If the mouse had a seeing-eye dog, we could relate the story like this: Hickory Dickory Dock – the seeing-eye dog looked at the clock. "Egads," the dog said, "no wonder I feel so hungry – it's away past my lunch hour!" And he dashed off for the kitchen where Old Mother Hubbard was searching through the cupboard for a bone.

"Here I am" said the dog, "Sorry I'm late. I'm famished – where's my lunch?" "Where indeed?" lamented Mother Hubbard. "I'm afraid the mice have beaten you to it – they're eating us out of house and home!" "What!" yelped the dog. "After all I've done for them!" and dashed back towards the grandfather clock in the hallway.

The mouse, whose eyesight had suddenly miraculously improved, saw the dog zooming in on him with eyes flashing and jaws gnashing. It realised the dog was not in a jovial frame of mind, and so quick as a flash it scooted up the clock for safety. Just as it reached the top, the clock, which hadn't rung since the old man died, struck the hour of one with a resounding gong.

The mouse which had never heard the clock strike before, suffered a massive heart attack from the shock, and slithered back down the grandfather clock to lay inert between the paws of the dog which didn't know what to make of this sudden turn of events.

Mother Hubbard waddled out of the kitchen. "I thought I heard something," she said. Then noticing the prone figure of the senseless mouse, she reached out and patted her dog Rover. "Oh you clever, clever doggie. Now perhaps there'll be more for us to eat and the cupboard won't be so bare!"

Don't you think the kiddies would have a lot of fun and at the same time learn something useful if more nursery tales were told like that?

Some of those old ones haven't changed in a millennium. In this case, it's about time – don't you agree? Isn't this a better nursery story to tell the little dumplings? Come on!

The Leewards Times, May 21, 1999

A Y2K Complaint

With the year 2000 barely six months away, it would be nice if the leaders of this country could assure the people of St. Kitts and Nevis that there is nothing much more to worry about aside from "the millennium bug", that pesky little critter widely known as the Y2K bug. Around the globe, individuals, businesses of all descriptions and governments are rushing to complete whatever adjustments are necessary to ensure that their technological equipment is "Y2K compliant".

It seems to me that I read somewhere recently, that the government and major businesses of St. Kitts and Nevis are not lagging behind in the effort, and may even be leading the region in this regard. If this can be factually proven, congratulations may be in order, but on the other hand it occurs to me that Y2K compliance for St. Kitts and Nevis ought to involve more than the upgrading of electronic equipment and operations dependent on certain critical computer chips.

Federal Elections are due for St. Kitts and Nevis in the year 2000. The thorny problems raised by the Nevis secession threat and the constitutional reform issue still loom large on the horizon with no clear remedies in sight. Despite sporadic and questionable efforts by the Constitutional Commission, Committee, and Task Force, nothing yet has emerged that looks the least bit promising and nobody even seems much interested in trying to find a fix for what ails this troubled Federation.

The election process for St. Kitts and Nevis may not be dependent on computers, but Y2K will bug us nonetheless in other ways if we don't do something soon to try to deal with our problems. I certainly find it interesting that we're trying to help certain other countries solve their particular problems while we've still got our own big ones to worry about.

At the International Whaling Commission meeting in Grenada two weeks ago, our representative voted in support of Japan's bid for (1) a secret vote amendment (2) expulsion of the Greenpeace observers from the proceedings, (3) permission to take 50 Minke whales, (4) abolishment of the Southern Ocean Sanctuary.

Scarcely a week later our government was rolling out the red carpet for dignitaries visiting from the Republic of China (Taiwan). The Taiwanese delegation brought gifts of money and expertise to assist with the development of our people and our country. Our country of course supports Taiwan's bid for re-entry to membership in the United Nations Organisation.

Having cozy relationships with other nations for mutual benefits should not be a problem and in fact, should be encouraged and applauded so long as it is clearly established that we are not being bought or sold. And let's face it – Japan and Taiwan do not really need our votes (secret or otherwise) on the international scene, as much as we need to straighten out our internal problems right here at home.

It is clear to me then, that while the Federal Government of St. Kitts and Nevis may have done a masterful job of establishing and maintaining good relations with Japan, Taiwan and other foreign countries, it has not been doing such a hot job closer to home. And while the technological aspects of the Y2K problem may be well under control in our country, something tells me that as far as the political and constitutional reform advancements are concerned, we will not be Y2K compliant. In fact, at the pace we are currently dealing with the difficulties between St. Kitts and Nevis, the next millennium may come and go sooner than constitutional reform, secession or any other resolution to the problem arrives.

The Leewards Times, **June 11, 1999**

ON THE TELEPHONE

I get strange telephone calls from time to time. Sometimes people dial the wrong number, but want to stay and chat anyway. And sometimes people hang up as soon as I say "Hello." Maybe they don't like the sound of my voice. But sometimes people hang up before I even say anything. I find that a little demoralising. I wonder if I've got bad breath, or something!

Some people obviously don't know how to conduct themselves with a telephone. It makes them act a little silly.

For example: my telephone rings. I answer it, "Hello…"

The caller says "Hello…?"

"Hello" I say again, "can I help you"

The caller says "Hello?"

"Who do you wish to speak to?" I ask, "this is Amba Trott speaking. Can you hear me?"

The caller says "Hello."

I tell them what number they have reached and suggest they have dialled the wrong number.

Sometimes the response then is just, "Oh…" Occasionally the response is, "sorry–sorry."

But I'm amazed at how often the final response is still, "Hello…?"

It's also surprising how often people call right back after I tell them they called the wrong number. Obviously they don't believe me the first time, so they try again.

Once somebody asked for the police when I answered the phone. "This isn't the police station – this is the Trott residence," I said.

"Well get off the line so I can get through to the police!" they practically shouted in my ear.

Perhaps the telephone company should organise a workshop on Proper Telephone Usage: Dialling, Answering, and Responding for Beginners and Others. Or maybe they could publish a little 'How To' booklet, a sort of Telephone Manual for Dummies.

Having said that, I have to confess that I've been guilty myself of dialling wrong numbers more often than I'd like to admit. Several times the party I'd reached knew the party I intended to call and gave me the correct number. My brain however sometimes does strange and not so wonderful things and instead of dialling the new number, I've dialled the wrong number over again. Embarrassing!

It's not a good idea to eat while you're having a telephone conversation. If the phone rings while you've got a mouthful of food and you don't want to miss the call, it's best to do one of two things: either spit the food out before you answer the phone, or slide the food into your cheek and ask the caller to "hold please." Then you can chew and swallow your food before starting the conversation.

I haven't always done this myself though. One time a long-winded friend called me just as I was starting my dinner. This person usually does all the talking, so I just brought the telephone over to the table and continued my meal. My end of the conversation was mostly "mm-hmm, uh-huh, uh-huh." The conversation went well until I inadvertently knocked a glass of beer into my plate and in my effort to catch it, knife, fork, plate and glass went clattering and my call became disconnected. My friend soon called back, wondering what had happened. Of course I told the truth, but it was really embarrassing.

Another time, my sister Sonia in California called to wish me "Happy Birthday." We hadn't been in touch for months, so there was really a lot to talk about and Sonia is one of the world's great talkers. Ordinarily, I'm a pretty good listener. But while it was only 9 p.m. in California, it was around midnight here and I was already in bed snoozing when she called.

The call must have lasted an hour or so, but I can't recall much more than the "Happy Birthday" part because I kept dozing off during her narration. Finally I was jolted awake by an insistent voice in my ear, "Amba – are you there…?" Groggily, I assured her that I was and explained that I must have dozed off a bit. If it had been anybody else but my sister Sonia, I'm sure I would have been much more embarrassed.

I've had a number of other funny telephone happenings too. Like the time I was going to make a call, but before I could dial, someone addressed me through the receiver. When I asked who it was, it turned out to be the person I intended to call.

Sometimes I disconnect my phone so that I won't be disturbed as I sleep, but occasionally I forget to reconnect when I get up. Once as I was taking a shower in the afternoon, I suddenly remembered that someone had promised to give me an important call in the morning and I had forgotten to reconnect the phone. I jumped out of the shower to plug in the phone, narrowly missing serious injury as I slid on the tiles and landed on my rump. As I plugged in the phone, it rang immediately. The caller was my friend apologising profusely for forgetting to call me in the morning. He had so many things to do that it had slipped his mind until that moment.

The telephone is a wonderful invention, a great convenience, and I'm usually glad to have it, except once in a while when a whopping bill comes and I don't have the money to pay it. That's embarrassing. It's not much fun then at all.

The Leewards Times, **July 5, 1999**

A Word, If You Please!

In an article I wrote last week, I used a word which many people find objectionable. I'm not surprised. I find it objectionable too. I have even campaigned in the press several times over the past five years against the use of foul language in our community. Few seem to have taken any notice, for the use of foul language has not abated and is commonly heard all over the islands of St. Kitts and Nevis these days.

You can hardly avoid hearing bad language anywhere you go. While waiting for the ferry or around the bus terminals or even certain areas at the airports, foul language is not the exception, but the norm. At beach bars and certain watering holes and eating-places around town, you can't escape it. And you don't have to venture very far from the police stations or churches to hear obscene language. It's just out there at almost every turn. And nobody's doing anything about it. Society just turns a deaf ear. But not a blind eye, apparently.

My simple use of one word last week has aroused more reaction than the hundreds of thousands of words I've used in all of my writings so far. I guess that's some sort of testimony about the power of the written word. One just has to find the right word. From many of the reactions though, it appears that some people believe I wrote that word with criminal or evil intentions.

It may be instructive for my critics to consider that one of the most highly regarded and reliable tools of modern medicine is the use of vaccines. In order to establish an individual's immunity against an infectious or contagious disease, a small carefully calibrated amount is injected into a person's body. The body's immune system is easily able to reject the tiny unwanted invasion and as a result, strengthens and fortifies its defences and remains ever alert to beat off larger invasions of that kind should it become necessary.

I submit that my use of an expletive last week should be seen in that context and no other, as it is the only model, which will even closely resemble my intention. Unfortunately, there are a number of people who do not accept that premise. They prefer to ignore the fact that I purposely published a piece of purple prose, which had been directed against me by a person associated with illegal activity near my home. And they ignore the fact that I've been trying to get the attention of the public and the authorities to focus and do something about the offensive behaviour and illegal activity including the burgeoning drug trade menacing the area and indeed, the entire community.

In other words, it seems that some people are more upset about seeing one bad word in print no matter what the intention, than they are about the fact that crude, coarse characters indulging in bad language, bad behaviour and illegal activity are threatening the peace and comfortable environments of the rest of the community. Pity.

Thank goodness though, that there are others who understand the issues and appreciate what I have been trying to do. Some of them have made it clear that they wish I hadn't felt it necessary to completely spell out the expletive. But they say they understand my intention and will support the cause by contacting the authorities and demanding that something meaningful be done to arrest this sorry situation.

These are the ones who encourage me to go on with the feeling that all is not yet lost. Which leaves me with one final word – hope. As long as people are able to understand and appreciate what I have to say, then there is still hope, and maybe my words are not in vain. Thanks for reading this far.

The Leewards Times, July 30, 1999

Trott Talks To Trott
(An Imaginary Interview)

Q: Mr. Trott, I'd like to interview you today. Do you have the time?

A: Well, it's almost time for my mid-morning nap, but for you I can always spare a few minutes.

Q: Thanks. Is there any truth to the rumour that you are anti-government?

A: That's just a nasty rumour. I can't imagine how it got started. I've always consented to government as a necessary evil.

Q: Oh – so you see this government as evil?

A: Which government are you referring to?

Q: The Nevis Island Administration of course, do you see it as evil?

A: Not necessarily.

Q: But you just said, and I quote, "I've always consented to government as a necessary evil", unquote. The Nevis Island Administration is the local government isn't it?

A: That's debatable. As a matter of fact, if you recall, we recently held a referendum to try to clear up that issue.

Q: But wasn't the referendum about secession. About whether Nevis would separate from St. Kitts?

A: It was about Nevis having its own separate, sovereign, independent government. The referendum failed, so the ambiguity still exists. Perhaps that's why the Premier was confused about where certain transactions took place and where certain stamp duties were paid, and so on. And also why the Attorney General of St. Kitts and Nevis will seek clarification in court about whether the NIA's bid to acquire certain private land is in breach of a certain section of the Constitution of St. Kitts and Nevis.

Q: You're being a little facetious, aren't you?

A: You don't have to take me seriously if you don't want to. But I assure you, I'm not the one who's making jokes.

Q: Are you trying to suggest that our government is being run by a bunch of jokers?

A: Which government are you referring to – the federal or the local?

Q: Why don't you take your pick?

A: The answer is yes.

Q: To which government are you referring now?

A: You may have your pick.

Q: Can I quote you on that?

A: No problem

Q: You don't seem to be too happy with either of the governments. Why is that?

A: If it will make you feel any better, I felt the same way about the previous administrations. As I told you before, I see government as a necessary evil. I'm not happy with any government, but I believe that in most cases, having government is better than having anarchy.

Q: Are you a cynic?

A: I don't think so. I believe I'm more of a skeptic, and even then , by nature rather than doctrine.

Q: Who would you vote for if an election was to be held next month?

A: If it was a Federal Election, there'd be nobody for me to vote for since I've been led to believe that none of the parties in Nevis will contest another Federal Election.

Q: And if it's a local Nevis Island Election?

A: If an election were held tomorrow in Nevis, neither of the two main parties would get my vote. The way they've both performed in recent years has only managed to "get my goat".

Q: Are you saying you would not go to the polls if an election were held?

A: I'm not interested in voting for a particular party. I could be persuaded though, to vote for an individual who I believe has the right ideas – the right agenda, and is not merely a "yes" man for any political party.

Q: So who's out there that you might support?

A: I can't even see anybody on the horizon at present. Maybe I'd have to "jump in the ring" myself.

Q: You mean you'd seriously consider running for public office?

A: Listen, if people can take all those other guys who've been running for public office seriously, why not me? At least then I could vote for somebody I want to support.

Q: What party would you consider running for?

A: I'd most likely be a party-pooper and run as an independent. I don't think I could stick to the "party-line" of the established parties.

Q: What would be the main planks in your platform?

A: Simple. A willingness to serve the people as best I can. A desire to make government more accountable to the people – more "user friendly". And a guarantee to step down anytime that more than fifty percent of my constituents sign a petition saying that they are unhappy with my performance. They needn't wait to vote me out of office in an election.

Q: And that's it – you'd expect people to vote for that?

A: People have already voted for a whole lot less. I know I have, and I'm tired of it. I'm not a professional politician, so they wouldn't be hearing from me all those phony promises that they ought to be tired of.

Q: So you're no phony – is that what you're saying?

A: Listen… I know zilch about political science, and economics and trade and all that stuff. And I won't promise a solution to the donkey problem, the monkey problem, or the monkeying around problem either.

Q: Well, there really isn't much left is there? What will you do for the public if you do get into office?

A: I don't know yet, but I'll tell you this much: If I make an error about anything and the public finds out about it, I'm going to say, "Ooops – I made a boo-boo. Sorry about that".

Q: Gee whiz! Isn't that kind of revolutionary?

A: And to top it off, I would call for a vote of "No confidence" if the government makes a boo-boo and doesn't clear it up.

Q: You're kidding, aren't you?

A: No way. I intend to be "up front" about everything, and I expect the same from everybody else.

Q: One final question – how long would you expect to last as a politician?

A: At my age, I'm not worried about it. You can quote me on that too.

Q: It's very refreshing speaking to someone who is so straightforward and "up front" about everything. Would it be possible for me to interview you again sometime?

A: No problem.

A Hamilton House Studio Publication, November 27, 1999

Happy Whatever!

Why, oh why is everyone acting as though the end of the year 1999 marks the end of the Twentieth Century? There is still one more year to go. The end of the Twentieth Century will not occur until next year, midnight December 31st, 2000, to be exact.

I only mention this because the number of people who seem to think that the 21st Century begins this coming January amazes me. The 21st Century can't possibly begin before the 20th Century has ended. So let's get things straight.

After any series of nineteen things, you will come to the twentieth. Since we are talking about centuries here, it is pretty simple and straightforward. Any primary school kid can tell you that after ninety-nine comes one hundred, Cricket fans are familiar with the term "Century" and know that in mathematical symbols it is written as 100.

A Century always ends with double zeroes. The batsman who scores 99 comes close but has not quite reached a "Century". If one century is written 100, it must follow that twenty centuries be written as 2000.

It appears to me then, that all those who are cashing in on the popular belief that midnight December 31st 1999 signals the end of the Twentieth Century and the beginning of the next millennium, are pulling off the biggest hoax in history.

After midnight tonight, the last year of the 20th Century begins. The 21st Century begins on January 1st, 2001. The end of this year only marks the end of the nineteen hundred and ninety-ninth year, that's all. I don't expect many people to pay much attention to what I say about it however.

Most people are anxious to go out and spend their money and have a good time. If it's not the end of the Twentieth Century or the beginning of the next millennium, they'll find some other excuse. I don't want to spoil their fun, so I might as well just wish everybody a Happy New Year – whatever it is!

The Leewards Times, **December 31, 1999**

BOOK   III

VERSES and SONGS

(The words on pages 247-260 are verses, and those on pages 261-271 are songs.)

MASQUERADE

Sound of de big drum "BOM-BOM-BOM!
Where is dat big sound coming from?
Crowds always gather when it's played.
Dey know it signals MASQUERADE!

Den hear de fife sound in de street,
Playin de tunes dat sound so sweet.
Feet runnin' cross de esplanade -
Folks rushin' to see MASQUERADE!

Tall peacock headdress reach de sky.
Colourful costumes catch de eye.
Dancers in such wild style arrayed.
Dis is de ting called MASQUERADE!

Kettledrum beating "rrrab-a-tat".
Forget yu worries, grab yu hat.
Join in de joyful escapade,
Yu know me meaning, MASQUERADE!

Den see de dancers go like so…
Dancing de Quadrille, stately – slow.
And other old-time dance displayed,
Whenever dem do MASQUERADE!

Den see de dancers start to flip,
When de dance-master crack de whip.
But yu don't have to be afraid;
Das all a part of MASQUERADE!

Dis is a form of culture we
Han' down from days of slavery.
What de white masters once had made,
We change an' call it MASQUERADE!

NONSENSE IN NEVIS

So when yu hear de big drum beat,
An' see dem costumes in de street,
Whether in sunshine or in shade,
You know we going see MASQUERADE!

***

(Written in July 1990, at the request of Anthony Pemberton, for a Culturama presentation.)

BABATUNJI

Babatunji and his pan
Played the happy tunes of Nevis
Played the sad, sweet songs of Nevis
Played the old, old songs of Nevis
Babatunji and his pan.

Babatunji on his pan
Beat such smooth pulsating rhythms
Sometimes joyful, bouncy rhythms
Sometimes solemn, soulful rhythms
Babatunji on his pan.

Babatunji on his pan
Played the high notes, played the low notes
Played the new and long ago notes
Played those rapid to-and-fro notes
Babatunji on his pan.

Babatunji with his pan
Reached the hearts and minds of people
Reached the heads and toes of people
Reached the joys and woes of people
Babatunji with his pan.

Babatunji with his pan
Searched for new ways of expression
Meshing old ways of expression
With his own unique expression
Babatunji with his pan.

Babatunji and his pan
Played the memories of old folks
Played the hopes and dreams of young folks
Played the melodies of all folks
Babatunji and his pan.

NONSENSE IN NEVIS

Babatunji with his pan
Concentrating on his purpose
Sharp, keen, focus on that purpose
Mindful only of that purpose
Babatunji with his pan.

Babatunji on his pan
Ping, ping, pinging like the raindrops
Pling, plang, plinging – plenty raindrops
Blang, blang, blinging – mighty raindrops!
Babatunji on his pan.

Babatunji and his pan
Coruscating in the moonlight
Clear and sparkling like the daylight
Warm and cosy like the sunlight
Babatunji and his pan.

Babtunji with his pan
Played his soul and played his heartbeat
Felt his people's dreams and heartbeat
Touched his country's mood and
heartbeat
Babatunji with his pan.

Babatunji with his pan
Took the measure of his music
Found a treasure in his music
Gave the pleasure of his music
Babatunji with his pan.

Babatunji and his pan
Such a match is very clever
Such a bond will never
sever
May they both play on
forever
Babatunji and his pan!

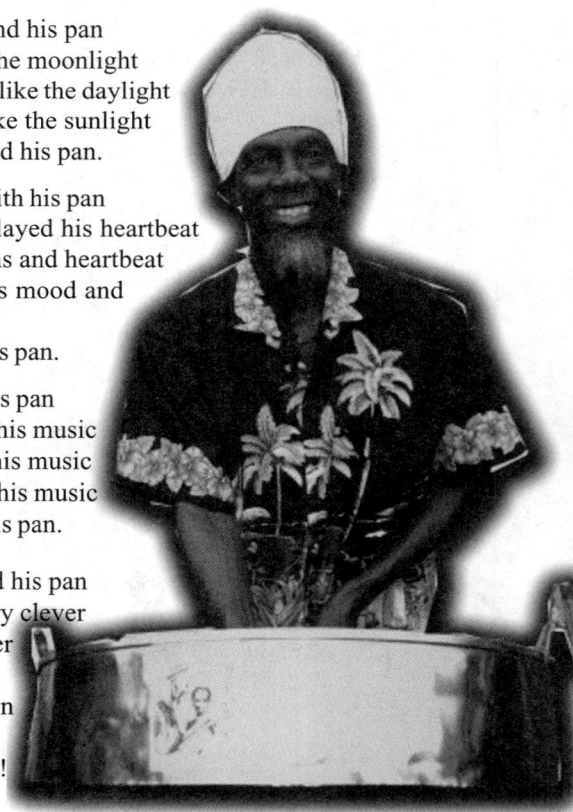

***

Babatunji Moore is a virtuoso steel pan artist from Barnes Ghaut, Nevis. This piece was written in celebration of his fiftieth birthday in March, 2004.

250

LOOKING AT LIFE AHEAD
(A POEM FOR GRADUATION)

As I stand here a thousand thoughts are swirling through my brain,
And long forgotten memories come back to me again.
I picture how it was when I first ventured off to school;
I was an awkward child then, feeling somewhat like a fool.
But then somehow, I managed to survive those early days,
Because my parents nurtured me with tender love and praise.
Because my teachers coaxed me, led me, taught me, so that I
Would want to learn to read and write, they showed me how to try.
And try I did, like other kids , to understand those things
That helped explain the world to me, that helped my thoughts take wings.
From simple little two times two, and childish A, B, C,
Those simple, little childish things were building up in me
A store of skills which I would need to master other chores,
Which in their turn, once mastered, would then open other doors
To knowledge, which until then had been just a mystery
To simple, selfish, careless, thoughtless, carefree kids like me.
So, slowly I was nurtured under watchful caring eyes,
Into a budding student with the thirst that never dies.
The thirst to soak up knowledge so that I could leave behind
The nagging, puzzling questions of an active, restless mind.
The thirst for education so that I could find the way
To stand and speak to others as I speak to you today.
The thirst for truth and wisdom, and indeed as I reflect,
The thirst to satisfy my ever growing intellect.
I guess I'll go on thirsting, and the reason I say so,
Is that the more I seem to learn, the more I need to know.
If I learned something new right now, you'd find that I'm perplexed,
Because I seem to need to know what's going to happen next!
And that's the way I am because this education biz
Has trained me up to be this way, has made me what I is.
"Good grief", you say, "his grammar's poor he hasn't learned enough!"
But there's no need to worry, 'cause I really know my stuff!
I've learned a lot through all those years from grade school up to now.
And though I don't get grades for it, I'm learning anyhow,

To face up to the challenges that life presents me with;
What once seemed so impossible, today seems just a myth!
I've learned to set high standards and to aim for nothing less
If I want to keep my footing on the ladder to success.
And so today, as I stand with my graduating class,
These thoughts rushed through my mind. And now I say to you at last,
To parents and to teachers, and to all who've gathered here
To bear witness at the closing of this academic year;
That you have done your jobs well, you prepared in every way
The graduating students that you honour here today.
And so we face the future without worry, without dread,
But with confidence and courage, as we look at life ahead.

***

(Written in July 1989, at the request of Halstead 'Sooty' Byron, for a graduation ceremony.)

GIVE IT A TRY
(A POEM FOR MODERN YOUTHS)

Dear friends there are some things I just have to say,
About what is happening with some youths today.
So many are swayed by the life of excess -
As if that's the way to the road to success.
They follow the leaders without thinking through
The consequence of whatsoever they do.
They live for the moment; the fun and the thrills,
Forgetting that some day they must pay the bills.
Instead of their family's kisses and hugs,
They seek out excitement in sex and in drugs.
They risk vile diseases like herpes and AIDS
As result of their wanton and wild escapades.
They consort with the devil and don't count the cost
Until they are senselessly, hopelessly lost.
They scoff at the warnings and run with the crowd,
Hell-bent on embracing the lewd and the loud.

They engage in mad dances by night and by day,
Forgetting they still have the piper to pay.
And when they're exhausted and beaten and hurt,
And too weak to rise from the filth and the dirt –
Instead of admitting their guilt and their shame,
They'll try to convince you that they're not to blame;
"It's society's fault!" is their cry and their yell –
If you won't accept that, they'll say "Go to hell!"
They'll say bad is good and that good is the worst,
Their folly is but an unquenchable thirst
To engage in immoral and improper acts,
And to lie, to conceal, or to varnish the facts.
My dear friends, believe me, whatever you do –
I know that's not me and I hope that's not you.
Our lives are too precious to ruin that way
In body and spirit and moral decay.

NONSENSE IN NEVIS

I spurn the embrace of the maddening crowd –
I uphold those virtues of which to be proud;
Of Hope, Faith, and Prudence, of sweet Charity,
Of Kindness, of Love, and of Integrity.
I'll try to live my life in meaningful ways
And set an example that others might praise.
I might fail in the effort, but until I die,
I'm sure going to give it one heck of a try!

***

(Written in July 1989, at the request of Chesley L. Davis, for Culturama Teen Pageant.)

LEGEND OF EDEN BROWN

Once was a lady fair
Living in Nevis where
A swain true love did swear
Her heart he seized.

The banns were soon proclaimed
Date place and time were named
How could the girl be blamed
For feeling pleased?

Her friends and kindred too
Planned gifts with much ado
And expectations grew
As days flew by.

And Eden Brown Estate
Topped all the gifts to date
The girl could hardly wait
Oh my – oh my…!

The great house built for her
Created quite a stir
Most of the people were
Highly impressed.

They gazed with wonder there
Mansions like this were rare
They said the lady fair
Truly was blessed.

And oh, how happily
And oh, how eagerly
She dreamed of blissfully
Her wedding night.

Nothing but joy in mind
Sweet dreams so well defined
True love can be so blind
Things seemed so right.

The day at last arrived
And every guest contrived
So's not to be deprived
Of the best view.

Not only that, but they
Connived in every way
To make sure that they
Could be seen too.

But be that as it may
Nothing could rue this day
At least that was the way
That things were planned.

The couple made their vows
The pastor made some bows
All the event allows
It was so grand!

And the reception too
Really was quite a do
Held in the estate's new
And great house hall.

Then came the grand soiree
Such as you'd never see
Or, put more succinctly,
They had a ball!

At the festivity
The lovers danced with glee
Everyone said that she
Looked so divine.

They marvelled as he too
While they danced, simply flew
Seemingly to a new
And strange design.

But stranger yet for sure
A dusky maid's allure
Fractured what seemed secure
Innocently.

She was of low estate
Servitude was her fate
She could not obviate
The tragedy.

Revellers drank their fill
And such occasions will
Loosen tongues willy-nil
And in this case

The groom's best man implied
That the groom's lovely bride
With dusky maid beside
Took second place.

The crowd then quickly quailed
Some of the women wailed
The groom's face blanched and paled
His fists were clenched.

And the fair lady swooned
At this most painful wound
The revelry was ruined
Her heart was wrenched.

The groom had gathered now
His wits and did allow
His solemn voice somehow
Though far from cool

To answer this offense
Demanding recompense
With honour's sole defense
To wit - a duel.

But see now, what is this?
Things have gone so amiss
From serene thoughts of bliss
To scenes so dread.

Two friends in duel engage
O'er dusky maiden; rage
Fans flames to set the stage
Two friends lay dead.

The guests in shock depart
Even the stoutest heart
No succour can impart
No aid extend.

No one could have foreseen
Such a disastrous scene
Such an untimely, mean,
And fruitless end.

As for the Lady fair
Now see her dark despair
More than her mind can bear
She has gone mad…

The many decades see
The empty great house be
Eden Brown legacy-
How sad – how sad!

**

N.B.   This poem is merely my own rendition of the Eden Brown story. I make no claims for accuracy and am aware that other versions may greatly differ from this one.   I attempted only to create a fairy-tale atmosphere, charming and romantic, in rhyming verse.

It can be offered as a short presentation with costumed actors portraying the main characters as a narrator does the reading. It can also be enhanced with appropriate music (simple harp or guitar chords) played between verses. Of course it can also be included with any printed matter developed about the Eden Brown Estate for tourism purposes.

■ *Written in 2002 for the Department of Tourism, Nevis Island Administration.*

INSECTY-SIDES

THE ROACH

Cock-a-roaches were here long before man came,
And will be here long after he's gone they say.
All I ask is that while I'm around,
They just keep outta my way.

Though my tolerance for most life forms
Is really well beyond reproach,
I've got no tolerance at all
When it comes to the cock-a-roach!

***

THE MOSQUITO

As far as I'm concerned
They're just hateful li'l varmints.
As objects of love
They don't meet my requarmints.
And whenever I kill one
I think it's quite neat-o
To know that at least
Thar's one less damned mosquito!

***

THE FLY

If you must know the truth about me and the fly
It is simply that we just don't see eye-to-eye
And if suddenly they should all become extinct
I would certainly see less of them, I should think.

***

THE ANT

Ants
Sometimes get into my pants
But there really isn't even the ghost of a chance
For any kind of romance
Developing with me
And those (slap, pow, scratch-scratch, x#^%xd) ants!

***

Insecty-Sides was not written at the request of anyone. It is just part of the reality of life in Nevis.

Tourist Visitors

Tourists visiting Nevis
Come expecting to see
Happy people and sunshine
Pristine beaches, and sparkling sea
And de money dey spend here
Some of it comes to me
Tourists visiting Nevis
Boost de economy.

Tourists visiting Nevis
Staying at de hotel
Like to get de best service
Like to be treated very well
Like de friendly Nevisians
Dat really is a fact
And we like to see friendly
Tourists keep coming back.

I am glad to see tourists
And it makes me feel tall
When dey tell me my island
Is so pleasant though very small
So I'm trying to do the
Very best that I can
To help my island of Nevis
Keep looking spic and span.

Everybody in Nevis
Don't matter what dey do
Benefits from tourism
That's why brother, I'm telling you
When I speak of tourism
I've got nothing to hide
When Tourist visitors come here
I show nothing but pride.

NONSENSE IN NEVIS

All de people of Nevis
Have a strong role to play
How we treat all de tourists
Can attract or turn dem away
If we need tourist dollars
And it's plain dat we do
Den treat de visiting tourists
Like it matters to you!

***

Written in 2003 for the Department of Tourism in the Nevis Island Administration.

SAMUEL HUNKINS SONG

What can you say about a man
Who reaches out with either hand
Who does the very best he can
For his small island

Who teaches others precious skills
So they can earn and pay their bills
And shout out proudly to the hills
"This land is my land!"

What can you say about the way
He soldiered on from day to day
Not for a moment did he sway
From his objective

He blazed a trail so others too
Could do the things that he could do
And the results I'm telling you
Are quite effective!

Samuel Hunkins played his role
As if perfection was his goal
He really put his heart and soul
In all his labour

His faith in God helped him to reach
The point where he could try to teach
The values that he held to each
And every neighbour.

And so when all is said and done
Though he's not the most famous one
I simply say that there are none
Whose deeds stand greater

Though he may take it all in stride
What he has done for Nevis' pride
Helps all Nevisians far and wide
To stand up straighter!

***

George Samuel Hunkins B.E.M. Born at New Castle, Nevis, on March 20, 1915. Passionate teacher, relentless pursuer of excellence, he established apprenticeship programmes for the woodworking and construction industries. Pioneered the use of privately owned heavy building equipment, large workshop machinery and modern business offices. Introduced funeral home services, and made numerous and varied contributions to churches, organisations and community. The thoroughfare along the Charlestown waterfront is named in his honour - The Samuel Hunkins Drive.

SMALL ISLAND COME BIG!

In Nevis or St.Kitts
Don't care where you go
De people so proud, man
Dey happy for so
Dey embracing strangers
An don't care a fig
Since Willett play cricket
Small island come big!

He play in Antigua
Dem people amaze
Dey say "Look dis boy, nuh!"
Dey chattin for days
He take all dem wicket
An den dance a jig
Dey say, "O me God oh,
Small island come big!"

When he reach Barbados
De people say "Mon,
Yu too small to play here
Go back where yu come."
He clean bowl de batsmen
Dem squeal like a pig
Dey say, "But bejeeze, man
Small island come big!"

He go to Jamaica
An den Trinidad
He take on de big boys
De best dat dey had
Dey can't do a ting, man
Except scratch dey wig
An shout in frustration
"Small island come big, big, big
Small island come big!"

A mathematician
While watchin de game
Said "I must be daft, man
I going insane
By my calculations
Without Pi or Trig
I reach de conclusion
Small island come big!"

A Latin professor
Look like he was stun
He said what he witness
Just should not be done
He froth at de mouth while
He cried "Infra dig
Dis shouldn't be happening
Small island come big!"

Some folks in St. Thomas
Sent Elco a car
He said "I can walk, man
I don't go so far"
Dey tell him their hero
Deserve a fine rig
Because he make Nevis
Small island come big!

Through all of de Leewards
De people gone mad
An all through the Windwards
De people so glad
De dance in de streets, man
Dey zag an dey zig
Dey say, "Now de world know
Small island come big!"

I went to a party
High society
An most of de people
Glance sideways at me

I so glad I manage
To get in a dig
I said "Have you noticed
Small island come big, big, big
Small island come big!"

Some ladies were chatting
Comparing their notes
Their likes and their dislikes
About certain blokes
One gal tell de next one
"Don't be such a prig
You'll like how it feel when
Small island come big, big, big, big, big
Small island come big!"

***

Elquemedo Willett was the first cricket player from small Leeward Islands in the eastern Caribbean to play Test Cricket on the West Indies Cricket Senior Team in 1973. His successful emergence paved the way for many others who have followed in his wake.

A BOY FROM CHARLESTOWN
AN ODE TO ALEXANDER HAMILTON

A boy from Charlestown
Who had to go away
Helped build a nation
The fledgling USA

He left his own land
The land where he was born
To build a new land
Red, white, and blue land

Across the ocean
An icon he became
His great achievements
Brought him undying fame

And so I wonder
Were there a way somehow
Just what he could do
And what he should do
And what he would do
For Nevis now.

***

Alexander Hamilton, who was born in Nevis in 1757, became one of the founding fathers of the United States of America, and was its first Secretary of the Treasury. His likeness adorns the US ten dollar note.

FANNY'S SONG FOR HORATIO NELSON

There's a reason why
I'm a little shy...
Horatio!

Trembling in my knees
Hope nobody sees...
Horatio!

I'm a little weak and tense and shaky
Cause my life is suddenly earthquakey
I'm a little scared
Though not unprepared

This is quite a thing
Just considering...
Horatio!

Who'd have thought that he
Could consider me...
Horatio!

Any woman would I'm sure get giddy
If he told her that he found her pretty
He said that to me
And I said "golly – gee!"
Couldn't find a thing
To be answering...
Horatio!

I was stricken dumb
And my mind went numb
Horatio! Horatio!

NONSENSE IN NEVIS

Wish my brain would give me better service
Then I mightn't be so doggoned nervous
On my wedding day
Should it be this way?
Still, I'm ready now
Shaking to the core
If my limbs allow
I am ready for…
Horatio! Horatio! Horatio!

***

Nevis-born Frances Nisbett married Captain Horatio Nelson at Montepelier Plantation in March 1787.

HAIL NEVIS!

Hail Nevis, land I love
Fair island – skies above
Show'r God's blessings over thee
Faith, love, honour, dignity

Our people standing tall
Answering freedom's call
Stand for Nevis proud and free
Hail Nevis, hail Nevis
Hail Nevis, our own country!

***